Endangered Fae

DIEGO

ANGEL MARTINEZ

Diego
ISBN # 978-1-78686-368-3
©Copyright Angel Martinez 2018
Cover Art by Emmy @ studioenp ©Copyright August 2018
Interior text design by Claire Siemaszkiewicz
Pride Publishing

Published in 2018 by Pride Publishing, United Kingdom.

DIEGO

Dedication

For Catherine, who pushed for this book to be finished, who told me when I was wrong, and who cheered when it was done.

Chapter One

Catalyst

"Don't go." Finn glowered down from his lofty height, arms crossed over his bare chest. "I forbid you to go."

"You...what?" Diego blinked at him in shock. "Since when did you decide you wanted to play lord of the manor? You can't 'forbid' anything."

Finn slumped against the wall and slid down until he sat on the floor. "Apparently not. I thought I might try it once. Would begging and pleading alter your ill-conceived decision, then?"

Diego crouched down to take Finn's long-fingered hand between his. "*Cariño*, what is all this? I'll only be gone a week. You left me once for five days and told me it wasn't long at all."

"But I wasn't doing the waiting, now, was I?" Finn said with a sharp bark of laughter. "Oh, love, I can't explain it. I have an ice spear lodged in my spine, and I don't know why."

"Please don't tell me you've got a bad feeling about this." Diego rolled his eyes. When he had first mentioned the trip to New York, Finn hadn't protested. Now, when it was too late to cancel his plans, his impending absence caused Finn such anguish.

"But I do. Have a bad feeling." Finn put his forehead on his knees, long blue-black hair falling forward to hide his face.

"So come with me."

"No."

"We could take a train. I don't have to fly. Or you could become an eagle or a peregrine and meet me there."

"I won't go back to the poisoned lands. Not even for you."

"I'm sorry. I shouldn't ask you to." Diego leaned in to nuzzle at Finn's jaw. "Are you afraid I won't come back? That I'm leaving you for good?"

Finn opened his arms and pulled him close with a gusty sigh. "It's not that sort of feeling, my love. It's more as if this journey of yours will act as a...catalyst. That we are at some strange turning point I cannot see beyond."

"Even you can't see into the future..." Diego stroked a hand over Finn's hard-packed chest. "Can you?"

"No. No, I can't. Frustrating sometimes."

"Whatever it is, *mi amor*, we'll work through it. Don't worry so."

* * * *

Finn stared out of the bedroom window at the larches. Tamaracks, they called them here. The soft burst of gold as they prepared to shed their summer needles amidst the dark green of the pines should have made his heart sing. They only made him think of

Diego's golden skin against the dark sheets and compounded his misery.

"Bloody, blithering fool," he muttered at himself.

Diego would return in another three days, a blink of an eye for someone who had lived for thousands of years. The thought didn't help. He yearned for his love with every scrap of his being, hating the emptiness of his arms and the empty spot in his mind where Diego's presence usually nestled. He was so cursed lonely without him, which was what made falling in love so gods-be-damned stupid in the first place. Only someone in love truly felt this consuming, hollow pain.

"I need to go out," he told the pillow he held, the one where Diego's scent still lingered. While he liked the new house nestled in the Montana forest, close to the wilderness for him but not too far from the little town for Diego, he had never spent five days sequestered inside a building of his own free will.

There, that was it. He was depressed because of confinement and lack of food. Not that the larder was empty. He just hadn't felt like eating. A nice fat trout sounded good, or perhaps whitefish, cold and shining.

He would swim, feed, and return by nightfall, when Diego might call. Good. Perfect. He hurried down the stairs, poked his head out of the back door and lifted his face to the breeze. No humans lurked nearby to see, so he stepped onto the wooden porch and wriggled out of his jeans. Clothes were fine now and then, and he wore them to satisfy Diego's sense of modesty, but the best part about putting them on was shedding them again.

The sun caressed his bare shoulders. The cool grass kissed his feet. He spread his arms to the breeze and closed his eyes. A faint blue glow danced over his skin as his body melted, his form condensing, his hair shortening and spreading to cover him in sleek black fur. A river otter soon stood where Finn had been.

Otter Finn galloped for the river, his heart singing as the tumult of its rush and tumble reached him. He stumbled and stopped as another noise drifted over the roar of the rapids—a scream, inaudible but in his mind. Terrible fear knifed through him—the cold panic of a human in mortal danger.

This is none of my business. I should not involve myself...

What would he say to Diego, though, if he came back and found out someone had died on the river? "Oh, yes, my love, I heard them dying. I simply decided not to act."

He cringed. Diego would disapprove in the worst way, and perhaps this was someone else's beloved, someone whose absence would cause terrible pain.

He shifted to hawk form and took flight. His powerful wings arrowed over the river, sharp eyes searching the water. *There.* A little bean-pod-shaped coracle rode the rapids, upside-down and unmanned. Not far behind, its former occupant struggled, head tugged under the whitewater again and again despite the orange vest humans wore to help them float.

Hawk Finn folded his wings and plummeted on an unerring course to intercept. The moment before he hit the raging rapids, he shifted again, his body elongating to a scaled, sinuous form. Dragon Finn caught hold of the unconscious human's collar with his teeth and knifed through the water to shore.

"Probably best not to have you see a dragon first thing," Finn muttered, and shifted back to his own shape. He sat panting a moment. All the swift and sudden shifts had taken a frightening amount of effort.

He cocked his head to the side to regard his odd catch. The scent was female and she still breathed. Her skin was fish-cold, though. Not normal for a human.

He shook her gently. "Do you hear me? Do you have companions nearby?" No response and, as he sifted through all the sounds his ears could reach, no companions either. *Dagda's balls.* He simply wasn't any good at dealing with ailing humans. *What would Diego advise?*

"Most likely to get her warm, you dunderhead," he muttered. With a sigh, he slid his arms under her and carried her back to the house.

The strap under her chin frustrated him, but he finally found the little catch to the clasp to remove her helmet. He supposed if one were to go boating in the rapids, which struck him as a supremely unwise idea, a helmet would be prudent. The wet clothes only pulled more warmth from her, so he removed those as well.

Pity, really. He traced a finger over the dark bruise forming on her perfect jaw. Such a beautiful human girl, full-hipped and plump-breasted. He would have liked… No, Diego put such stock in exclusive pairings, like swans did. For Diego, he would refrain.

He frowned. The girl still wasn't any warmer. Bed. Diego had a blanket that warmed itself. It should help. He carried her up and wrapped her in the magic blanket, then stared at the white box with the buttons that told it what to do. Which button did one push? The one with the red circle looked threatening so he chose the yellow as a happier color.

She remained stubbornly unconscious. He sat beside her and stroked the dark tendrils of damp hair from her face. Such soft hair, he fought the temptation to bury his fingers in it. *Still so cold. Damn and damn again.*

He would simply have to warm her himself.

Finn lifted the blanket and slid underneath with her. He pressed his skin to hers, wrapped his limbs around her and pulled warmth from the surrounding air. Slowly, her body temperature began to rise, and he smiled, pleased at his success. Of course, something else began to rise, as well, but he steadfastly ignored the erection pressed against her lovely bottom. He was no brainless slave to his mating urges. He could control them, despite what some might say.

* * * *

"No, really, Miriam, I don't mind," Diego said into his cell. The plane eased up alongside the gate, thumps and thuds coming from outside the door. "It's just one book signing. There are bound to be cancellations here and there, right?"

Miriam's snort was neither ladylike nor polite. "You just want to get home to that handsome beefcake of yours so you can screw like bunnies."

"I won't say the thought didn't cross my mind." Diego laughed as she swore softly. "But seriously, one promo event canceled in a dozen? I'd say that was pretty good."

"All right. But when you're bigger than Michener, those idiots'll regret canceling on you."

"Maybe. Thanks, though, for setting all that up in the same week."

"All to make me more money, hon. Don't ever think it's anything else," Miriam growled. Then her voice softened. "You done good, Sandoval. Though I always knew you would. When's my next book coming?"

"*Dios*. Don't I get some time off?"

"No. Not at the snail's pace you write. Tell me you've started the sequel."

"Started, yes." Diego shifted to pull his laptop from under the seat in front of him. "But finished is still months off."

"Get cracking, then. You tell that man of yours to take care of you so you can work."

"He watches out for me. I haven't had an episode since Canada." Diego cringed. Bringing up the seizure that had landed him in the hospital for two weeks was a bad idea.

Miriam only snorted her disbelief. "All right, kiddo. Talk to you soon. Kiss Finn for me."

Diego smiled, knowing she would have much rather claimed the honor herself. He said goodbye to the flight attendants, one of whom blushed, clutching her newly signed copy of *A Pooka's Life* to her chest. The notion of fans still amazed him, people who gushed and stammered upon meeting him and said absurd things such as 'you're so much cuter in person'. Officially, the events in New York had all been for the *Dragon Rites* release but many of his readers had fixated on his first book. One girl at a book signing had had tears in her eyes when she'd confessed she wished the pooka was real.

If only she knew.

He had given Finn a pseudonym, Thistle, for the book, but all the material came from recorded interviews about Finn's life, and the artist had used photographs of him for the illustrations. More than one plea had come in from agencies and advertisers for the model's name and phone number. Miriam said it added to the book's mystique when Diego steadfastly refused to divulge any information, and though Finn would never reveal himself to the world, he found the whole thing incredibly funny.

A spring in his step, he hurried to the parking garage, eager to get through the three-hour drive home. Finn had been so despondent over his departure; he hoped the surprise of coming home early would make up for any heartache.

* * * *

The girl struggled toward waking. Her thoughts took form as she fought clear of her dreams. Mother of waters, though, she was loud. Finn's forehead creased as another mental shout battered the shield he had thrown up against her psychic noise. The birds singing outside were drowned out by her.

Of course, some humans were naturally loud, like mental blue jays, but some only reacted to trauma this way and fought their way back screaming. She would most likely quiet when she woke. He hoped. Diego was never this loud, not even in his moments of greatest anguish.

"Fire and storm, Diego," he muttered. "Why did you choose this week to leave me on my own?"

* * * *

The house was still standing. Good. Finn hadn't had any major battles with household appliances. Diego pulled the truck into the freestanding garage at the back of the house. He smiled as he caught sight of the black jeans discarded in an untidy pile on the back porch. Finn was out, then, swimming and hunting.

A terrible thought had struck him on his way home. What if Finn had truly been pining, neglecting himself? He had sounded cheerful enough when Diego called each night, but he was a practiced liar and could have been covering up to keep Diego from worrying. A Beauty and the Beast scenario had crept into his thoughts, where he would come home to find Finn stretched out in the garden, dying. Stupid, of course, since Finn could go years without food, but knowing that he was doing what came naturally and not sitting inside sulking lifted a shadow from his heart.

He picked up the jeans and draped them over the porch railing. Finn might want them when he came back. "All right, *cariño*, you've had to wait days for me. I can wait a few hours while you're fishing."

The house was in order, no mess, no plates of half-eaten chicken strewn about and no oil paints smeared on the living room rug. A completed canvas leaned against the wall, a new one. Diego frowned at it, head cocked to one side. Predominantly black and gray, with anguished streaks of red and yellow, it screamed emotional distress. *Perhaps not doing so well after all.*

He climbed the stairs to take his bag to their bedroom and stopped cold in the doorway. A young woman lay in his bed, wrapped in his electric blanket and in his Finn's arms. As he watched, she turned with a little cooing sound and nuzzled at Finn's throat.

"Holy. Shit."

Finn's head jerked up, expression frozen in horror. "My love, I didn't hear you arrive —"

"I guess not," Diego said softly. "You're a jackass." He dropped his bag, hurried down the stairs and out of the back door.

"Diego, wait!" The anguished wail followed him but he didn't stop until he hit the gravel drive.

Finn shot through the door, stark naked, still half-erect. *Great, wonderful, go ahead and throw it in my face.*

"Diego, please." Finn spread his hands, looked down at himself, and at least mustered the sense to reach for his jeans draped on the rail. "Let me —"

"No. Don't." Diego held up a hand to stop him. "I don't want to hear your excuses, your justifications. Not just now."

Finn's mind reached for him, a soft, tentative touch, while he took a step closer, holding a hand out to him.

"No, damn it!" Diego flung up the mental wall to keep him out and backpedaled three steps. "You need to leave me alone right now. I came home early. I was worried about you. Stupid me."

"But I —"

"I don't care why you took her to bed! I don't want to hear what happened!" He ran his hands over his face, chest constricting with anger and pain. "I knew. I *knew* what you were when I fell in love with you. A liar and a satyric who's let his dick lead him around for centuries. But why make me promises you knew you couldn't keep? *Dios*... Finn..."

"My love —"

"Leave me be for a few! Let me think without you hammering to get in!"

He spun away and strode off into the woods.

* * * *

Finn shivered in the wake of Diego's fury and yanked the jeans on, marking the path of his retreat. Diego was so hurt, so angry, Finn could sense the lightning beginning to spark in his head. If he let it go too far, he would have an attack of the falling sickness. Out there in the woods. Alone.

Of course, if Diego was angry enough, he might turn the lightning on Finn.

He chewed his bottom lip and came to a decision, taking the steps two at a time to race back to the bedroom. The girl was just sitting up, befuddled and groggy. She looked up as he skidded to a stop in the doorway.

"You were drowning. I pulled you out. There's a phone beside you. Call someone to collect you. You are in a house at Box 22 on Old Route 249. They should find it by that."

He didn't stop to see if his rapid-fire instructions were heard or followed. Heart pounding against his ribs, he flung himself back down the stairs and after Diego. The trail was as much physical scent as thought scent. Diego's anguish could have been heard for miles by any creature not head-blind and the little sparks of magic leaping from him crackled more and more loudly.

"Don't turn me into fried pooka, love, please, please," Finn muttered as he ran. Diego had never been able to use his enormous potential while fully awake, but once he seized, the unleashing of his mental lightning was daunting.

The hairs on the back of his neck stood straight up, the sudden pull on the flows of surrounding magic nearly sucking all the air from the woods. Finn broke into a full-out sprint.

"Diego! Diego, no!"

A wall of force slammed into him and hurled him through the air. His back smashed into something with a sickening crack. The sun went dark.

Chapter Two

The Children of Danu

"Let me kill it. It should not be here."

"Hush, Morri. Of course it shouldn't. We should at least find out how it came."

"Human sorcerers. They have found a way through. This one is proof. It will bring more."

Diego struggled toward waking. The dream voices refused to go away even when the crippling aches and stiffness that followed a fierce, prolonged seizure took hold. His head pounded. Nausea crawled in his stomach.

He blinked his eyes open and squinted, unable to focus. Three people stood nearby, but they were fuzzy blurs. Soft light seemed to shine from them, most likely some optical disturbance left over from the seizure.

Who are you? Where am I? Found a way through what? He tried to ask the questions but only managed a low, pitiful moan.

"Oh, poor little thing. It hurts," the softest of the three voices said.

"No! Don't touch it," the rasping one spat out. "It is dangerous. Better I slay it now, while it is weak."

The third voice vibrated the air in a deep bass. "Only She has that right. We will take the little man to Her."

A rattling hiss of displeasure followed this command, and Diego no longer wanted to see what made that sound.

The hiss sounded closer to his ear, the voice full of bitter sarcasm. "Very well, Shining One. It will be as you wish. But I will take it so that no one else is imperiled. And I will kill it if it offers threat."

A hard hand clamped on the back of his neck, claw tips pricking his skin. The hand hauled him roughly from the soft bed and held him dangling so only his toes dragged on the floor. Fire needles of pain shot through his body, and he heard himself cry out.

"Morri, it's ill. You will kill it that way, and then She won't have anyone to question," the soft voice admonished.

Strong arms slid around Diego, and he found himself cradled against a hard-muscled, bare chest. "Finn?" he whispered.

The deep voice rumbling from that chest was definitely not Finn's, though. "It has expended its strength. There is no danger while it is so weak. Come. No more foolishness."

Diego let his head rest against a broad shoulder and closed his eyes, certain this was all some strange dream. When he woke up, most likely in the hospital, he would have to figure out what to do about Finn.

What was he going to do? He couldn't simply kick Finn out. He had no one else in the world and nowhere to go, except the river. The image of Finn wrapped around that girl surfaced again and sent a jolt of pain through him. How could he ever trust him again, no matter what promises he made? The thought bored a hole in his heart.

The surrounding air and light changed, so Diego opened his eyes again. A breeze ruffled his hair, and trees towered high above in a cathedral canopy. Vegetation ran riot with huge ferns, climbing vines and fantastic flowers of all descriptions competing for space. Everything seemed bathed in a soft, green glow, and a fine mist hugged the ground.

This is the forest primeval... So it seemed to him, as if the world were fresh and new again. He never recalled having such a vivid, sensory dream before. It had to be a dream, of course, because the progress of his little party through the woods was completely silent, without a single rustle or cracked twig. If only his dream would stop hurting so damn much.

Voices drifted to him from up ahead, the sounds of laughter and soft conversation. Suddenly the voices surrounded them, strange ones, some tiny and impossibly high-pitched, which whizzed by his ear and were gone, some melodious and fluid like cascades of bells.

His bearer stopped and placed him on the ground with the whispered command, "Stay down if you value your life, little man."

I couldn't get up if my life depended on it.

Diego nodded, trying to focus on the scene in front of him. He lay in front of a giant oak, its trunk massive enough to hide two tanks set side by side. Its exposed roots had curled and twisted into fantastic shapes, creating the illusion of statuary and furniture. Shining beings, mostly naked, perched on some of the benches and in the midst of them, on an elevated root gnarled into a throne shape, lounged the most striking woman Diego had ever seen.

A mass of fern-green hair crowned delicate, cool features, one decidedly pointed ear tip visible. A wispy bit of cobweb-thin material covered her from shoulder to hip, leaving one perfect breast exposed. The nipple, pale against her golden skin, had no aureole. Even fully clothed and covered, her eyes would have given her nonhuman origin away. Deep brown with black centers, they resembled a bear's eyes, without whites or visible irises.

Her voice, rich and husky, filled the clearing. "What have you brought me, my Lugh? Is it present or prisoner?"

"Grandmother, this is the one Morrigan found by the rent in the Veil." The male who had carried Diego spoke.

Diego turned his head for a better look, expecting another of the tall, slender beings. Lugh was tall, easily as tall as Finn, and had the same tipped ears and animal eyes as the others, but he was deep-chested and heavier built. When he moved a step forward, Diego had a shock. His muscular legs ended in cloven hooves.

"Morrigan? Is this human the sorcerer who ripped through what should have been impenetrable?"

"It was not the act of any fae, Light of the World," the rasping voice answered. She, too, was different from the others—ice-pale and sharp-featured, with long claws on her fingers that clicked together as she spoke. "An act of slovenly destruction, completely without finesse or beauty. Only a human would do such a thing."

"Yes. But was it this human?" The queen's tone implied she thought it unlikely, and Diego felt a flush rise up his throat.

She flowed from her throne toward him, her tread so light she did not bend a single blade of grass. Warmth and compassion shone from her eyes, and Diego felt his apprehension melt. She sat down beside him and ran a soft hand through his hair.

"I am Danu," she said, her voice the murmur of leaves through the trees.

Danu…*Tuatha de Danaan*, the Children of Danu, was what some of the Celts had called the *sidhe. Not woman, sidhe, the faerie Queen.*

"Poor thing. I could take the pain. Do you want that?"

"Yes, *majestad*," he croaked out. "Please."

"So polite. Are you certain you are human?"

She drew his head to her breast, crooning softly, caressing his face and arms. The pain sluiced from him — the throbbing in his head, the fire in his muscles and joints. He moaned in relief, sagging in her arms. Her hand moved lower to rest on his stomach, and his cock stirred. Odd, since women didn't usually do anything for him, but since it was a dream…

"Now, my sweet, let's see what you have hidden from me," she whispered, a sudden chill in her voice.

He struggled to pull away, but her slender arms held him tight, frightening in their strength. She tapped at his mental walls, the ones Finn had always declared impossible to penetrate, then she yanked them down as if they were children's blocks.

"No, no, please, *majestad*, don't, please —" He squirmed and broke off with a scream as she reached inside and plundered his memories. Childhood memories of his mother, fumbling teenage sex, lovers and friends all tumbled by in dizzying succession. It felt as if she ripped through the compartments of his mind and turned them inside out, tossing things aside as she went. The pain she had taken away was nowhere near the agony of having his memories forcibly invaded.

The whirlwind of memories stopped abruptly on one of Finn. He lay in bed beside Diego, finger tracing his nipple. "My hero, you are so beautiful in the moonlight," Finn whispered before he leaned in to take the nipple in his mouth.

The queen dropped him and rose with a sharp cry. "Fionnachd! He has been with Fionnachd!"

Whispers erupted around the glade, rustling as of a thousand wings. Diego curled into a ball with his arms over his head. He felt violated, stripped bare and flayed.

Rough hands grabbed hold of his T-shirt and shook him. "Where is he?" Lugh shouted in his face. "What have you done with him?"

"I don't know, I don't know," he choked out. "We argued. I walked away. I don't know if he followed. *Dios*, I hope he didn't follow…"

"Lugh, go. If his human lover is here, Fionnachd may be on the other side still or has followed him through the tear." The queen's voice trembled. "By the Mother, to learn he lives after so long… Find him!"

Not a dream, not a dream. Carajo. *I'm on the other side of the Veil? How the hell…*

"Carry him back to the bower," she went on softly. "We will make some sense of all this."

Dizzy and exhausted from having his mind torn into, Diego let them take him without a struggle. He had the vague notion he was on shaky and dangerous ground. The *sidhe* didn't have human reactions or motives—

even Finn found them difficult to fathom at times. Any word or thought might cause offense, and an unintended insult could mean his death.

They placed him down on the same sort of bed where he had first woken, a green mound of soft moss. The queen came and sat down next to him, her head cocked to one side to regard him with a thoughtful expression.

"You are not head-blind like most humans. It would not have hurt you so if you were," she said softly.

Not quite an apology, but I guess that's the best you get from royalty.

Diego pulled in a slow breath, the agony in his head already receding. "I'm not good with having someone in my mind, *majestad*. Maybe there are things I could just answer for you?"

Her alien eyes blinked slowly. "You have been with him. Not for merely a night, I think. He has shown you how to share a memory?"

"Not...really, no." Diego scrubbed his hands over his face. "He took me into his Dreaming. No, that's not really right. I wandered in there myself, looking for him. He had memories there and he showed me how to reach for them, to see them."

"You followed him there?" A note of wonder crept into her voice. "You should not—" She took his hand, her skin cool and rose-petal soft. "There have been humans born, perhaps one or two in a century, with such power. If you can do this, you can easily make a gift to me of your memories of Fionnachd."

"Please, *majestad*, would you answer a question first? How did I get here?"

"That is a question I must have answered as well." She squeezed his fingers. "Concentrate, little one.

Think of how you met him and separate that memory. Surround it and contain it."

"What do I make the container out of?"

"Whatever you wish." She laughed. "It is your memory."

Diego chewed on his bottom lip as he brought to mind the first time he had seen Finn, filthy, starved and despairing on the rail of the Brooklyn Bridge. Lost in the Dreaming for seven hundred years, he had woken to a terrifying world he no longer recognized. With the way to the Otherworld shut, Finn had believed himself alone and exiled, in a world devoid of magical beings.

With this memory held at the forefront of his mind, Diego struggled to surround it with a film of clear thought, a bubble of bright, shifting hues.

"Now push it toward me." Her voice slid into his thoughts as silver notes.

He struggled a moment with the impossibility of physically moving a thought but soon he had it, the bubble encased memory drifting to her.

"Well done," she murmured as she examined the encapsulated thought. "Oh, my poor Fionnachd. If I had known…and what then?"

He continued to send her gifts of memory, small spots of time in iridescent bubbles until she had the whole of it, how Diego had discovered his refugee was a pooka, ill and half-mad from the city's pollution, and how they had gone north for Finn's health, where he had inadvertently woken the wendigo. He shared with her the wendigo's defeat as well, how the light of the world had helped him fill the frigid void of the monster's soul until it tore itself to pieces. Finally, he showed her the promise of faithfulness Finn had made him, his betrayal and the argument that had resulted in Diego's seizure.

"The lightning... I can't control it without him to guide me," he concluded miserably. "If he was following, I may have hurt him."

"You are his Taliesin," she told him with a soft smile. "You could not truly harm him." Her brow creased. "But your lightning has torn a hole in my Veil, a thing that should not be possible. You are more powerful than you know."

"So he's said many times, *majestad*," he answered bitterly. "But without control, it doesn't amount to much." *Without Finn...Dios...*

A taurean snort came from the thicket behind them. Diego expected to see a bull charging toward them, but it was Lugh returning.

"He is gone, Grandmother," he said.

Diego's heart gave a painful thud as he surged up. "No...no, please. He can't be dead."

Lugh gave him an odd look. "I said nothing about dead, little man. He was there, near the tear you made in the Veil, and now he is gone."

"And where has he gone?" Danu asked with exaggerated patience. "You tracked him?"

"I tried. There was no trail. Echoes of him lingered. But he has vanished."

Chapter Three

Balor's Court

Finn swam back to consciousness through murky dreams full of thunder and pain. The heavy stiffness along his spine told him the vertebrae had healed after a hard blow. Good thing his back knitted so quickly, as many times as it had been broken over the centuries.

He pulled in a deep breath. The air...

Puzzled, he tried another. *Clean. The air is clean.* His eyes flew open and showed him a world tinged in green, with sunlight filtered gently through a profusion of leaves.

With a soft cry of wonder, he leaped to his feet and buried his nose in the leaves. They held no taint of pollution, no sharp scent of iron, no hint of humans.

"I'm home," he whispered to the leaves. "Sweet goddesses of stream and pool, I'm ho—"

A hard blow took him from behind and a heavy body slammed him to the ground. Finn snarled and twisted around to grapple with his assailant, only to be clubbed over the head from various angles. The need to shield his head with his arms rendered him unable to see how many or who hit him.

This losing consciousness is becoming a nuisance.

"Cover the trail. Herself will come before long," a rough growl ordered.

That voice... Finn struggled with the familiar sound, but failed to come up with an answer before the dark closed back in.

* * * *

Hollow echoes of grunts and snorts reached him first, his impression of a cavernous space confirmed when he opened his eyes.

Hang it all, I despise caves.

His head ached. Everything ached. When he tried to move to curl into a ball, his arms and legs refused to obey him. Lying on his side, hogtied and bruised on a cold, rock floor was simply not a pleasant way to wake.

He would have to become something tiny and hide until he puzzled out what had happened. Eyes squeezed shut, he tried to shift to darkling beetle. Pain skittered over his skin instead of magic, though, and he twisted to see what bound him. Braided grass lay against his skin, wrapped tight with thicker, iron-shot rope. The iron prevented his shifting and explained why he felt so dreadful.

Now what had he fallen into? He lifted his head for a frantic look around, worry for Diego overcoming his native caution.

"The traitor wakes," a voice hissed nearby.

The cavern erupted in howls and squeals, squawks and growls, repeating the words over and over, the cacophony creating a psychic ram battering against Finn's mind.

"Diego!" he cried out in desperation, unable to locate him through the din.

"Silence!" a canyon-deep voice bellowed.

The cacophony faded to a few disgruntled mewls and peeps. Finn lifted his head again to search for that voice, the one from his capture, and found the speaker with little effort. The throne of polished granite, though large enough for three Finns to sit side by side, barely contained his massive frame. A crest of boar bristles crowned the huge head rather than hair, fists large enough to crush a skull in each palm clenched on the stone. Two tusks, not terribly attractive but quite menacing, curved up from the corners of his mouth. Even after being knocked senseless, Finn knew the enthroned figure well, and if the rest of the identifying features had not been enough, the emerald-encrusted eye patch would have informed him in his most addled state.

"Balor." Finn hitched around so he faced the throne. "I suppose, given current circumstances, that you are not pleased to see me after my long absence?"

The Fomorian king's roar vibrated through the stone Finn lay on, and he winced as a stalactite crashed down in the open space between them.

"How dare you speak, filth!" Balor pointed a claw at him. "Rip out his tongue!"

Howls and lowing split the cavern's air into a thousand jagged pieces as his court took up the litany "rip out his tongue, rip out his tongue!" A Fomorian with a scale-covered head and fingers far too long for his palms crouched in front of him, hissing.

Finn swallowed against a suddenly dry-as-dust throat. "Please, if it's all the same to you, please don't trouble yourself." The tongue would grow back, of course, but the agony was something he could well do without.

"Lie still, Fionnachd. I will be quick." The scaled Fomorian's voice held a note of regret. "Bite, and I shall take your eyes as well."

"But what have I done?" Finn reared back from the reaching hands, not ready to submit to pain. His thoughts raced in desperate circles, trying to latch onto some incident, some bit of foolishness that would have caused Balor to be so angry. He had been furious with Finn before, but for seven hundred years? He failed to recall anything quite that deserving.

"What have you done?" Serpent-pale eyes blinked and the scaled head turned toward the throne. "Balor, he wishes to know what he has done."

An ominous crack echoed through the cavern. Balor rose slowly, a chunk of broken granite clutched in each fist. "Lying, treacherous, murderous scum," Balor growled, each word increasing in volume until he reached a bone-jarring roar. "Your honeyed words will not be allowed to sway hearts this time!"

"Heart of the Earth, what have I done?" Finn cried out, ignoring the command not to speak. "But tell me, and I will atone in whatever way you choose!"

Balor's one visible eye pinned him, crimson fire and more than half-mad. "Can you bring my son back? Do you have some new trick that will restore the dead?"

Finn blinked, as stunned as if someone had slammed a rock between his eyes. "Nuada...has died?"

A moment too late, he realized his mistake as Balor charged. A huge clawed hand closed around his throat and lifted him so he hung, hogtied and fighting for air in the Fomorian king's grip.

I saw this on the picture box once...

Not a fortuitous thought, since that dangling person had expired with eyes bulging and a snapped neck.

"You killed him!"

The spit from Balor's rage was perhaps the least of his problems, but he did wish his breath wasn't quite so foul. *The things that run through one's mind at a moment of imminent death are completely irrelevant and unhelpful.*

"I did not...kill him..." Finn rasped, his sight darkening. "He was...my friend."

"Which is why your treachery was so abominable! He loved you and you led them to him!"

Perhaps it was the shaking that accompanied the strangulation and the creeping nausea of the iron sickness, but Finn failed to find any sense in the explanation.

"Who?" he choked out.

"The cursed humans!"

The scaled one — *goddesses, he has a name, but I can't remember it* — cocked his head to one side and hissed. "They shot him through the heart with iron arrows. Then staked him to the ground so he could not slip through the Veil for help. Nuada died screaming. Your scent was on the humans when Balor found them to rip them apart."

"When?" *So blasted dizzy.*

"The day you disappeared." Yellow eyes, vertical pupils dilated, regarded him with more curiosity than hostility. "Herself called and called for you. You were nowhere to be found. Even she thought the worst."

Finn stopped struggling, shock and horror overriding pain. Nuada the Beautiful was dead, had been dead for centuries and had died at the hands of the same humans who had tortured him and ripped his heart out, metaphorically, then quite literally.

He gathered the memory of that day to the forefront of his mind, all the anguish and torment, the soul-shattering agony of watching his love burned as a witch and the equally horrifying agony of being hacked to bits with iron hatchets. With his last bit of fading strength, he hurled the memory at Balor just as the darkness closed over him.

A grunt and a muted roar told him he had hit his target. The grip on his throat loosened, and he fell for what seemed an inordinate amount of time. Falling, falling… Oh, no, perhaps not. His cheek rested on cold stone again.

"…a true memory?"

"Without a doubt, Father," a feline purr answered Balor. "You have accused Fionnachd wrongly, and he has suffered so."

Eithne.

"And why did he live?" Balor growled. "Your brother is dead, and that *pooka* lives."

"And tormenting him with iron will help? The idiot humans threw the pieces of him in the water, Father. He lives only because of their stupidity."

Balor issued a grunt and a long sigh, followed by, "Let him loose."

Most likely the closest Finn would get to an apology from the Fomorian king, but he would make no complaint. Relief flooded through him as the ropes were removed, but he stayed on the floor, curled into a ball with his arms over his head, fighting the urge to whimper. His head throbbed and his throat hurt, and where in all hells was Diego? Not that his absence was an entirely bad thing, given Balor's disposition toward humans at that moment, but Diego waking up alone in an unfamiliar place after a seizure worried him. Unless they held him somewhere else in their honeycombed caverns, which could be much worse.

"Fionnachd?" A furred hand caressed his hair. "Why do you come now? And how did you pierce the Veil?"

They don't know. They don't have him. He walled off his thoughts and resolved not to give them any more information until he understood the lay of the land better. He coughed, cleared his throat and found a rasping version of his voice. "I emerged from the Dreaming. I was alone."

He uncurled far enough to see Eithne, her lovely pointed black ears swiveling atop her head as she listened. One never lied to Eithne, she would know, but one could tell bits of truth. "I called and called. No one came and the way through was closed to me."

She took his head in her lap, purring to comfort him.

"There was a magical storm. It hurled me through." He ended on another cough, wondering how long his throat would take to heal.

A snort came from far above him. "He still reeks of humans."

"The whole outer world reeks of humans, Balor. And their machines. And their poisons." One cough led to another, and he soon lost the ability to speak entirely.

"Poor Fionnachd." Eithne let out a little growl. "For shame, Father. Leave him be."

"He has changed." Balor's deep voice another degree. "He has a certain strength that was not there before."

"Let him recover, and I'm sure he will tell us everything that has happened."

Balor's snort was still angry, but Eithne, as she always did, would get her way.

Chapter Four

Lugh

"I think I'll stay here, if that's all right." Diego patted the rock beside him.

The two winged beings, 'pixies' he supposed would be the best word, collapsed into each other's arms in gales of laughter.

"I'm sorry, did I say something funny?"

They sputtered, looked at each other and lost it all over again. "You can't bathe from there!" the blue one finally hooted, holding his—*her…their?*—sides.

"I'm not sure I want to bathe right now."

The green one tossed long wet hair over one shoulder. "Herself said to have you bathe. And you stink. So you should." She—the movements, the tone, suggested 'she'—fingered his shirtsleeve. "Do you bathe in your overskin?"

Heat rose up his throat. "I don't, ah, usually take my overskin off in front of strangers. I'm sorry. I'm just not comfortable."

"Strangers? But we met, oh, ages ago." The green one's smile seemed indulgent.

"Yes, this morning, right. But for humans, that's still strangers."

The two exchanged an odd look. The blue one's wings drooped in a dejected way. "You don't even remember our names, do you?"

Did you give me your names? "I'm sorry, please don't be offended. If you told me, I don't remember."

The green one whispered in the blue one's ear. He giggled and brightened, which normally might only have been an expression, while for the pixie it was a phenomenon of light and color. A soft glow suffused his skin, his blue ratcheting up the spectrum from cornflower to cerulean.

"Humans," he said with a nod and put a hand over his heart. "Scath."

The green one nuzzled at Scath's throat while she pointed to herself. "Croi."

They forgot him for a moment as they twined around each other, her leg sliding up around his hip, his hands cupping her firm little butt. Their lips met in a desperate kiss as if they had been separated for months.

Tiny bell voices had woken Diego that morning, words just beyond human hearing tugging him from sleep. Two firefly lights had danced before his eyes when he opened them, a feeling of well-being surrounding him despite his sore muscles and his aching head. The little lights had vanished and these two charming creatures appeared in their place, roughly human in shape and size, with delicate features and translucent wings. They'd brought him berries and water, teasing him gently while he ate, then had taken his hands and dragged him to a lily-strewn pool, clear as glass, with a little waterfall chuckling at the far end.

Now Diego took an avid interest in the trees and tried not to blush harder. Not that he could imagine them actually doing anything together since the mound between their legs was identically smooth and sexless. They possessed nothing to have sex with unless…

What if their mouths are *their sex organs?*

He rose to return to the bower, unwilling to play the voyeur. They abruptly broke off their tender immersion in each other and flew to him, gossamer wings whirring hummingbird fashion.

"Come, we are not strangers," Croi whispered in his ear as she tugged Diego's shirt from his jeans.

"We know you, Taliesin," Scath murmured with a nuzzle to his jaw, his fingers making quick work of Diego's fly.

The name forced the puzzle pieces into place. "You…know me? From before? From a different life?"

"A different form. Always the same life. We would know your life if you were a stone." Croi kissed the tip of his ear.

They had taken advantage of his distraction to pull his T-shirt off. Scath's hands slipped below his waistband and slid Diego's jeans and boxers down to his knees.

"Please don't—" Diego's breath hitched when Croi's delicate fingers traced his nipple. *How do I tell them no without offending them?*

Scath laughed, a shimmering of silver bells, and seized his hands. "Come! We are here to bathe you, and you still haven't put a toe in."

Forced to either step out of his clothes or fall on his face, Diego stumbled after, leaving sneakers, jeans and boxers in a little trail down the bank.

"Wait, wait!" he called out, laughing, as they reached the water's edge. Gently, he retrieved one of his hands from Scath's and slipped off his socks. "Nothing worse than wet socks."

"You won't need your foot coverings," Croi assured him.

"I think I'd rather have them when we're done. Thorns and stones and things. I can't fly like you." Diego took her offered hand and stepped gingerly into the pool, expecting cold water and mud between his toes. His breath caught as his foot sank into warm, soft sand, the sensation so unexpected he lurched sideways into Scath's arms. The pixie's chest felt cool, like Finn's would have.

Finn…

"Oh, something hurts him! What is it?" Croi stroked his hair, crooning to him.

Diego swallowed against the lump in his throat. "Nothing, please, I'm fine. I just thought of something. Someone."

"Fionnachd," Scath supplied for him. "He wrenches your heart." He moved behind Diego, blue glow visible as a trail for the eye.

A splash and a soft susurration later, Scath's hand touched Diego's back, stroking something into his skin like a fine-grained exfoliate accompanied by the scent of lilies.

"What's that?" Diego tried to twist his head to see.

"The sand." Croi's eyes sparkled with gentle mirth. "It will cleanse you. Take the human stink away."

"I smell that bad?"

Croi bent to gather a handful of sand from the pool bed and began working on Diego's chest in slow circles. "It is...different than how humans used to smell. Sharper. With many strange notes in the scent. As if you were poisoned by many small, evil spells."

Her hands moved lower to caress the muscles of his abdomen.

"You don't have to —" Diego choked off with a gasp and jerked forward as Scath's hands cupped his backside, his fingers sliding into the crease in an intimate caress. "Stop that!" He reached back to grab Scath's wrist, brought up short again as Croi cupped his balls. "*Dios!* Stop! Please..."

He staggered sideways, trying to evade their ever bolder hands, tripped over someone's foot, and fell headlong into the water. Gasping and sputtering, he resurfaced to the sound of deep, resonant laughter from the bank.

"The *féileacán* do not understand your reticence, little man." Lugh leaned against a tree trunk, grinning as he wiped tears of mirth from his eyes. "For them, there is no distinction between a friendly touch and one meant to inflame desire."

No distinction? So when I held their hands... Diego stayed where he was, sitting on the sand, submerged to mid-chest. "Holy shit." He looked up at Scath, his blue head tilted to one side in a puzzled way. "I didn't...that is, I don't...I didn't realize. I'm sorry. I can't..." He trailed off as Lugh began to laugh again.

"Go, little ones," Lugh said with an undignified snort. "Leave him with me. You confound him."

"We were only doing as She asked," Croi said in a small voice.

"And he enjoyed our company," Scath added, chin raised. "His root grew stiff."

Diego covered his crotch with both hands out of reflex, trying to will his cock out of its semi-erect state. Naturally, thinking about it had the opposite effect.

"Still, he is human and will be unhappy soon if you persist." Lugh pushed off the tree, arms crossed over his massive chest. "Fly away, pretties. You will see him again soon."

A blue hand and a green one ran quickly over his shoulder before Scath and Croi vanished, replaced by the firefly lights. Now that he understood their nature, Diego could just make out the tiny winged forms within the lights as they darted away.

"Thank you," Diego said, though he made no move to get out of the water. Lugh had been kind to him, had defended him from the *sidhe* with the claws and stood by him in the glade. Caution threaded through his gratitude, though. *What does he want from me?*

Lugh picked a cloth up from the ground and shook it out. "Come. I know you are body-shy. Wrap this around you. I would speak with you."

Here it comes, then. Diego forced himself to take a deep breath and stepped from the pool into the blanket Lugh offered. The material settled light and soft around his shoulders, a weave so fine he wondered if it was woven at all. Lugh settled on a nearby rock, no longer looming, so Diego followed suit and sat down on the next rock over with the blanket held tight around him.

"You have forgotten everything." Lugh's tone was steady but resigned.

"I suppose I have. You mean past lives, don't you? Who I was and what I knew before?"

"You are Taliesin, who has lived as much among the fae as among your own kind. Sometimes you recall, other times not." Lugh shrugged, a casual lift of his shoulders that caused one of his four braids to fall forward onto his chest.

Diego found his eyes drawn to the glossy black sheen of it, his mind wandering to what it might feel like. "Yes, I've forgotten. I only know what Finn told me and showed me."

"I did not recognize you with your flows so muted and your spirit so wounded." Lugh's voice grew soft. He leaned forward, arms on his knees. "There was a time you found joy in my arms."

"Oh. Um." Diego tugged the blanket closer. The short green kilt Lugh wore did nothing to hide the huge bulge of his erection. His whole body was huge, his hands large enough to crush a pumpkin. If he wanted to force the issue, there wouldn't be a lot of choice. "I... Look, you're incredibly handsome—"

"Don't be afraid. I won't harm you. My word of honor." Lugh moved closer and reached out to put a hand on Diego's knee. "Your heart is full of pain. Let me help."

"Please, I'm sorry." He broke off in confusion when Lugh moved over to his rock and wrapped strong arms around him. It would be so easy to lean into that embrace, to close the distance to the lush, full lips above him, to give in to this powerful, beautiful otherworldly being. "I can't. You're hot as hell, but I can't. I'd just be going through the motions, and I think you want more than that. Finn—"

Lugh pulled back with a sharp laugh. "After he betrayed you, broke your heart? You still remain faithful to him? To a pooka who has no more understanding of faithfulness than a honeybee has?"

"Yes," Diego whispered, ashamed that he trembled and that the backs of his eyes stung.

"Poor little man." Lugh leaned forward but only to plant a soft kiss on his forehead. "Poor, beautiful little man." One hand lifted to cup Diego's chin, black eyes searching his face. "I could—"

With a sharp cry, Lugh broke off and jerked away, doubled over with his arms wrapped around his stomach.

Did I hurt him somehow? Diego sat stunned, watching the powerful body writhe on the ground, the black hooves beating against the nearest rock. No, he would have felt the magic run through him and no lightning had sparked from his fingers. He slid off his rock and knelt beside Lugh, one hand on his shoulder. "Easy, easy, what can I do? What hurts?"

"Sweet mother," Lugh gasped out. "Gods...eaten alive..."

Desperate, unable to think what else to do, Diego concentrated on an image of Danu, thinking as hard as he could of her, calling out to her in his mind.

The answer came soft but clear, *"I am coming."*

Chapter Five

Challenge

Finn lay on a round cushion filled with eiderdown, wonderfully soft for his aching body and just the right size to curl up comfortably. Eithne stayed with him, worry etched around her amber eyes.

"I am feeling much improved, truly," he tried to reassure her, but another fit of coughing ruined it.

She stroked his hair and waited until he quieted. "How did you come back through the Veil, Fionnachd?"

"I have told you."

"Mm, yes. In part."

She knows me too well, damn the luck. He gazed up into eyes with vertical pupils. She had loved him long ago, though with a comfortable, now-and-then sort of love. It was her compassion he needed to appeal to instead — the very core of her nature.

"I will tell you a thing, but you must not tell your father. Lives may be at stake." He let his rasping voice waver. "Eithne, I have done a terrible thing."

Her ears dropped flat against her skull. "What have you done? If you hurt my family…"

"No, no, it was in the outer world. Before I came here."

"Who is Diego?" she asked abruptly.

"Pardon?"

"The name you called out when you woke. You cried out 'Diego!' Such anguish in a single word."

Of course she had heard, despite all the noise in the cavern. Ah, well, best simply to plunge in. "He is my Taliesin. The goddesses of storm and tide brought me across the ocean to find him when I woke from the Dreaming. I did not know it then, but there he was. His name is Diego in this life." He reached out to take her hand. "Was there a human found nearby? Where I crossed?"

Eithne's brows drew together. "There was human scent, but it was on you. So we thought."

He told her about the argument and Diego's seizures, which released the lightning. "He is more powerful in this life than ever before. Though he has no skill to use it. It must have been his own storm which ripped through the Veil."

She took her bottom lip between her teeth. "There was no sign of anyone near the tear but you. Fionnachd—"

"No! He must be there. We must look for him!"

"There was no one. The trackers would have found him had he lain anywhere nearby." Her voice dropped to a tender murmur. "His storm was so powerful, and if he had no control, he most likely destroyed himself."

"It cannot be! I would have felt him die!"

"You were unconscious."

"But I would know! Eithne!" Crushed beneath the terrible realization, he curled into a ball and wailed. "No, no, no, no, *no!*"

"Fionnachd, he was human. They have such brief lives, as it is." She held out her arms to him and he shifted into wildcat form to crawl into her lap, where he howled pitiably. "Hush, hush, my poor dear." She held him close, her rough tongue washing his face and ears to comfort him.

"But we were to have years together this time!" He sent his frantic thoughts to her. *"The witch hunts were over, and he found a house for us in the woods, and I made him promises! I told him not to go to the poisoned city. Oh, gods, why did he go?"*

"Time does not stop even for us, dearheart," she murmured. "A day, a week, a year — if you have a human lover, you must accept the time you are granted."

Finn mewled and cried, kneading at her arm with both paws in his distress. It was too soon, too bloody soon, and to have his Taliesin ripped away so violently again, in a moment of pain and anguish, was too much.

With an ear-splitting howl, he shifted back to his bipedal form so he could bury his head in her lap and weep. "Oh, my heart, my light, my hero…how can this be? Mother of us all, I cannot bear it…not again…"

She held him and rocked him, sending the flows of her magic over him in waves, pressing him down into sleep.

* * * *

When Finn woke again, his heart still felt as if someone had torn into it with rusted shears, but he steeled himself against the pain, determined not to give into despair this time. A possibility occurred to him that Eithne had not considered. Diego might still be in the outer world. The opening of the Veil did not mean both of them had been hurled through.

He had to believe Diego still lived. He would know if his love, his light, had died, wouldn't he? Though he would be hurt and ill after his seizure, Diego would have his little speaking machine with him, *the cell phone*, and he would summon help. Finn simply needed to find a way back to him.

Yes, simplicity itself, you idiot. First get out from under Balor's watchful eye, then find a way to break back through the Veil, which has since closed, then find where Diego has gone and beg his understanding and forgiveness... Oh, yes, simple as swimming upstream in a spring flood with boulders tied to your feet.

Not that he truly needed forgiveness. Blast it all, he hadn't done anything wrong. It had only appeared so.

He sighed into his cushion. He must take one gnarled problem at a time. The first thing to discover would be whether he was ailing guest or prisoner. The former was unlikely, since Balor would have ordered him placed in a pool or stream if he truly had been concerned about Finn's health. How much freedom did he have?

Moving silently, he slid from his cushion and poked his head out of his little cavern niche. *Nothing to the left.* He turned his head right and jerked back when he encountered a pair of golden, reptilian eyes.

"Nathair." Yes, that was the scaled one's name. He had little scent, or he would not have been such a surprise.

"Fionnachd." The forked tongued flickered out, tasting the air.

"You haven't come for my tongue, have you?" Finn smiled and leaned against the wall, carefully nonchalant.

"Not today. I have been charged with your safekeeping while you are with us." A soft, repeated hiss escaped him that could have been a laugh. "To keep you from your usual mischief, Balor says. Where do you wish to go?"

Home, to Diego and my forest and our house. "I am hungry, and find neither rocks nor feathers agree with me."

Yes, the little hisses were laughter. Amusement rolled off Nathair in little wavelets. *More of a guardian than a jailer. Or what is that word? A babysitter.*

"It seems a mite quiet today," Finn began, to try to get his escort talking.

"Oh, yes. Everyone is in the Great Hall."

"Some celebration?"

Nathair turned his scaled head to give him a long look, tongue flicking. "Eithne has told you nothing?"

"What should she have told me?"

They walked in silence a few yards, down a narrow hallway of gleaming black rock, carved in complicated designs that made the eye dizzy.

When he finally spoke, Nathair's voice was hesitant and contemplative. "Balor has sent an ultimatum to Herself. He has had enough of negotiations. They await Her answer."

"What question is she to answer?"

"The one he has asked her since she closed the Veil. Balor wants the outer world back. He will either have the way opened and make war with the humans to take it back, or he will have war here with the *sidhe*."

Finn shivered. War with humans had evolved in terrifying ways since the days of swords and crossbows. Balor had no idea...and yet, if he meant to force a way back, perhaps there was a way to Diego in it as well, terrible as it sounded.

"You are not pleased with the thought of battle?"

"I am no warrior." Nathair's nostrils shut tight, then opened on a soft exhalation. "Leave me to my flowers and my herbs. We have had enough bloodshed over the centuries. I do not relish more."

They turned a corner, and Finn's breath caught. The tunnel suddenly opened before them into a massive cavern, the sun streaming in through its uncapped roof. Flowering trees grew here, surrounded by patches of golden wheat and rye, fields of scarlet poppies and delicate feverfew, fennel, kale, beans and root vegetables, all in neatly ordered rows. The scent of lilac and apple blossoms drifted to him on the breeze.

"Your garden?" Finn murmured in wonder.

Nathair nodded. "Eat as you will, but have a care that you don't trample the plants."

With an offended sniff, Finn shifted to raven and flew straight for the apple tree with the plumpest fruit. He landed, shifted back, and settled comfortably in the crook of a branch to munch on his prize. Nathair sat down amidst the tree's roots to wait for him, seemingly content to bask in the sun, his face turned up toward the light, green scales gleaming.

"Nathair?"

"Hmm?"

"Why would Balor wish to war with the humans? If he wishes to return, why not live as we always did?"

Golden eyes blinked up at him, puzzled and solemn. "Did you not just return from the outer world, Fionnachd?"

"Yes."

"And did you not say it was poisoned?"

"Yes, though some places more than others." Finn considered the line of questioning for a moment. "How long ago did Danu close the Veil?"

Nathair stretched out in the sun, hands behind his head, the position showing the sleek muscles of his arms and torso off to good advantage.

Goddesses, he is lovely...

"A little more than a hundred years ago." Nathair let out a soft hiss. "The humans began to build these horrible boxes that belched foul smoke into the air. The skies grew dark. Some of the *féileacán* fell to the ground, ill and unable to fly. Danu called us all home. She said the humans were too numerous and multiplied more every year, and that the outer world would soon be the death of us all. Balor did not like it, but she gave him little choice. She closed the way, and did so in such a manner that she claimed it could not be undone."

"And yet I am here."

"So you are."

"And Balor thinks if he slays all the humans, the world might be clean again?"

"Not immediately, but someday, yes."

Finn finished his second apple before he leaped down to the ground. "I think I must have a long, earnest talk with Balor about the nature and number of modern humans."

Nathair rose and stretched in one graceful, sinuous motion. "Come. I have someone else I must see to." He plucked two ripe peaches from a tree and a wheat stalk from the patch as they passed, and led Finn from the garden.

They wound their way back through the maze of passages. Without the sky above him, Finn's sense of direction soon went awry. If he tried to get out of the caverns on his own, he would wander forever. Nathair stopped at a sleeping niche larger than the one Finn had been given.

The dim light afforded by phosphorescent stones provided more than enough for nocturnal eyes to make out the room's occupant. A wolf-headed Fomorian lay sprawled on a nest of blankets. His large frame could have rivaled Balor's, had it not been for his wasted state — his arms and legs resembled long sticks, and ribs were painfully visible.

"Faolchú?" Finn whispered in horror. "Oh, sweet Mother, what has happened to you?"

"Our champion fell ill some months ago," Nathair explained. "He grows worse each day. Yesterday, I could not even force water between his teeth."

The clamor of a hundred voices shouting reached them from farther along the passageways in what could only have been the direction of the Great Hall.

"What would you wager — ?"

Nathair shook his head. "I can't take time to guess now. Come. Help me with him." He leaned down to speak into a gray-furred ear. "Faolchú, you must wake now. Fionnachd is here. He has come back to us."

A weak growl rumbled in a chest Finn recalled as broad and finely chiseled in better days. Sharp teeth showed as Faolchú whispered, "You lie, little serpent. The pooka is dead."

Finn knelt by his bed and ran a hand over the soft fur of his muzzle. "Truly, then, I do wish someone would tell me these things. I had no inkling I was dead."

"Is it you?" Fevered eyes opened to search his face, eyes that had been the color of a winter sky, now yellowed and rheumy. A trembling hand with broken claws came to rest on Finn's arm. "Fionnachd?"

"It seems to do him good when you touch him," Nathair said, a speculative expression on his face. He stripped his wheat stalk and broke it at both ends to make a straw that he stabbed into one of the peaches. "This is more than he has moved for days. Sit behind him for me, prop him up against you."

"My poor friend, what have you done to yourself?" Finn murmured as he moved behind Faolchú and took him in his arms.

"You feel...different," Faolchú whispered. "Stronger." He nuzzled under Finn's chin, a subservient gesture the wolf champion would never have lowered himself to when he was whole and well.

"Here, take it." Nathair handed over the straw-pierced peach. "See if he will drink for you."

Faolchú's muzzle wrinkled in distaste and he turned his head away.

"Come now, braveheart." Finn bent to kiss his nose. "It's not deer's blood, but you need aught to keep you with us, eh?"

The lupine eyes closed, and Finn felt a sting of defeat. For a long moment, Faolchú lay still, his breathing ragged and weak. Then he drew a deep, shuddering sigh, and another. His hand closed over Finn's wrist, broken claws digging into his skin. He turned his head and fastened his lips around the straw to drink, little growls of satisfaction rumbling in his chest.

Voices sounded in the passageway outside.

"How would she know, Father? She would not do such a thing!" Eithne shouted.

"Of course she knows! Why else send such an answer?" Balor roared.

They rounded the corner and stopped short in the niche's archway with identical expressions of shock.

"He woke for Fionnachd. Reached for him. Drinks for him," Nathair explained calmly. He cocked his head. "What has happened?"

Balor recovered first, gnashing his tusks. "She sends an answer and it is no answer at all. I demand that she choose one thing or the other and instead she issues challenge! She must know my champion lies near death, or she would not have done so!"

"I still hear well enough, Heart of the Earth," Faolchú said in an unhappy whisper.

"He speaks." Balor's one visible eye blinked. "He looks at me and knows me. How is this when this morning he could only growl in pain?"

"As I said, it is Fionnachd," Nathair repeated in his even, soothing way. "Some magic I have not seen. A strength I have not encountered."

A wicked gleam entered Balor's eyes, and his smile made Finn's stomach lurch.

"Good, then," the Fomorian King said on a throaty laugh. "I think we have found a new champion."

Chapter Six

Unlikely and Reluctant

To Diego's consternation, Lugh's head ended up in his lap. Not that he minded helping someone in such obvious pain, but it was a little disconcerting having that powerful body so close with only a thin blanket between them.

Arms wrapped hard around his ribs, Lugh lay with his eyes squeezed shut. Tremors ran through him while furnace heat radiated from his skin. He seemed to derive some comfort from Diego's touch—at least, he had stopped writhing and thrashing.

A rustle of leaves drew his attention. Diego squinted in the soft, green-filtered light, trying to make out a figure hurtling toward them through the trees. Quick glimpses gave him the impression of something huge and...shaggy? When he blinked, it was gone.

"My poor Lugh."

Diego jumped at Danu's voice so suddenly by his ear. She knelt beside them, running her hands over Lugh with a worried frown. "How long?"

"It just started, *majestad*," Diego murmured, afraid that even a loud sound might hurt Lugh. "One moment he was fine, the next he was on the ground."

Two more *sidhe* appeared as if they had dropped from the sky. *Maybe they did.* Both tall and slender, they looked too graceful and willowy to possess much strength, but they scooped Lugh up between them without any apparent effort.

With a sharp cry, Lugh twisted in their arms, reaching for Diego. His eyes rolled, more white than black.

Like a wounded bull. Diego fought against the unbidden image of the end of a bullfight, the beautiful animal on his knees with rivulets of blood running down his shoulders.

Danu's voice nudged him back to reality. "Take his hand, Diego."

He closed his fingers gently around Lugh's, and immediately the massive body relaxed. "Is it serious, *majestad*?" He looked up to find her watching him with an unreadable expression.

"Come. He needs rest. You will stay with him."

The non-answer worried Diego more than anything else had that odd morning.

With his hand enveloped in Lugh's grip, Diego walked beside the *sidhe* as they wended through the trees and up a rise. They climbed until they reached a shallow cave carved out of the hillside just large enough for someone Lugh's size to sit up comfortably. Honeysuckle framed the entrance, suffusing the air with its bright fragrance.

The *sidhe* placed Lugh on the moss bed just inside the cave and stepped back to give Diego room to settle beside him.

"My clothes are still by the pool."

"You have little need for them," Danu told him softly.

I have plenty of need for them. Damn it, I feel so exposed. "What should I do?"

"You do what is necessary without thinking. Something in your flows soothes him, and you send streams of comfort to him without thought. You are your own sun when you feel someone in need."

He wasn't sure what she meant, but if his simply being there helped, he would stay.

"You can grant him sleep." Danu took his hands and placed them on Lugh's chest. "Open to him. Not too great a breach or his pain will overwhelm you. Just enough. Do you feel it?"

Diego gasped as pain crawled through him, heated needles that stabbed a thousand tattoos along his nerves. A sledgehammer pounded behind his eyes, and his stomach lurched.

"Careful, careful. Shore up your walls," Danu murmured. "You have it…yes, just enough to reach him."

The pain still threatened, but Diego found he could distance himself from it. Lugh's heart raced under his hands and a moan vibrated in his barrel chest as another wave of agony swept through him.

"So. Now feel the pulse of his blood, the scatter of his thoughts, and will them both to slow. Slow. Slower still…yes." Danu granted him a smile and patted his shoulder. "You have it. You learn so readily. Lie down with him, and he will sleep awhile. Perhaps he will be better when he wakes."

Perhaps? "But, *majestad*, what's wrong with him?"

"It will pass," she said. Then she stood and vanished.

Diego stretched out beside Lugh. "That's an annoying habit your grandmother has. Popping in and out."

Fast asleep, Lugh grunted and nestled closer to rest his head on Diego's shoulder and throw an arm over him.

Wonderful. Now I'm stuck. He rearranged his blanket to cover himself decently and tried not to think about the lonely knot under his heart. Was Finn somewhere safe? What would he have thought of this? Would he have discovered jealousy, or was the emotion too alien for him? It certainly would have been easy to misunderstand the situation, if Finn came up on him snuggled with Lugh in his bower.

An unhappy thought crept up on him. What if Finn had been in a similar predicament when he had surprised him with that girl? His memory brought up odds and ends he hadn't noticed in his jealous rage — a life jacket, the pile of soaked clothes.

"*Dios.* He wouldn't have..." Most likely not, since Finn wasn't given to playing hero. Still, there might have been something else going on, and he hadn't given Finn a chance. Angry, yes, he'd had every right, but he'd overreacted and caused all this. If he'd just acted like a sensible person, they might have made up by now and been together, at home. *Damn it, Finn, I'm sorry.*

Lugh whimpered in his sleep, and Diego fought to clamp down on his misery or risk telegraphing it. With the black ball of pain firmly lodged under his heart, he eventually drifted off as well.

He woke what could have been hours or minutes later, from a dream of Finn kissing him senseless. A large hand cupped his butt, squeezing and caressing his cheeks, and in his momentary disorientation, he moaned and pressed back.

"Are you awake?" The deep bass, so decidedly not Finn, jerked Diego out of his doze.

"Lugh, stop." He pulled back when he realized he lay snuggled all too intimately in powerful arms. It didn't help at all that he was rock-hard, his body obviously enjoying the attention.

Lugh shrugged and ceased his caresses. "It was you who kissed me, little man."

"I'm sorry. I was dreaming about Finn."

"Ah. Disappointing."

"You feel better?"

"Yes, a good deal. I think because of you." Lugh stroked a finger down Diego's nose. "Thank you."

Diego caught his hand before it wandered lower. "Look, I think we need to get something straight. You're gorgeous and I like you. I'm happy to be your friend, but that's it, all right? Not your lover. My heart's taken, even if his attention wanders sometimes."

"And if you never find him again?"

"God." Diego flopped onto his back. "I don't know. Never's a long time."

"I am patient."

The gentle humor in Lugh's smile made Diego chuckle despite himself. "You'll have to be. I'm glad you feel better. You scared the hell out of me."

"I am sorry for that."

They lay quietly side by side for a few minutes, until the backlog of curiosity caught up with Diego. "Lugh? You're not like the other *sidhe*. Is it too personal to ask why?"

"Personal? I'm not certain I understand the turn of phrase. Does the question offend me? No." Lugh propped his head on his hand. "My father was *sidhe*, my mother, Eithne, is Fomorian. It was the cause of the first war between the two courts, their love."

Diego chewed on that, dredging up all he could recall about ancient Irish myth. "So Fomorians really are beastly and misshapen? With goats' heads and things?"

"Beast-gifted, not beastly," Lugh said with an indulgent laugh. "The *sidhe* carry their animal spirits within—the one they are able to shift to. Fomorians carry the animal part of their nature in plain sight and have only one form."

"Oh. So you have hooves…but you can also shift?"

Lugh nodded.

"And what animal is part of you?"

"I think you know, little man."

The bull. He would be a beautiful, gleaming black bull… "Yes." He sifted things around for a moment. "And Morrigan?"

"She is the battle bird, the raven."

"I mean, she's half-Fomorian, too?"

"We have never gleaned who her mother was. And her father will not say. She is our Morri, fierce and proud." Lugh's head came up as if he listened to something. "Grandmother calls. We should go to the grove."

"You sure you're up to walking?"

"If we do not go…" Lugh flashed him a devilish grin. "Tongues will wag."

"Um, I'm not exactly dressed for company."

Lugh reached behind him for a carved wooden box out of which he pulled a length of red cloth. "It is strange to me that you feel your body will horrify others. You are beautiful, and would only be admired."

"I'd rather not be stared at naked, thanks."

With Lugh's help, he managed to wrap the kilt around his waist and fasten it securely. Since he was considerably shorter, it reached his knees, rather than ending mid-thigh, for which he was grateful.

Though he made a brave show of waving off Diego's help, Lugh needed a shoulder to lean on before they reached the bottom of the hill. By the time they reached the grove with the huge, ancient oak, he was pale and shaking.

"You should sit down," Diego whispered.

Out of breath, Lugh only nodded, and pulled Diego down onto a rock outcropping with a good view of the rest of the gathering. The *sidhe* had assembled — scores of them, tall and graceful. Scattered among them were other fae — smaller, gnarled-limbed beings, and the *féileacán*, always in pairs, and ethereal, translucent women who seemed to fade in and out of sight as they moved. Diego searched the crowd for anyone resembling Finn, but there was no one who looked like he could have been a pooka. He wondered if Finn was unique among the fae.

"Let him come among us," Danu proclaimed, and the crowd parted to admit a being who made Diego stare in wonder.

Thick, russet hair tumbled in waves to his waist. Sparkling eyes the color of new leaves swept the gathering with ironic confidence. His beauty was undeniable and would have set him apart, but that wasn't the half of it. Russet fur covered him from the waist down, behind him waved a luxurious, white-tipped tail, and where his feet should have been were delicate, black-nailed paws. He swaggered toward the throne, giving cheerful greetings as he went, even though the *sidhe* watched him with suspicion.

"Who's that?" Diego whispered.

"My cousin, Sionnach," Lugh answered. "He is the Fomorian king's herald, and most likely does not bring good news."

In a practiced, fluid motion, the herald knelt and laid his head on Danu's foot.

"You may speak, little fox," she prompted in a clear voice that reached the far edges of the grove.

Sionnach sat back, his tail curled around his knees. "Light of the World, King Balor Bane-Eye, He of the Hundred Spears, the Heart of the Earth, sends greetings." His melodic tenor paused. Whether for dramatic effect or to gather his courage, Diego was uncertain.

"Speak freely, little fox. The messenger is not the message. What would Balor Bane-Eye have of me?" Danu leaned her head on her palm.

"He states it is his final asking of that which must be asked." Sionnach shifted restlessly, raised his head, and closed his eyes. When he spoke again, another voice so unlike his own rumbled from his throat, the strangeness of it made Diego's heart pound.

In a gravelly bass as deep as the roots of thousand-year-old trees, he said, "What's it to be, Danu? Will you find a way to open the Veil for me? Something tore through it, so you can no longer tell me it's impossible. Or do I gather my warriors and meet you on the Field of Brón?"

Sionnach slumped, panting. One of the *sidhe* women brought him a wooden goblet and helped him drink, since he trembled from head to foot.

"Brusque and to the point, as always." Danu's voice remained even and calm, but Diego recognized the slight chill that signaled her displeasure. She sat motionless on her throne for several minutes, every being's attention riveted on her. Finally, she asked, "Are you recovered, Sionnach?"

The herald's smile could have melted glaciers. "Enough for your tender attentions, Light of the World."

Holy shit, he's flirting with her. Diego held his breath, suddenly afraid for him as Danu leaned forward and wrapped her hand around Sionnach's throat.

A soft white glow enveloped them both as Sionnach brought his hand up to cup Danu's and she began to speak. "Here is my answer, then. I will not willingly open the Veil for you, Balor of the Hundred Spears, for you only wish to bathe the outer world in blood. I will not meet you on the Field of Brón, for both our people have wept enough. I call challenge, a Champions' Match at Cian's Ford, five days hence. You must prevail there to have what you wish."

"Glorious Light," Sionnach murmured when the glow faded. "I hope you do not send me to my death with such a message."

Danu placed a soft kiss on his lips. "You are given a sacred trust, Sionnach Silver-Tongue. He will bellow and snarl, but he will not harm you."

"I will deliver your message faithfully, your voice to his ear."

"Go, little fox, and may you grace our glade again in happier days."

Sionnach rose and loped off, much less cheerful than when he'd arrived. Murmuring peppered the grove as all heads turned to Lugh.

"Grandmother, I am yours to command, as always." Lugh stood up, pale and unsteady. "But if this does not pass—"

Danu waved a hand to cut him off. "Not you, my brave Lugh. You are ill, and can hardly keep your feet."

"Who will take my place at the ford, then? You have no other champion and no one who can stand against Faolchú. And if you have no champion to field, there will be war the likes of which we have not seen in five thousand years."

Her laugh had a brittle edge. "Ah, but we do have one now. Diego Sandoval will take your place."

"What? *Majestad, está bromeando*? Are you crazy? I've never fought before! I wouldn't know which end of a spear is which, and I'm only half the size of most of the fae! I don't stand an ice cube's chance in hell!" Diego choked off when he realized he had surged to his feet, shouting. Everyone stared at him.

"Little one, a Champions' match is not fought with weapons," Danu explained in a patient, amused tone.

"What then? Do they play chess?"

Several of the fae laughed, and Diego's face flushed hot. At least some of the tension had drained from the air.

"It is a contest of magic," Lugh said as he sank back down onto his rock. "Of raw power, wit and skill. You do have the strength, Diego. More than any other here."

"But unless you plan on inducing a seizure and bonding with me to guide the magic, I can't do anything with it." Waffling between frustration and anger, Diego fought against telling Danu what she could do with her brilliant plan.

Lugh took his hand, his grip gentle and comforting. "Away from the poisons of the outer world, you have already healed so much, learned so much. I will teach you."

"Lugh's Five-Day Formula for Beginner Sorcerers?" What the hell was he supposed to do? Agree to this madness, or sit back and watch the fae slaughter each other... "She doesn't leave me a lot of choice, does she?"

"She rarely does," Lugh said with a rueful chuckle.

* * * *

"Heart of the Earth, it is a grand jest." Finn tried to laugh, but it caught in his suddenly dry throat.

"I have never been more serious," Balor growled. He seized Finn by the hair and dragged him into the corridor. "You will fight for me."

"You forget, Balor, I'm not yours to command." Finn shifted to water moccasin and sank his fangs into the King's hairy arm.

Balor roared and flung him against the far wall, where Finn shifted back to his own form and lay dazed.

"You are not mine, pooka, but you will fight for me." Balor raised a clawed hand, and a fist-sized rock flew across the corridor at Finn's head.

Finn jerked aside, and the rock landed a glancing blow on his shoulder. "Wrack and storm, Balor! I'm not one of you! I hide when the battles begin. I hate the whole valor and honor mess. I'll most likely shift to mudskipper and burrow into the riverbed with the first bolt of lightning Lugh sends at me."

"There is more to you than you pretend, Fionnachd." Balor's voice dropped to an ominous rumble as he raised both hands. "You will do this because you do not wish to see friends and lovers lying dead and dying. You have been apart from us all these centuries and have returned changed, or you would have already run away."

Another rock whizzed past Finn's ear and another struck his thigh with bone-bruising force. "Balor, please! Stop this!"

The barrage intensified until Finn found he could no longer dodge all the missiles. Larger and larger stones smashed into him. With a frustrated cry, he flung up his hands, wind whipping his hair into wild serpents as he hurled a wall of air at the boulder heading for his chest. It stopped mid-flight and fell harmless to the floor. More hurtled toward him. He blocked them in rapid succession. Distantly, he was shocked at his own actions, unable to recall having done such a thing before. It felt like something Diego would have done.

"Father, stop! How can he fight for you if you maim him?" Eithne shouted, but the attack only doubled in intensity.

Some of the smaller rocks got through, striking Finn's shoulder and side. Desperate, knowing he could keep shielding himself for only so long, he thought of Diego and drew on the memory of his beloved's magic flowing around him, through him. The air around him crackled, his hair stood on end, and he closed his eyes as lightning flew from his fingers.

A thunderclap rattled the caverns, followed by a heavy thud. Finn opened his eyes to see Balor sprawled on his back a hundred feet down the corridor. He stared at his hands, unable to believe what he had done, then sank to his knees to curl into a ball and whimper.

"Hush, Fionnachd, don't fret." Nathair wrapped cool, green-scaled arms around him.

"I didn't want to hurt him," Finn whispered, feeling absurdly close to tears.

"He pushed you to show you what you could do."

"I don't want to do this. I don't want to hurt Lugh."

Nathair pulled Finn's head to his shoulder. "I know, I know. But you need not harm him. Only best him. And you hear what will happen if you refuse."

"And what if I do this, and I lose?"

"Perhaps they will begin to talk again. Perhaps there will be war, after all."

"And if I win?"

Balor's deep bass rumbled down the corridor where he sat, dusting rock slivers from his arms. "If you win, my brave Champion, then you may claim any boon you please of me. And Herself will be honor-bond to open the Veil."

So I can go through and find Diego. Then I must, for him.

"Just this once, Heart of the Earth, I will fight for you."

Chapter Seven

Memory

"Do you feel ill, Fionnachd?"

Nathair's gentle question startled Finn from his brooding. He held Faolchú propped against his chest again while Nathair coaxed him into eating slivers of rabbit but Finn's thoughts had wandered far afield.

"I am well enough," he answered. "Considering the state of things."

"I only ask since you are so pale suddenly."

"Bloody caves. If there were somewhere to swim, a river or a pool, perhaps I might not feel so...."

"Confined?"

Finn nodded, not trusting his voice.

"Ah, well, if that's all it is." Nathair wiped the blood from Faolchú's muzzle and stood. "There is a place that might suit."

Finn slid back to return Faolchú to his blankets, but a rough-padded hand gripped his wrist.

"Take me," Faolchú whispered.

"Take you where?"

"With you. To the pool."

"Ah, someone else feels confined." Finn kissed his ear and knelt beside him. The magic danced over his skin in warm, blue eddies. His body stretched and shifted until a coal black horse knelt on the floor of Faolchú's sleeping niche. "If you can climb on my back, I will bear you there."

Faolchú drew in a deep shuddering breath and threw an arm across the arched equine neck. Every small effort a struggle, he panted and grunted as he forced his ailing body onto Finn's back. Nathair had to help him the last bit of the way, but at last he lay sprawled atop Finn's back, clawed fists tangled in his mane.

As smoothly as he could, Finn rose, an ache around his heart as he realized how easy it was to bear Faolchú. As if he prepared by decreasing in mass to release his tenuous hold on his long life until the first strong breeze would suddenly carry him away, all the strength and fire that had been Faolchú reduced to thistledown in the wind.

"Hold on as tight as you please," Finn told him. "But no snacking."

"Snacking?" Faolchú whispered.

"Don't bite my neck."

Faolchú let out a soft snort. "You used to like it."

"That, bucko, was a different sort of biting."

Nathair walked beside them, his hand on Faolchú's hip to steady him, and led them through the maze of corridors. When the scent of water reached Finn, his ears pricked forward and his step quickened. They turned a corner and once again the rock opened before them to reveal a massive cavern, like the Great Hall and Nathair's garden, but this one made Finn prance sideways and whicker in wonder.

A dark pool stretched out before them, smooth as polished obsidian. Gentle, moss-covered slopes bounded three sides of this pool, while the far wall rose in a sheer cliff of glittering rock, a mosaic of smoky hematite, rose quartz and mica. Phosphorescent minerals dotted the cavern's roof like stars on a winter's night, bathing the space in a soft, enchanted light.

"Do you like it, Fionnachd?" Nathair asked.

"Oh, I think it might do," Finn allowed in an airy tone.

Nathair chuckled and coaxed him down the bank to a spot where the moss grew thickest at the water's edge. Here, Finn knelt again and leaned to the side to help Faolchú roll off. As soon as his passenger lay safely on the ground, he tossed his head, shifted to salmon, and leaped into the water.

The dark pool was cool and soothing along his scales, as he let the water sluice away some of his misery. Under the surface, a different world lived and breathed—the soft music of the sightless fish, the endless fascination of the play of light filtering through the water.

I could stay here with the cavefish. Their world is beautiful and simple…if I could live without Diego.

He flipped his tail and shot upward, sleek body breaking the mirror surface of the pool. Ever-widening collisions of ripples fanned out from his impetuous movements. Finn stopped to watch, salmon head poking out of the water, and caught sight of Nathair and Faolchú on the bank. The massive wolf-head lay cradled in Nathair's lap, Faolchú's eyes closed as Nathair stroked his ears.

They are lovers. More than lovers. I have been so blind.

The epitome of the Alpha wolf, Faolchú had always made love where and with whom he pleased. He chose lovers as some chose breakfast, as his whims suited him, and few ever refused him. That he had finally found a mate in this gentle, scholarly garden snake astounded Finn, but the evidence lay before his eyes. He swam to the shallows and shifted back to his own form, sitting waist deep in the water and staring at the glittering cavern roof.

How hard it must have been for Nathair to watch his powerful champion failing, how heart-wrenching to know he could lose him soon. Why did the heart insist on love when inevitably loss followed?

A bit of song tugged at his memory — a winter's day when the winds howled around the house. Diego had insisted Finn remain inside and had turned on the boxes which played music. A woman's voice, rich and haunting, had filled the room.

"Who is it, my love?"

"That's 10,000 Maniacs."

Finn had blinked in astonishment. "Surely she is only one person. And she sounds quite sane."

"No, querido." Diego laughed. "That's the name of the musical group."

"Odd name."

"I guess. Lots of bands give themselves strange-sounding names so people will remember them." Diego crossed the room and knelt on the sofa, straddling Finn's lap. He leaned in to plant a soft kiss on Finn's lips. "I don't suppose you feel up to a little bit? Or are you too sleepy still?"

Finn slid his hands under Diego's shirt to caress up the smooth muscles of his back. "I think I could be persuaded."

Diego smiled that heartbreaking, beautiful smile and yanked Finn's T-shirt off over his head. He closed the distance again, soft lips pressing against Finn's insistently, begging for entry until Finn opened to him with a moan. Desperate fumbling had them both naked within moments. Wrestling for top, they tumbled to the floor. Finn ceded control in deference to his love's fierce need, rolling to his back and letting Diego part his thighs.

Their cocks rubbed together in delicious ways as Diego moved above him. Suddenly Finn found himself seized in a crushing embrace, Diego trembling against him.

"My hero, my heart, what is it? What distresses you so?" he murmured into Diego's thick, black curls.

"I love you so. My heart feels like it might shatter sometimes," Diego whispered.

The woman's voice sang about the man in one-nineteen taking tea all alone.

He stroked the smooth skin of Diego's buttocks, those lovely, rounded globes that fit so well in his hands. Soothing, encouraging, he waited until Diego pushed back toward his hands, rolling and grinding against him. Diego's lips fastened on his pulse point, and the room spun in dizzy, lurching circles as all the blood rushed to Finn's core.

"Take me, my love. Now. Make me howl."

Still shivering, Diego shifted, and with a fierce cry, impaled Finn on his rock-hard shaft. Finn arched and gasped, the momentary pain fading into a heated wave of need.

"Did I hurt you?"

"Hush. Don't stop."

Diego slowed, though, each thrust deeper than the last. He curled over to take Finn's nipple between his lips in a hard suck.

"Love, please…"

"Hmm?"

"More, faster, don't torture me so."

Finn cried out as Diego fisted his cock and drove in hard, hammering into him. The tight pressure built in Finn's groin until he did howl. The world exploded in a thousand bright *suns as he came, the woman's voice rising to a crescendo on the score to* Aida…

A cry echoed through the cavern as the memory overwhelmed Finn. Tears coursed down his cheeks, and he buried his face in his hands.

A splash behind him signaled Nathair's approach. His hand fell on Finn's shoulder. "This place was meant to cheer you, Fionnachd. Instead, you weep. Forgive me."

"No, no, the cavern is wondrous and soothing," Finn choked out. "I… There is someone I miss so terribly."

"Ah. Is it someone we can find for you?"

Finn shook his head. "No. I thank you, but he's on the other side."

Nathair stroked his hair. "Come lie down with us. You are heart-sore and weary." He tugged at Finn's hand until he rose out of the water and waded to the bank. Faolchú held out his arms, and Finn nestled into them, Nathair settling at his back. Naked and melancholy, the three of them clung together, afraid for each other and anxious over what might be. They slept huddled close like a litter of new pups, needing comfort and warmth most of all.

* * * *

"You block the flows, still," Lugh explained patiently. "You must reach out, open yourself to the magic, as you did with Fionnachd."

"I can't, damn it! You make it sound so easy, but I can't!" Diego flung back in frustration. The rock he had been trying to warm stayed stubbornly cold. "I can do little things here, but I can't just make the magic do whatever I want."

"You defeated an evil being of great power, pulled the flows in from all around you—"

"With *Finn*. During a freaking seizure. I was in the hospital for two weeks afterwards."

"It is pain you fear, then? Incapacitation?"

Diego ran his hands back through his hair. "Maybe that's part of it. I don't know. I know what it felt like with Finn, and I can't get it to work like that now."

"He acted as your guide."

"Yes. He...he made love to me. He said my barriers were lowest then. That it was easier to reach for my mind to help me."

Lugh reached over and ran a fingertip down his arm. "Diego...I would do that for you. Guide you in that fashion if you wish it."

Anger surged up the back of Diego's head in pinpricks of heat. "Damn it, stop it! How many times do I have to tell you no! Is that why you're helping me? As an excuse to get in my pants? *Carajo*, Lugh, you are worse than any human I ever met in any bar!"

"Your pardon, please." Lugh gripped his hand, his eyes pleading. "I only meant—"

Diego snatched his hand away. "Yes. I see what you meant. Goddamn it, leave off! Just let me alone awhile!"

He stalked off into the trees with no idea where he was headed. After stomping about in the woods for half a mile or so, he found himself back at the little lily pond. Scath and Croi skimmed the surface like enormous dragonflies, chasing each other's wakes.

Why am I so angry? There had been persistent would-be lovers over the years. He'd always been patient with them, firm but patient. In the face of an unfamiliar problem, Lugh was trying to do the best he could without even a hint of irritation. Frustration fueled the largest part of his fury, Diego suspected. He was supposed to face someone skilled in handling the currents of magic in a few days, and he had no inkling of how he would do anything but curl into a frightened, whimpering ball. It didn't help, of course, that Lugh was gorgeous and Diego was anguished over what had happened with Finn and where he might be.

He sighed and sank down on one of the flat rocks by the pond. Anger at himself, sexual frustration and the absence of Finn had all simmered and stewed together to erupt in a tantrum. He tried to reach out once more, as he had several times that day. *"Finn? Mi amor, are you out there?"*

No answer came, again, no touch from that beloved mind to his. Lugh had suggested that Finn was hiding. Apparently, he often hid for a time when hurt or upset, but *his* Finn had never done so. When Diego needed him, he had always come. Even critically injured, Finn had always come. Either he couldn't hear the call, or he was in such bad shape somewhere he couldn't answer. Not a happy thought.

Scath held his hand over the water, and a shape formed, a little horse, which galloped to Croi and splashed against her shoulder. She laughed, clapping, and sent a water butterfly to him. Back and forth their play went, both pixies giggling and splashing. Magic came to them so effortlessly.

"Diego, make the car fly again!" his little sister crowed. At four and five, they had been very close, always together.

He laughed and thought at the toy Camaro again, his eyes narrowed in concentration as it rose from the sand and flew to Carlita, who shrieked in delight.

"No, Diego!" His mother had come and snatched him from the sandbox. "You mustn't do things like that! The fairies

will see and come and take you away!" Mama had held him tight, her fear transmitting to him, until he grew fearful, too, and wept and promised never to do such things again...

"*Dios...*" Diego whispered. The ability had manifested when he was small, but he had suppressed both the memory and the magic. He stared at his hands. It wasn't because of the seizures — it had always been with him.

"Diego!"

He glanced up and a water rose smacked him in the face. Sputtering, he wiped the water from his eyes in time to duck the water swan that followed. Scath and Croi had fallen into each other's arms, laughing so hard they could no longer fly.

"Very funny. Hilarious," he muttered.

"Come play with us!"

"I'm probably not very good company right now, I'm sorry."

They flew to him, and he found himself embraced from either side.

"You are so unhappy today," Scath murmured against his shoulder.

"What hurts you so?" Croi nuzzled at his arm.

No difference between a friendly touch and a sensual one for them, he had been told, but there was something so open and innocent about them, he couldn't push them away. "I don't even know if Finn's still alive. It's... I hate this. Being apart."

Croi blinked at him, green on green eyes puzzled. "But you have been apart from him many times. Years. Centuries."

"Maybe. But how would you feel if you were separated from Scath? If you didn't even know whether he was alive or dead?"

Her emerald hue drained to an unhealthy chartreuse. She backed away from Diego, her breaths coming short. "I would know," she whispered. "I would know."

"Croi!" Scath cried out and opened his arms, pulling her close when she flew to him. She clung to him, sobbing, both their coloring faded to near gray.

"I'm sorry." Diego wrapped his arms around both trembling bodies and their shaking lessened.

Scath drew a whole breath first. "We are never apart. When we hatch, we must find our *leath*, our second half, within moments, or die."

"If one dies" — Croi sniffed — "the other follows."

"Oh, God, I'm sorry. I didn't know. I would never have said something so cruel."

"We know, Tali— Diego." Scath fluttered his wings, his color ratcheting up to a cadet blue. "You have never been cruel. Come. Make water-*bréagán* with us."

The return to play was more serious and subdued, but Diego understood it was to cheer Croi up, so he went with them to the water's edge. Scath made her a flock of birds that swooped and collided until she began to glow green again. She joined in with a little smile and sent Diego a palm-sized water bear. It trundled about on his hand, snuffling, and he thought, perhaps, he felt something through it.

He extended his other hand over the water and reached out for the magic he knew flowed so freely there, Finn's magic. A sphere rose from the pond at his urging, and Croi laughed as he shaped it into a rough cube, then a cylinder before he let it fall with a soft splash against Scath's leg.

They continued with simple shapes, coaxing Diego into more and more successful imitations. When they were both laughing again, he hugged them and felt he was ready to return to Lugh.

Unfortunately, he had picked the worst possible time for storming off. When he returned to the field, he found Lugh curled in a tight ball on the ground, teeth gritted against the pain.

"Lugh, hey..." Diego knelt beside him, one hand on his shoulder. *What a shitty thing to do, leaving someone when he's sick.* "How long have you been down here?"

"Not long," Lugh forced out through his teeth.

"Okay, it'll be okay. I'm so sorry." Diego took Lugh's head in his lap and let him bury his face against his stomach, knowing by now it was his touch the big guy needed to ease the pain.

"You are calmer," Lugh whispered as his shaking subsided.

"I guess I am." Diego stroked the gleaming black hair, still feeling like a heel. "Someone reminded me about how important play is in learning." He sat quiet for a moment, concentrating on helping Lugh slow his breathing. "Maybe when you feel a little better, you can show me how you make those lightning spears."

Chapter Eight

Cian's Ford

"You will wear it," Balor growled. "It's tradition."

Finn turned the enormous obsidian helmet over in his hands. Carved of a single piece of smooth stone, it even had the bad form to be topped by branching antlers. "But it's bloody heavy, and how in blazes am I supposed to see?"

Wrapped in blankets and propped up against the wall, Faolchú made a derisive sound. "If you don't wear it, you idiot, you risk brain injury and allow him to force his way into your mind," the ailing champion whispered. "Do you wish to have visions of being eaten alive by wolf spiders distract you?"

"Is that any way to speak to someone who has taken such good care of you?" Finn asked in a pained voice.

Faolchú bared his sharp teeth in a wolf grin. "Your pardon. I only wish to have my nursemaid returned in one piece." Still weak as a new duckling, he had at least improved enough to take an interest in proceedings.

"Put it on, Fionnachd. You'll find you see well enough, and it is not eyesight you will need."

"Is there, perhaps, a helm that's a mite lighter?" Finn tried again to hand it back to Balor.

"There are, but they are not made for what you need." Balor crossed his arms over his chest and glared down at him. "The stone was shot through with spells during its carving. As long as it is on your head, it will keep any opponent, no matter how strong, out of your mind."

"And the dragon hide? Truly, I will suffocate."

"It's to protect *your* hide, dear pooka," Faolchú insisted. "Lugh's imagination is limited. Press him, and he'll throw lightning spears."

"Ah." Finn shuddered. "Perhaps I could just speak with him? Or go to Herself? She did always have a soft spot for me."

"Challenge has been issued. It must be met. You have given your promise, Fionnachd," Balor insisted.

"Promises. Yes. Seems to have become a bad habit of mine. Bloody nuisance."

* * * *

Diego shook his head. "It doesn't matter what I put on. One look and they'll know it's not you."

"True." Lugh eased down onto the nearest rock. He tired easily, though the attacks held off as long as he rested and Diego stayed nearby. "But you will make Faolchú wonder who he faces. That bit of doubt is to your advantage."

"And it's your helmet and armor. It'll never fit."

"Magical armor, little man. I forged it myself. It has enough sense to mold to its wearer."

"Oh." Diego stared at the silver, winged helm. "Is it okay to say I'm scared out of my mind?"

Lugh squeezed his arm. "A bit of fear keeps you sharp."

"Are you ever? Afraid?"

"Yes." Lugh held his gaze, dark eyes filled with worry. "I have never been more afraid than now. For my people, for my life, for both our worlds."

"I'm sorry. I feel like I've brought all this with me."

"The storm was brewing ere you came, Diego." Lugh shook him gently. "You merely arrived on the first thunderclap."

Lugh helped him with the armor, a bodysuit of silver overlapping plates lined in the lambskin-soft, lightweight cloth that seemed ubiquitous among the *sidhe*. It laced up the front from crotch to throat in an arrangement he might have found delightfully kinky under different circumstances. At that moment, it simply felt odd.

"I look like some weird species of flying fish, don't I?" he said dryly as Lugh settled the helmet on his head.

"No, you look like the Queen's Champion. Stop deriding yourself."

A sharp blow to the side of Diego's head sent him staggering.

"Get your head out of your ass!" the now familiar, rasping voice demanded.

"Leave off, Morri. He needs encouragement, not to have his ears boxed," Lugh said with a weary sigh.

"No, he needs you to stop coddling him! You treat him too gently because you want to fuck him!" Morrigan's sharp teeth clicked together in her exasperation.

She turned on Diego and seized his chin in her claws to yank his head around. He stared into fathomless eyes, cold silver, like a grackle's. "But I have no interest in your body. Only as a vessel for magic. You have power in your blood the likes of which I can only dream on. And all you do is whine. You're afraid. You don't want to harm anyone. You want to go home. You can't, you can't, you can't. Pah! You are Taliesin! Remember that and be the warrior bard you were meant to be!"

Diego shivered hard and closed his eyes, unable to meet hers any longer.

"Let him go," Lugh snarled and rose from his rock.

"No." Diego held out a hand. "No. She's right. You need me, and I've just been feeling sorry for myself. You've taught me everything you could in a few days' time. It's a hell of a lot more than I could do before I came here. I have the lightning as a last resort. I just have to stand on my own now."

"Then do it," Morrigan rasped softly.

"Yes, ma'am." Diego gave her what he hoped was a brave smile.

She released him with a sharp laugh. "There, Shining One! Now he is ready!"

Lugh snorted in answer and gave the silver laces at Diego's throat a last tug. "Keep the helm on, no matter what happens. The silver and the spells will keep him out of your mind. Remember that Faolchú favors the flows in the earth and water. Expect the river to rise against you and the ground to tilt beneath you."

"Got it. Floods and earthquakes. Great. So long as there are no plagues of locusts and frogs, I shouldn't have any trouble at all." When both Lugh and Morrigan opened their mouths to speak, Diego raised a hand. "Joke. It was a joke."

"Humans have a strange sense of humor." Morrigan shook her head.

"Hmm, true," Lugh agreed. "Much of the time, I have no inkling what he's saying."

Danu's court gathered near the edge of the trees, at a spot where a wide, lazy river meandered through the forest. Movement on the far bank heralded the arrival of the Fomorians, but both parties stayed back, waiting. An air of ceremony hung about the whole arrangement.

Sionnach finally emerged from the trees on the Fomorian side, and Angus, the queen's herald, golden-eyed and flaxen-haired, stepped forward on the *sidhe's* bank.

Angus filled his lungs and shouted toward the opposite bank. "Challenge has been issued."

"And answered," Sionnach's voice floated to them across the water.

"Your champion cowers in the underbrush," Angus sneered. "He has the courage of thistledown and the strength of a snail too long in the sun."

Diego moved to step forward to prevent humiliating his hosts, but Lugh stopped him, a hand on his shoulder. "Patience. It is traditional. Do not disgrace Angus by interrupting."

"I see no sign of yours," Sionnach flung back. "He is as brave as any tadpole and as powerful as rose petals on the water."

This continued for some minutes, the insults to honor and courage becoming ever more poetic, until Sionnach flung up his hands in concession, laughing. "Your tongue is as golden as ever, Angus Far-Seer. May your champion be worthy of you today."

Angus swept him a graceful bow. "You are a true poet, Sionnach Silver-Tongue. May yours prove brave and true." He straightened and raised his arms. "Let the champions come forth, and let no fae break oath when it is done."

On that last word, he rose onto the balls of his feet, his body glowing golden as his limbs melted and reshaped. A golden eagle rose into the air on powerful wings where Angus had stood, and this seemed the signal to begin. Both sides surged forward, the *sidhe* shifting to their animal forms, the Fomorians roaring and howling as they came.

Lugh walked beside Diego as the bull, powerful muscles bunching and flexing under gleaming black hide. Who all the others were, he couldn't be certain, since he had been watching Angus transform when they all shifted. A brown bear, larger than any Kodiak, ambled nearby. A raven flew circles overhead with the eagle. Stags, wolves, foxes, badgers, songbirds and raptors all surrounded him.

Neither side made any move to cross the river, though there was a great deal of threatening noise and posturing.

"Go forward, Diego." The bull's great head nudged him. "To the water's edge. Faolchú will do the same."

"Lugh…"

"All will be well, little man. If it reaches a point where you cannot continue, the match will stop."

"Comforting," Diego muttered, and lowered the visor on his helm as he walked toward the bank on shaking legs.

The Fomorian champion mirrored his actions — a tall, lean figure dressed in black, crowned by an ominous, horned helmet.

Behind him, Diego heard Lugh's puzzled murmur. "That is not Faolchú."

Finn hesitated in his march to the bank and turned to pretty Sionnach. "Unless he has lost considerable mass in my absence, *that* is not Lugh."

"Courage," Sionnach said gently. "It can only mean that Lugh is unable to take his rightful place today, like our Faolchú. They have no one stronger to take his place. You will be victorious, Fionnachd."

"You suggest that Lugh is ill as well? A champions' plague?" Finn shook his head and realized what a bad idea this was in his ridiculously heavy helmet.

"I couldn't say." Sionnach shot him a wink and a grin. "But you may have a kiss after you win."

"Ah, well, something to look forward to, at least." Finn watched the *sidhe* champion advance slowly, his steps as hesitant as Finn's own. Something familiar struck him in those movements, something...but he could not place it. *The things I do for you, Diego. But I will see you soon.*

Not Faolchú. Wonderful. All the advice Diego had been given about strategy and defense had just been rendered useless with those anxious words. The Fomorian who faced him didn't seem any more eager, his steps down the bank cautious and slow. *All right, so we're both scared.*

Then he felt the tug on the currents of magic as the Fomorian gathered for a strike, and he had no more time to wonder. The river, so tranquil a moment before, sprouted whitecaps, its gentle murmur growing to a roar. A wall of water reared up and raced across the river toward him.

With a terrified cry, Diego flung up his hands, reacting out of pure instinct. The wind rushed to him, a boom sounding as his displacement of air created a vacuum. A shield of air met the oncoming fifteen-foot wave. For a moment, the wave halted, churning mid-stream like some bizarre, nightmare fountain, then it collapsed with a crash back into the riverbed.

Panting, Diego fought against the urge to flee. This was a whole lot scarier than he could have imagined. Unlike the fae, who could regenerate to a certain degree, if he drowned or had his back broken, he would be dead. Not merely dead, but really, most sincerely dead, as the Munchkin coroner had so eloquently put it.

The Fomorian champion stood with his arms crossed over his chest. He seemed to be waiting, so Diego had to assume it was his turn. He reached out for the magic of the Otherworld, more accessible and of a different flavor than the human world, and gathered the air to him more gradually. He fashioned a ball the size of a wheelbarrow, heated the air until the ball burst into brilliant red flames, then hurled his fiery missile at his opponent.

For a moment, Diego thought it might hit when the Fomorian cringed and retreated a step. But the dark champion caught himself in time and flung up a ball of water to intercept, extinguishing the fireball.

The Fomorian stood with his fists clenched at his sides, unmoving for several long breaths. *Dios, I wish I knew what he was thinking…*

Both black-clad arms jerked up as if flinging something. Diego heard the whistling and glanced up in time to see the rocks hurtling toward him. He backpedaled and threw up another shield of air. The basketball-sized rocks tumbled into the water, and

Diego drew a breath, only to find another pair of rocks heading for his head.

After four of these barrages, a prickle of adrenaline-charged anger rose up his spine. This was ridiculous and getting them nowhere. He shaped his air shield into a dome around him and reached into the currents for the strongest flows, pulling the energy to him from the trees and the river and the very ground beneath his feet. There were things that had to be settled between the fae courts, things that had to be seen to. It was time to end this.

Finn huffed in frustration as the *sidhe* champion pulled the air all the way around him. He thought surely some of the rocks would have found their target, that if he threw enough at once, he could distract the *sidhe* enough to get in a good strike. Perhaps he could reach under the river and shake the earth beneath his feet, knock him off balance.

Then the *sidhe* champion pulled on the flows so strongly, Finn's heart lurched. He had never felt such frightening power, not since...

His opponent began to form the lightning, not in a spear as Lugh would have, but in a lance. Only one lightning lance-maker existed in his long memory. It had to be.

"*Diego? Diego!*" He called out in his mind but there was no response. "Ach, thunder-blasted helmet!" He fumbled with the strap and flung it away from him just as the figure across the river hurled the lance.

Diego flung the lightning at the same moment the Fomorian tossed away his helmet, too late to call back the strike. He watched in horror as a thick fall of blue-black hair tumbled from that helmet and a familiar, beloved face appeared amidst the wind-whipped tresses.

"Finn! Dios ayudame, no!"

The lance struck even as he cried out. The far side of the river disappeared in a blinding flash of light. When Diego's vision cleared, Finn lay sprawled against a tree trunk twenty feet back from where he had stood.

"Oh, God, no," Diego whispered, unable to draw a full breath. He threw his helmet off as he ran down the bank and through the knee-deep water. *"No, no, no, no!"*

The Fomorians made way for him, milling about in confusion, as he raced up the bank to Finn's side.

"Querido, mi amor, speak to me," he pleaded as he dropped to his knees and put his ear to Finn's chest. *"Mierda!"* Either there was no heartbeat, or he couldn't hear it through the armor Finn wore.

Water, he had to get Finn to the water. Whatever was broken, he could put himself back together as long as he had water. Diego slid his arms under Finn's limp frame and lifted him, opting for speed over caution. Only when he knelt in the river with Finn mostly submerged across his lap did he dissolve into tears.

"Oh, God...what have I done? Finn...my poor Finn..."

Whispers reached him from the riverbanks. "He weeps for his opponent. It is like Cuchulainn and Ferdiad. What have we done?"

Diego lifted his tear-stained face and looked around at all the stunned expressions. Anger and sorrow welled up in him until his body could no longer contain it. "You selfish bastards! All of you! Your stupid squabbles, your insistence on tradition and your damn, stubborn pride! No one could ask the question? *Is Finn with you? Have you seen a human?* No one thought there might be other solutions than this?"

Danu, back in her *sidhe* form, spoke from the bank. "Diego, we—"

"No! I don't want to hear it! Go away, all of you! Leave us in peace!"

He turned back to Finn to gather him in his arms, rocking and weeping. The leaves rustled on either side of the bank as both fae courts slunk away.

Chapter Nine

Surrender

Diego knelt in the river holding Finn's broken body for what seemed like hours. The lightning had torn up the right side of his body, a gaping rip in his black, scaled armor from his hip to his shoulder. Charred, bloody skin showed through the tear and covered the right side of his face. His torso had twisted in an unnatural way, indicating a broken spine, and his right ear had been ripped in half.

"They told me it was someone else," Diego whispered into Finn's whole ear. "It was supposed to be this huge, powerful wolf-warrior. Someone born for battle. Finn...my poor Finn..."

"My love, do you suggest I was lacking as a champion?"

Diego nearly dropped Finn in shock at the gentle touch on his mind. "Oh, God...*caro*, I wasn't even sure you were alive." He heaved a shaky breath and hugged Finn closer.

"Hmm, well, I'm still not entirely certain, myself. My heart, my light, I need to go for a bit. Will you be all right?"

"Go? Go where? No…don't leave me, not when I just found you!"

"Hush, now, my hero. You know where I will be. It won't be so long this time. At least I'm in one piece."

Finn's body shuddered and faded into the water, leaving Diego holding the empty black-scaled armor. "Damn…oh, damn…" Yes, he knew where Finn had gone, into the Dreaming to let his body heal. It was just too much to bear to have found him only to be separated right away again.

He crawled up the bank and curled up on the grass with the armor clutched tightly to his chest. No more. His heart couldn't take any more. Diego closed his eyes and reached outside himself in a desperate attempt at what he had been told should be impossible. The eddies and tides of magic flowed all around him, but he ignored all the tugs on his concentration, searching for that one bright spark that was Finn.

* * * *

A featureless twilight stretched before him without color or substance. Diego turned his attention in the direction he thought should be up and, yes, there they shone, the multitude of stars in the midnight blue firmament. He had found his way into the Dreaming.

"Finn?"

"There you are, love. I thought you might never arrive." Finn's image manifested on the empty plain, a dream image, whole and well.

"Brat. You just did this to see if I *could* follow you without the seizures," Diego grumbled.

"It had occurred. And I certainly could heal wrapped in your arms in the physical plane, but it would take days." Finn's mental image looked away. "This will speed things."

Diego settled by him. "Ah."

"Am I to have my hearing now? Since you no longer seem furious with me?"

With the connection between them so close, Diego didn't need to ask what he meant. "You don't have to."

"It would ease my thoughts if I could share the memory of that day, my heart."

"I guess I owe you that much for almost turning you into pooka-kebab."

"Kebab," Finn said wistfully. "I like kebab."

"How the hell can you think about food right now?" Diego hovered between amusement and revulsion.

"I'm hungry."

"You're half-charred and broken like some discarded toy, and you're hungry."

"It has been an anxious few days. I haven't eaten. And now you appear miraculously. Does wonders for the appetite."

Diego smiled. "I missed you, too, *mi vida*." He waved a hand at the stars, each one of them representing one of Finn's memories. "Which one is it?"

"There." Finn reached up and pointed to one near his right hand.

It took three tries, but Diego managed to pull the memory to him of the day he had surprised Finn with that girl. The whole, heart-pounding day rushed past him from the moment Finn had woken that morning, the girl's desperate cry for help and Finn's valiant rescue, to the moment Diego had stormed out of the house.

"*Cariño,*" Diego murmured. "I'm so sorry. Here you were trying to do something good. You wanted me to be proud of you. And I—"

"I have thought on this long and hard, love," Finn cut him off. "And despite good intentions, I still must beg your forgiveness. I broke my promise."

"No, you didn't."

"I promised I would never take another to my bed. And she was, without a doubt, in our bed."

A laugh leaped from Diego. "Finn, *mi amor*, that's an expression. A euphemism."

"I know. I do recognize some of them by now." Finn's image huffed in irritation. "Still, I think it was the shock that made it so terrible for you. I should have found a way to prepare you."

"Would have been nice to have a call." Diego wrapped mental arms around Finn. *Dios*, this was all his fault. If he hadn't overreacted…if he'd insisted Finn learn the numbers on the phone… Though teaching Finn numbers and letters had proven frustrating. Pooka concentration didn't lend itself to such things.

"When we get home, I'm ordering you DVDs of *Sesame Street*. Maybe then we can get you to use things besides speed dial."

"Tell me I'm forgiven?" Finn said plaintively.

"If I am."

"I will think on it."

Diego snorted.

"Love? Where are you lying?" Finn asked after a long silence.

"I'm on the riverbank."

"Ach. Soaking wet, in Lugh's gods-be-damned armor. You will be ill." Finn stood and held out his hands. "Come. We're going back."

"Isn't it too soon?"

Finn shrugged. "Perhaps. Come. I won't have you back only to have you catch your death."

Diego returned to his body to find that Finn was right. He was chilled, his teeth chattering. Finn sprawled naked nearby, his body half on the bank, legs trailing in the river. The open wounds had healed to angry red patches, his spine had straightened and his ear had regained much of its shape. Amazing what Finn could manage in a few hours. Human doctors would have given their right arms for such things.

"*Caro.*" Diego smoothed the tangled hair back from Finn's eyes. He got a weak moan and fluttering eyelids in response. "Let's get you somewhere comfortable."

He lifted Finn again, cradling him against his chest, always grateful that he weighed less than his size implied.

With a sigh, Finn opened his eyes and found him with a smile. "There's my handsome hero," he got out in a scratchy whisper. "I will say you look grand in Lugh's armor. Quite virile."

"Great, thanks," Diego grumbled as he trudged up the bank. "I want it off. My balls itch, and I can't scratch."

"I have several itches I want scratched." Finn nuzzled at Diego's jaw.

Diego snorted. "You're barely back in one piece."

"I don't recall that being an impediment before."

An ancient willow provided the best available shelter, its trailing leaves acting as a curtain against the breeze. Soft moss grew thick under its branches and here Diego laid his passenger down. He stroked Finn's hair and bent to kiss his forehead.

"Will you be taking the armor off?" Finn asked. "Or did you intend to play the conqueror and keep it on while you take me? I suppose you could simply unlace the crotch. I'll have no difficulty playing the helpless, vanquished foe for you if you like, but —"

Diego cut him off with a soft kiss. "I think I've missed your touch too much for games."

"Could I still be helpless?" The husk of desire in Finn's voice was unmistakable.

"I don't think you have much choice." Diego ran a finger down Finn's long, perfect nose before he took his hands back to undo the silver laces. Damnably frustrating things, Lugh had done them up so tight, but he managed to get them loose enough to slither out of the silver scales.

"My conqueror is so beautiful. I think I shall surrender gladly," Finn murmured, his eyes traveling up and down Diego's body.

"Good." Diego ran a hand down Finn's uninjured side, tracing over his ribs and hip. Already half-erect, Finn's uncut shaft expanded at the gentle caress. "You tell me if anything hurts, okay?"

"Okay," Finn repeated, the modern phrase still sounding strange from him.

With gentle nudges, Diego urged Finn's thighs apart so he could move between them, keeping his weight on his arms. His cock was already hard and aching, and a shuddering groan tore from him when it brushed up against Finn's. It had been too long, the urge to just thrust in and hammer away savagely was so strong it frightened him.

Instead, he curled over to brush Finn's lips with his. Finn's left hand slid up his shoulder, fingers tangling desperately in his hair to pull him down for a more serious kiss. *So much for helpless.* But Finn didn't press further, waiting for him to lead. Diego ran his tongue over those soft, full lips, and plunged within. The heat of Finn's mouth, the answering thrust of his tongue sent a spear of searing longing through his groin.

"Here, *mi amor*." Diego broke off the kiss to offer Finn his fingers. "Get some of these wet for me."

Finn's prehensile tongue wrapped around his forefinger, hot and incredibly flexible, and he thought he might come right then and there. Diego bent his head to lap at Finn's nipple, breathing in the soft scent of his arousal as the nub pebbled and hardened under his strokes.

A moan vibrated around Diego's fingers where Finn had stuffed three in his mouth. "My heart, my own," Finn whispered. "I'm in dire straits. Please don't tease too long."

"You and me both." Diego hissed a breath as Finn licked his palm. "All right, *caro*, give that back. I need it now."

He bent Finn's leg up on his uninjured side and slid his wet fingers between his cheeks. Flexible in so many ways a human wasn't, Finn needed far less preparation than a human lover. Still, Diego hated to rush. He teased at the puckered entrance and Finn tilted his hips, pressing into the touch, silently pleading. Diego's forefinger sank inside his tight channel and Finn let out a soft moan, hands gripped tight on Diego's shoulders.

"More?"

"Yes, more, please." Finn writhed on that one finger, head flung back, lips parted.

Diego inserted a second finger, slowly working his way inside to press against the gland shared by fae and human males alike. Finn whimpered, his erection jumping with each stroke.

"Tell me you want me," Diego murmured, taking some advantage of his role as conqueror.

"Oh, goddesses of stream and spring," Finn moaned. "I want you so. I want you buried inside me, joined with me, one with me, please, love, oh…"

Diego leaned over to kiss the glistening head of Finn's shaft and withdrew his fingers so he could replace them with the head of his cock. Finn spread his thighs wider and lifted his hips to give him better access, black eyes shining with desire. Slowly, deliberately, Diego sank inside his tight heat while Finn begged and pleaded for more, faster. It was the first time since he had first made love to Finn that he truly felt in control, an unfamiliar but intoxicating sensation.

When he had buried himself to the hilt, he wrapped his arms around Finn's torso and lifted him to sitting so he ended up impaled on Diego's lap. Finn's eyes went wide in surprise, then closed on a deep groan as Diego thrust upward. The position apparently stimulated every sensitive nerve bundle at once for Finn, his ass thoroughly filled and stretched, his cock caught between their bodies against the hard ridges of Diego's stomach. His head fell back, his hair tumbling down in a wild, black cataract.

Diego felt the long, lean muscles relax under his hands as Finn surrendered completely and let Diego move him up and down as he pleased. Finn's legs locked around him, and Diego groaned as he was pulled in deeper still.

"Finn, I won't last."

"It's all right, my hero." Finn cupped Diego's face between his hands. "Neither will I. I'm—" He kissed

Diego softly, his breaths coming short. "Oh...gods... Diego!"

The hot splash of Finn's seed hit Diego's chest at the same moment his channel clamped hard around his cock. Diego slammed in twice, and the white-hot pressure exploded up from his balls. He cried out, loud enough for his ecstasy to echo off the opposite shore. Finn jerked and bucked in his lap, the movements and the erotic sounds he made tearing hard aftershocks from Diego's core, the nova intensity of his orgasm sending black spots dancing before his eyes.

Finn's head flopped down on his shoulder, and they simply held each other gently, panting hard. After a moment, though, Finn's breaths began to hitch.

"What is it? Finn? Did I hurt you?" Diego stroked his hair and tried to lift his head.

"I thought I'd lost you again," Finn got out in a choked whisper. "I thought you were dead. I've been so miserable, so frightened."

"*Mi vida, mi amor*," Diego murmured against his hair. "I thought so, too. About you. I'm here now. Don't cry." He had never been able to fathom why those gentle words often guaranteed tears but, right on cue, Finn began to sob. "Hush, hush, I'm here, I'm here. I'm sorry...I'm so sorry."

The storm passed quickly and Finn soon quieted in his arms, apparently content to be rocked and held.

"Finn." Diego kissed his cheek. "From everything I've heard, we may never make it home again. The Veil shut behind us. We could be stuck here."

"I have you back," Finn said on a heavy sniff. "Naught else matters. I am home."

Chapter Ten

Outbreak

Diego opened his eyes to the morning sun filtering through willow leaves and Finn snuggled against him, fast asleep. He gazed at the handsome face resting on his shoulder, this frustrating troublemaker who had swept into his quiet, miserably lonely life and turned it upside-down, and heat pooled around his heart. His troublemaker, his Finn…at last he felt whole again.

Finn appeared whole as well, the delicate shell of his right ear unblemished and perfect, all traces of the lightning strike melted away as he slept.

And now what? He hoped Danu and Balor were negotiating peacefully, that they worked through some solution that was best for both their people, but from what he had seen so far, he thought it might be a bit much to hope for. The Fomorian king wanted back what he felt rightfully his; the *sidhe* Queen wanted to keep all the fae safe from the evils of the human world. Where a compromise lay, he had no idea.

With a sharp intake of breath, Finn snapped his eyes open.

"I'm sorry, *cariño*, did I wa—"

Finn's hand clamped over his mouth. He whispered, "Hush. Can you shield us, love? Keep them from hearing us?"

"Keep who from hearing us?" Diego whispered when Finn took his hand away.

"The damn—"

"Fionnachd! I know you are near!" a voice called nearby. Sionnach's head thrust through the willow branches. "Oh, there you are. Good morning!"

"Too late," Finn grumbled and hid his face against Diego's neck. "Go away, little fox. You interrupt my morning nap."

Sionnach made a show of sniffing the air. "I think I may be interrupting more than napping."

"Perhaps you are. Now go away. Tell Balor I have done what I promised, and will do no more."

"Fionnachd." The grin fell from Sionnach's face. "It is not Himself who asks for you, but Nathair. He asks if you will come. Faolchú is failing."

Finn sat up, scrubbing his hands back through his hair. "Bloody hells...he was sitting up yesterday morning. Taking breakfast. Laughing. How is this?"

"I wish I could say." Sionnach twisted his tail in his hands. "It is not so today."

"Faolchú's sick, too?" Diego's mind turned things over in ways he liked less and less. "That's why Finn was there instead?"

"Yes. Balor made threats and promises and flung rocks at my head until I agreed to take his place," Finn muttered into his hands. Then his head shot up. "What do you mean 'too'?"

Before Diego could answer, another voice cut across their conversation, a rich, melodic baritone. "Diego! Diego are you there?" Angus' blond head poked through the willow branches opposite Sionnach. "Ah, I thought I heard you here."

Sionnach's hands stilled on his tail, and a little twitch curled his lips before he dropped his gaze to his paws. "Angus."

"Sionnach." The one word conveyed so much longing, Diego felt his cock stir.

Those two pig-headed rulers have kept them apart, too. Hell only knows how long, poor things. Diego cleared his throat. "Did you need me for something?"

"Yes." Angus tore his attention away from the lovely fox-fae, his brow crinkled in concern. "Lugh calls for you. Bellows for you, if truth be told. He is…in terrible pain."

A low growl rumbled from someone, and it took Diego a moment to realize the growl was Finn's.

"Diego stays with me," Finn snarled. "He will not be taken from my sight again."

"And Finn has said he will go to Faolchú's side." Sionnach raised his chin, eyes glinting.

"I said no such thing, little fox."

"Then come with him to see Lugh." Angus pressed his momentary advantage. "He needs—"

Finn stabbed a finger at Angus' chest, snarling directly into his face. "I have had quite enough of being shoved about by those who think themselves my betters. You will both leave us in peace, and I will decide what is to be done."

The peaceful morning dissolved into a shouting match with all three snapping and snarling, past hurts dredged up, old insults recalled. Diego rolled his eyes.

Nice to see him stand up for me, but he could ask what I want...

His irritation cut off when a thin cry of anguish pierced his mind, the mental voice achingly familiar.

"Croi?"

"Taliesin, please..."

A soft whir of wings sounded outside the willow's shelter. Diego shoved through the branches in time to see Croi land awkwardly, burdened by the body in her arms. All the color had drained from Scath, leaving him a deathly ivory. His wings drooped and he huddled in Croi's arms, whimpering.

"What happened?" Diego stroked the now-ivory hair back.

"He fell." Croi's voice trembled. "We flew to the thicket, where the berries grow. And he fell, his wings unable to hold him. He hurts so."

"I know, *pequeña*, I feel it. Give him to me. Maybe I can help like I did Lugh." Diego gathered the pixie to him, not surprised that he weighed no more than an overstuffed briefcase. The shouting continued unabated behind him, and he had had enough.

He shoved his way back through the leaves with Croi stuck tight to his side. "Shut the hell up, all of you! Good God! This isn't about any of you or about territorial male imperatives. Look at poor little Scath! While you and your rulers argue and sulk and threaten, your people are getting sick, and I don't see anyone doing a damn thing about it! All the centuries behind you, all the mysteries of the universe at your fingertips, and you have no *sense*! None of you!"

Sionnach at least looked ashamed. Finn chewed his lower lip, eyes still glazed with anger. Angus managed a good impression of a hungry fish.

"This is what we're going to do. I'm going to carry Scath, and we're going to go see Faolchú since it sounds like he's in worse shape." Diego shot Angus a quelling look when he raised a hand to speak. "Chill. You take Sionnach and go tell them to bring Lugh to me. That way, everyone gets taken care of, and my Finn doesn't get all bent out of shape."

Angus stiffened. "None of the *sidhe* have entered the Fomor caverns for centuries."

"Perhaps…" Sionnach reached out to take Angus' hand, twining their fingers together. "Perhaps it is past time, then."

"All right, I was wrong," Diego said. "One of you does have some sense."

Angus lifted their joined hands to brush his lips over Sionnach's knuckles. "I will see if Lugh is willing."

Sionnach closed his eyes with a sigh. Then his breath caught, and he collapsed as if someone had cut a string holding him up. Angus caught him, reflexes too fast to follow, and eased him to the ground.

"You always did make my head spin, Angus Far-Seer," Sionnach said when he opened his eyes, his silver voice wavering. "But this is taking it just a mite too far, don't you think?"

"Don't jest, dearheart, not now," Angus admonished softly. "Are you hurt?"

"No, simply dizzy. And my head aches."

"On second thought, give him to Finn," Diego said. "We'd better take him with us, too."

"But I'm not ill," Sionnach insisted. "I must be overtired." He made a brave attempt to stand but cried out in pain when his knees buckled. "I can't be ill."

"Why not?" Diego asked.

"Because I am the herald."

Obviously that meant something to the fae—their expressions were uniformly distressed—but this was not the time to unravel the significance of ceremonial positions. "Sorry, bud, you obviously are sick."

Angus swept his Fomorian counterpart up and handed him into Finn's arms. "Diego will look after you." He leaned in to brush a soft kiss over Sionnach's lips. "I will come soon."

A vision of Angus lying somewhere helpless and alone ambushed Diego. "You sure you'll make it back?"

The look Angus shot him screamed offense. "I will fulfill my duties to my last breath. Your request will be delivered." He stepped away from them, shifted to eagle and leaped into the sky on a rush of powerful golden wings.

They made a strange little troupe, a naked human carrying one *féileacán* and supporting another, and a naked pooka carrying a lovely, lithe fae with a bushy red tail.

"Diego..." Finn began as the ground rose and the caverns hove into sight.

"I'm not angry with you, *mi vida*. I'm sorry I snapped."

"I know." Finn shot him a shy smile and cleared his throat. "It was...exciting to see you so, ah, confident, though."

"Was it?" Diego chuckled despite his worry. "You like being yelled at and ordered around?"

"Not...as such. But it did make my blood run hot to see you so masterful."

So Finn enjoyed it when he played Alpha sometimes, not that big a surprise after his reaction to their little conquest scenario the evening before.

A beautiful Fomorian female met them at the entrance, her human shape clothed only in her sleek, black fur, her pointed ears swiveling atop her head.

"It is you." She addressed Diego in a rich, purring alto. "At the ford, I was uncertain."

"And who do you think I am, ma'am?"

The answer, by now, was expected. "You are Taliesin."

"So I hear."

"Welcome home." She leaned over Scath and rubbed her cheek, as soft as any Persian's, against Diego's. "Come. Perhaps you might ease Faolchú where I cannot."

As they followed her, Diego dropped back to whisper to Finn, "Who is she?"

"That is Eithne, Balor's daughter. You were lovers long ago."

Diego missed a step and Croi had to steady him. "*Dios*. Please don't tell me I have fae children."

"No. Never fear, my heart. Eithne does not cling to her lovers. And she has only one child. Lugh."

Fae genetics would have given poor old Gregor Mendel a fit. Cat Fomorian plus *sidhe* equals bull didn't make a lot of logical sense. A more important thought hit him and he hurried to catch up to her.

"Eithne, they're bringing Lugh. I don't know if anyone told you. He's been sick, too."

"I thought he might have fallen ill." Her voice wavered on a sigh. "When you took his place, I knew. But to bring him here might be unwise. His grandfather holds his grudges long and hard."

Diego dredged through his recollections of ancient Irish literature. *Oh, yes.* Lugh had, in some versions of the stories, put out Balor's deadly eye on the battlefield, either with a spear or sling. Human versions, though, usually included Balor's death, and so were less than reliable.

"He might be pissed, but I think it's time for everyone to pack the old issues away. You've got boys keeling over right and left on both sides of the fence. Time for a truce in the face of what could be a pandemic for all of you."

She tipped her head in acknowledgment. "Perhaps when he sees his herald ill, his ire will abate."

"I'm not ill, healer!" Sionnach protested, though he shivered hard enough to make his sharp teeth chatter.

"Stubborn," Finn muttered.

A murmur of voices drifted down the narrow corridor to them. The murmur grew to a hum of echoing conversation, and when they turned the last corner, Diego gasped. Before him lay the most enormous cavern he had ever seen. The caves he'd visited years before in Puerto Rico, *las Cavernas de Camuy*, were rabbit holes in comparison. Shining stalactites grew down to meet their stalagmite brethren, forming graceful, undulating pillars, as if Gaudi had decided to build a vast underground cathedral. The walls' phosphorescence gave off enough light to make out shapes nearby, but darkness shrouded the far end of the cavern.

Out of the gloom roared a terrifying voice, deeper than the lowest notes on a pipe organ, rough and dangerous. "Who has brought a *human* to my domain?"

"Father, open your eye," Eithne shot back, unafraid when everyone else in the cavern had shrunk back to the walls. "This is no mere human. Our Druid-Bard has returned to us."

"Taliesin?" The deep voice quieted. "Is it you, boy?"

"You could've warned me," Diego whispered to Finn, then turned to the darkness where he knew Balor sat, trying to keep his voice steady. "I have to believe it is, *majestad*. I came with Finn to see your ailing champion. And brought your herald back home, since he's come down with whatever it is, too."

Balor remained silent for so long, Diego was certain there would be another explosion. Instead, a soft chuckle came from the darkness, one that grew into a mighty roar of laughter. "Taliesin! Of course! I knew Fionnachd could never have pierced the Veil on his own!"

Beside him, Finn bristled and Diego shot him a quelling look. "Hush, *mi vida*. Pack the ego away."

"And the little ones?"

It took a moment for Diego to realize Balor meant the *féileacán*. "He fell ill suddenly this morning. She seems fine so far."

"Then it has begun. As was foreseen. I am too late." Balor came forward into the light, and Diego fought the urge to run.

Carajo, that's the biggest, ugliest, meanest looking fae I've ever seen. He gulped a deep breath and croaked out, "What's too late, *majestad*?"

"It is the end. We are dying."

Chapter Eleven

Veil

Since no one protested and no one seemed to have a better suggestion, Diego turned the Great Hall into a sick room. Finn sat with his back against a stone pillar, Sionnach curled up beside him, pride threatening to make his heart burst as he watched Diego marshal the Fomorians.

He knew, in an intellectual way, that this side of Diego existed, knew he had stepped in to run homeless shelters back in New York when they needed him, had often taken charge of the Code Blue efforts on those nights when the cold became dangerous for the ones who lived outside, but Finn had rarely witnessed these things.

Diego's soft, gentle requests sent people scurrying for blankets, for water and for food. He organized a search party to scour the caverns for anyone else who might be ill. When the *sidhe* arrived, with both Lugh and Angus carried on litters, Balor began to roar again, and Diego's quiet, reasonable words calmed him.

Ask him to do something for himself, and Diego would delay and defer endlessly. Put someone in need before him, and he became the warrior-chieftain he had been in earlier lifetimes.

Balor himself carried Faolchú up from the living quarters and set him down beside Sionnach. Dear goddesses, he looked worse than the first time Finn had seen him lying ill. He struggled for every breath, the air rattling in his lungs.

"Pretty fox, I need to hold him. Go see Angus." His touch had comforted Faolchú before, though he had no notion why. He could only hope it would ease him again.

Sionnach crawled the few feet to Angus' litter and curled up close. In the clutches of a raging fever, Angus wrapped his arms around Sionnach, though his eyes darted fretfully as if he no longer tracked on anything in the physical world.

"Apparently, he managed to deliver his message and collapsed." Diego crouched next to Finn. He had pulled on only his jeans, even though the *sidhe* had brought all his clothes. "Fever, shaking, severe stomach and joint pain, dizziness." He stroked Faolchú's head. "And this guy's obviously been sick the longest. God, he must've been gorgeous when he was well."

"He was." Finn ducked his head to hide his tears and gathered Faolchú to his chest. "He will be again."

Diego stared out into the middle distance, chewing on his bottom lip. "They found one more in his bed. The court's seer, they called him. Cute little guy with a ferret's head."

"Pine marten."

"Sorry?"

"He's a pine marten, love. His name is Easóg."

"Oh, sorry. Not up on my weasels. But, look, there are so many things that don't make sense here. Why don't they go into the Dreaming to get better? And why are they all male? Why isn't there any pattern to the infection? You're not sick. Nathair's not sick. No one who said they'd slept with Lugh lately is sick."

"As for the Dreaming, Faolchú said he could not cross over. That he could not reach it. For the rest, I don't know, my hero." Finn shook his head. "And there is no hospital for the fae, no doctors with tests and books who could glean something useful from all this."

"Finn, you hate doctors."

"For myself, yes. But they have helped you." He shifted Faolchú to a more comfortable position. Had his breathing eased, or was it wishful thinking? "Tia Carmen would know. She always knew how to ease what ailed me."

"She's on the wrong side of the Veil, *mi amor*. Doesn't help us much."

"Diego," Finn began. Oh, gods, he didn't want to say this, didn't even want to think it. But someone would say it eventually. "You opened the Veil once."

"Yes, during a tantrum, that brought on a massive seizure. Are you planning on driving me into a jealous rage again?"

"No, my heart." Finn stroked Faolchú's ears when he moaned. *Definitely breathing easier.* "But you could not call the lightning lance before without a seizure, either. You... Diego, do you recall how I've always told you your channels were closed? The magic blocked by your own mind?"

"Yes."

"They are open now, love. I felt it last night. You have as much access to your magic now as I do mine."

"Oh."

A few feet over, Lugh began to bellow and thrash again. He had been bound hand and foot to prevent his fists and hooves landing blows indiscriminately. While he had accepted the necessity, the waves of pain took his reason and he raged against the ropes.

Diego ran his hands back through his hair. "We'll talk about this later, *mi vida*. Let's get our patients stable first." He brought Easóg and Scath to Finn, the little pine marten's head ending up in his lap and both the *féileacán* snuggled against his left side across from Faolchú. A bizarre arrangement, but the three little ones soon fell fast asleep.

When Lugh's bellowing ceased, Diego spoke softly to him and untied him. He sat back against a pillar a few feet away and let Lugh lie between his thighs, head on Diego's stomach, arms wrapped around his waist. Then he coaxed Angus and Sionnach to him, one on either side, and they soon ceased any restlessness and whimpering as well.

Odd, for Finn to see his Diego wrapped up in someone else's arms, even if that someone was deathly ill. That should have been him, nestled there between those strong thighs. He didn't quite know what to make of the sensation gathering around his heart, a painful heat, reminiscent of anger but different in flavor.

"Jealous," Faolchú got out on a spare whisper.

"Stuff and nonsense," Finn protested. "I've never been jealous."

Faolchú snorted. "Smells...like it...to me."

"Go to sleep, bucko. You're talking rubbish."

When Faolchú had taken some water and all their charges had fallen asleep, Finn eased out from under the slumbering forms and met Diego halfway between.

"Did you ever get breakfast?" Diego's brow wrinkled in concern.

"Nathair brought me some cave crickets."

"Sorry I asked."

"They were roasted. Nice and crunchy."

"Please, *querido*." Diego patted his arm. "I don't need to hear any more."

Finn tactfully changed the subject. "You have thought on what I said?"

"I have...but I don't know how. I mean, I don't even know where the Veil is or what it looks like or feels like. How do I open something I can't find?"

"You are my hero, my Taliesin. I have faith in you."

"This belief that I can do just about anything because of who I was in a past life is getting a little tiresome."

Finn chewed on his bottom lip a moment, then said, "It is Diego Sandoval I believe in. This version of you, here and now."

"Oh." Diego pulled in a slow breath. "I'm not sure if that's more or less disturbing. Not that it matters. We have to do something. I have no idea why you and I are able to help when their own healers can't, and it's fine for now, but what happens when there's not six, but ten, and twenty, and two hundred sick? There's not enough of us to go around."

"And I would rather find a different solution before someone decides I need to be cut up into a few dozen pieces again so there would be enough to 'go around', as you say." Finn shuddered. "The Veil is...not a place, love. Or not in one place. It is something you move through, like the air, like water."

"So how could it be closed? That doesn't make any sense."

"I'm sorry, my heart." Finn shook his head. "It's difficult for me to explain something I simply know. Perhaps it would be easier to show you."

He rose and offered his hands to Diego, a wave of desire rushing through him when those strong, graceful hands settled in his. *Not now, you idiot.* His cock still stirred and expanded despite his efforts, so he did his best to ignore it.

When he led Diego out of the caverns and the sunlight glinted off his golden shoulders and raven-black hair, Finn gave up entirely. He pulled Diego into a fierce embrace and tilted his head to press their lips together in a searing kiss. He moaned as those beloved hands roamed over his bare back. Finn let his tongue caress Diego's and explored every sensitive ridge and plane of his mouth. The moan turned into a whine of frustration when Diego pulled back.

"*Cariño*, we have things to do."

Finn barely suppressed the urge to stamp his foot. "But I want you. Here. Now. Please, love, just a few minutes…"

Diego lifted both hands to cup his face. "I wish we were home, snuggled on the sofa, watching bad TV, with a pizza in the oven. I wish this would all go away and I could just have you to myself. But we're not, and I can't right now. People need us."

He pulled Finn's head to his shoulder and held him tenderly while Finn tried to hide both his body's trembling and his roiling thoughts.

"What is it, *mi vida*? This isn't just about sex."

Storm and sea wrack. They were too closely attuned now to hide much. Finn thought of a dozen things he wanted to say, such as "I love you so" and "I will stand by your side always". Instead, to his utter horror, he heard himself blurt out, "Did you mate with him?"

Diego pulled back and blinked at him, coffee brown eyes wide in confusion. "Mate with…oh, Lugh. No, *querido*. He asked several times, and we did sleep together but only sleep."

"Ah." Finn pulled in a shuddering breath. "Even that seems too much."

A smile lit Diego's face, the one that always made Finn's heart race. "Finn! You're jealous."

"No, I'm—perhaps I am. A bit." He rubbed at the ache in his chest. "Is this what it feels like to be jealous? As if a heated stone is lodged in your gut and a sudden urge to violence washes over you?"

"Well, yes. Something like that."

Finn huffed. "I don't like it."

"It's not a pleasant feeling." Diego stroked his cheek. "You don't need to be, though. I'm yours and no other's. All of me. Even when I'm not with you."

"I love you so."

"I love you, too, *mi vida*. You don't have anything to worry about." Diego kissed him softly. "Now, show me how to find this thing that's not a place."

With a soft sigh, Finn moved behind him and wrapped him close. Not that he sought an excuse to nestle his erection against that firm, denim-clad backside, but he wouldn't complain about the necessity, either.

"Deep breath, my light," he whispered as Diego closed his eyes. "Reach for me. Mind to mind. Feel what I feel."

Diego leaned back against him, his hands covering Finn's, and suddenly his brilliance nestled against Finn's thoughts, so bright Finn forgot to breathe.

"You are blinding, my hero."

"I'm sorry. Is there any way to tone it down?"

Finn chuckled. *"No, no, I only meant I have never seen you so clearly before. Now...reach with me. Between the worlds. Between the air and the magic. Between the smallest dust motes you can imagine and smaller still. Everywhere. As the magic is. You could cross the Veil through a space tinier than a gnat. Do you feel it? Can you push against it?"*

"Yes, I...feel something. There's a humming. Almost a call. Pulling. Something just out of reach..." Diego went stiff in his arms, then broke off with a frustrated cry and buried his face in his hands. "I can't. I can't feel my way through. Damn it. It's like giving a Rubik's Cube to a chimp and expecting him to figure it out."

"Did the word 'can't' pass your lips again?" The rasping voice made them both jump. Morrigan stood before them with her hands on her hips. "Must I knock sense into you as before?"

Heart hammering, Finn shrank back a step so his anxiety would not transmit to Diego. The sudden urge to shift to something small and flee nearly overwhelmed him. When her cold, sharp eyes met his, he panicked and shifted to the black dog Diego liked so much. Her disdain for him, her disgust over seeing him hammered at him like a hard rain. He curled up at Diego's feet, silent and unobtrusive.

Apparently too distracted, Diego answered as if nothing had passed between them. "I meant it. I can't figure it out, how to get through. I wish you'd all understand. I'm not a sorcerer. I can't do these things instinctively."

Morrigan's voice softened a hair. "If that were true, you would not be here."

"But—" Diego fell silent a moment. "I suppose so. I can't see hurling lightning at it randomly, though. Who knows what kind of damage I might do, here or in the outer world?"

"So. It is no longer the power you doubt, but your control." She nodded and held out a clawed hand.

Finn shivered when Diego, wide-eyed and trusting, settled his hand on her palm. *"Be careful, love."*

"Why?"

"Because she's...Morrigan."

"She won't hurt me, cariño. *Don't worry so."*

"Why do you seek to cross?" she asked sharply. "Do you wish to desert us when we need you most, Taliesin?"

"Of course not." Diego gave her a wry smile. "I just can't help enough. There's someone on the other side who might be able to. A woman who knows things most humans don't understand."

"Ah. A wise woman."

"So I need to see if she'll come here. And if I have to resort to seizures and lightning, then I guess that's what I'll have to do."

"You think in large things, little man," Morrigan went on. "Magic is not always so. Small things can be more powerful."

"Like a virus," Diego muttered.

A little warm ball of satisfaction nestled against Finn's heart when Morrigan looked puzzled. *He* knew about viruses.

"But why me, at all? If the Veil was closed forever, if no one's supposed to be able to get through, why could I?"

Morrigan let out a dry, hacking laugh. "You are what no one considered. The spells were laid, in an intricate web throughout the Veil, so no fae might break the strands."

Diego bent to ruffle Finn's dog ears. "*'Laugh to scorn the power of man; for none of woman born shall harm Macbeth.'* And still he dies. I'm the loophole, the thing unlooked for. Since I'm not fae…"

"Yes." Morrigan nodded. "Humans had no more knowledge of magic. So we thought. And you…you, we thought lost forever."

"So the spells didn't take humans into account. I guess even a ten-thousand-year-old fairy queen can't think of everything."

The gods will have their jokes, Finn thought, though he kept it to himself.

"Since you fear the large, make it small," Morrigan said again.

Diego closed his eyes and stretched out his palm. A blue flash crackled. The air hissed as a lightning ball the size of a mouse hovered over his hand.

"Smaller still. The tiniest thing you can imagine."

Finn lifted his head to watch the lightning shrink. The hiss and crackle remained, lifting the fur along the back of his neck, but the ball faded from sight, presumably to the size of a virus.

"Now, Taliesin. Hurl it through."

"I don't think—"

"Do not think! Now!"

Diego's forehead creased in concentration. His chest heaved a few desperate breaths. Then with a ferocious cry, he flung the miniscule lightning ball from him, not into the visible world but at the fabric of the Veil. A thunderous boom shook the ground beneath their feet. The wind of the Otherworld whipped and howled around them. Diego would have collapsed to his knees without Morrigan's arms around him.

There…oh, sweet goddesses…there…

A scene appeared as if painted over the surrounding woods, a circle of incongruous landscape no larger than one of Finn's own canvases at home. His heart ached. It was home, their snug little house crouched among the larches. Finn surged to his feet, barking, drawn inexorably toward that other place.

Diego sagged against Morrigan, and the scene snapped shut, leaving only the woods of the Otherworld again.

"I couldn't hold it," Diego panted. "I got through, but I couldn't hold it open."

"You will need borrowed strength for that." Morrigan laid him on the grass. "Sleep now. You will need all of your own strength, as well." She passed her hand over Diego's face, and his breathing evened out, his features softening in slumber.

Eyes colder than ice turned on Finn. "You."

With a yelp, Finn scrambled back and shifted to horse to gain some advantage in height.

"Why do you linger here?"

"You know why, Morrigan. Please don't torment me."

"Thief."

"I gave it back."

"The orb was not yours to take."

Finn shook his mane in agitation. "What do you want from me?"

"Liar."

"Yes. I can't help that."

"Coward. Craven, sniveling coward."

"No!" The protest came out as much whinny as word. "I am no coward!"

"You hide whenever battle is joined. You run when those who call you friend need you most."

"I am not *sidhe*! I could not take sides when I loved people in both courts!"

"You think you are the only one? And yet, others chose their loyalties carefully. Others knew where their obligations lay."

"I'm not like you!"

"No. No, you are not, Fionnachd. And you do not deserve to be with him. Honorable, courageous warriors wish to throw themselves at his feet and he refuses them. Because of you."

"He loves me." Finn cringed at the whine in his voice.

"And should not. You only bring him pain, treacherous mischief-tempest that you are."

"It's not true."

"Why did it take so long for him to return to his next life? Why is he so damaged this time?"

"Because of the humans who betrayed him, who tortured him and burned him alive."

"Because of you." She clacked her teeth impatiently. "Do you think they would have branded him and whipped him and burned him if they had not come upon you with your cock up his ass? You who never saw any needs but your own selfish ones. You who found it easier to pretend you didn't understand humans than to admit the danger."

"I tried to protect him," Finn whispered. "I nearly died for him."

"If you truly love him, as you say, you should go away. Let his heart break while he is among those who will soothe him. Let him have the honorable love he deserves."

She stormed off, leaving Finn trembling so hard he thought he might shatter. He shifted back to his own form and stretched out beside Diego to hold his hand while he slept. *It's not true. All those things. I would only leave you if you said I must. If you showed me you needed something else, and even then... Please don't ever tell me to go.*

Chapter Twelve

Wise Woman

"Finn? *Querido*, you've been crying." Diego woke in the warmth of the afternoon sun with a red-eyed Finn curled up against his side.

"Not a bit of it. Don't be ridiculous."

"Yes, you have. What's happened?"

"I was worried for you."

The lie was so obvious that Diego didn't pursue the question. If Finn was simply trolling through memories better left alone, he didn't want to make things worse, and if it was something important, Finn would tell him in his own time.

Diego's stomach growled and Finn bent to kiss the bare skin above his jeans. "I will fetch you something to eat."

"Not crickets, please."

"As you wish." Finn made no move to get up, though, stroking his long fingers through Diego's hair. "They wish to try again this evening. With those who can help you keep the way open."

Something's off here. "*Mi amor*...if I'm holding the Veil open here, who's going to go talk to Tia Carmen?"

"I have thought on that." Finn rose, brushing grass from his hip. "It must be me. There is no one else who knows how to find her. No one else she might give a hearing."

"What? No! I can't send you into the city alone! What if you have an asthma attack..."

Finn had already strolled away, though, dismissing Diego's protests with a vague wave of his hand.

"Damn it." Diego sat up to scrub his hands over his face. His muscles ached as if he'd run up forty flights of stairs, making him wonder whether Morrigan's enforced sleep had been the only thing holding off a seizure.

As if the thought conjured her, she settled beside him on the grass, tearing at a freshly caught trout with her sharp teeth. She held out the partially mangled fish. "Are you hungry, Intrepid One?"

"Um, thanks, no." Diego tried not to gag at the sight of exposed fish guts. "Finn's bringing me something."

She shrugged and returned to demolishing her catch.

"Finn says he's going through if I can open the Veil again."

"Do you trust him?" Morrigan mumbled around a bite.

Diego turned that over, certain the question came from some history between them. "Do I trust him to come back, to do what he says he will? Yes. Do I trust him to be safe doing it? Not so much."

She growled into her fish.

Diego changed the subject. "Have you gone in to see Lugh?"

"A hole in the ground is no place for a raven," she said with a snort.

"It's hardly a hole. And Angus is in there. Caverns aren't all that natural for eagles, either."

"He had no choice, and would gladly follow Sionnach's bushy tail into a morass if need be." Morrigan bit the head off her fish, crunching through the bones with evident relish. "I will lend you my strength this evening. Mine for the *sidhe*, Eithne's for the Fomor."

Hungry a few moments before, Diego wasn't certain he could ever face fish again. Madre de dios, *who knew fish bones made so much noise?* "Because you like me so much?"

She let out one of her strange, hacking laughs. "I do like you, little human. But aside from Danu and Balor, Eithne and I are the strongest, the farthest-seeing still standing."

On the last word, Finn wandered back out, carrying, of all things, peaches and grapes. Morrigan abruptly took her leave.

"You go into a cave, *mi vida*, to find fruit?" Diego hummed in delight at the scent of fresh peach and bit eagerly into the one Finn handed him.

"Nathair has a garden, love. I'll take you there sometime." Finn stared after Morrigan's retreating back, tense and distracted.

"She doesn't think much of you, does she?"

"Ah…no."

"Want to tell me about it?"

Finn shrugged. "There is not much to tell. It was long ago. I borrowed her orb. She took offense and beat me to within a hair of my life. I gave it back. Since then, she would find fault with me if I sat still as stone for a thousand years."

"Maybe you shouldn't, um, borrow things without asking."

"It was pretty and shone. I was simply curious and had no intention of keeping it. Not as if I could see with the blasted thing."

"See what?" Diego lay back with his head on Finn's thigh, wanting both his touch and a good view of his face.

"Some fae…" Finn hesitated, the little crease forming between his brows that appeared when he tried to find the right words. "They don't truly see the future. But they speak prophecy when the fugue takes them and they see…places we don't. Easóg uses a silver bowl. Morrigan uses an orb of some lovely yellow stone with tiny branches trapped in it…" He drifted off, apparently lost in the memory of this fascinating object.

"Dendritic agate?"

"More than likely."

"You've no idea what I just said."

"Not the slightest notion."

This was what Diego had missed more than the sex — this easy companionship, the way each could draw a smile so readily from the other. He reached up to curl his hand around the back of Finn's neck and pulled him down for a tender kiss. Finn hummed against his lips and licked the peach juice from his chin before he pulled back to gaze at Diego's face, desire sparking in his black eyes. "Tease."

"Sorry." Diego tugged on the leg of his jeans, which were suddenly uncomfortable. "Balor seems to think this illness has to do with a prophecy. You wouldn't know what he means?"

Finn sat back on a deep breath. "We all know the one, my heart. It is a dark one, one which struck Morrigan and Easóg in the same moment, though they were miles apart at the time."

"And? What was it?"

"I don't suppose I could persuade you to ask someone else?"

"Not if you know it." Diego put the peach pit on the ground and wrapped his arms around Finn's neck. "Tell me, *querido*. It's all right."

With a shudder, Finn rested his cheek against the top of Diego's head, his voice rumbling soft and low in his chest as he recited,

"The strongest lie wasting
The many-voiced stilled
Silken wings tumble earthward
To halve the whole
Leaves only silence
No earth
No song
No light
No life."

"Rather...ominous." Diego swallowed hard. "What does it mean? Halves of what? Is it a reference to the fae being divided?"

"If anyone knows, they have not spoken." Finn shrugged. "Seems a lot of nonsense to me."

The dismissal showed Diego how unsettled Finn was by the recitation. *Too damn tense. Neither one of us thinks straight that way.* He slid down to nuzzle at Finn's hard-packed stomach, his scent a siren call to his tightly strung nerves.

"My heart, my light," Finn said in a strained whisper. "Please don't, unless you intend to do more than dip a toe in the water."

"Hush, *mi vida*, don't worry. I want total immersion."

Finn stroked his hair, encouraging him lower, until Diego's tongue reached out to tap the crown of his erection. With a low growl, Finn rolled down onto his back. "My love, could you— Oh, sweet mother of—" He broke off with a gasp when Diego plunged halfway down his shaft.

Wild and enticing, the flavor of Finn's skin only made Diego want more. He sucked harder, taking him in until the head hit the back of his throat. The way Finn gripped his hair and writhed beneath him sent shockwaves of pleasure to his groin. A sensual being, even when he felt poorly, Finn had never been hard to please, and his delight at every touch, every lick and caress, held more eroticism than some lovers' entire repertoires.

"Diego," Finn whispered. "Turn for me. I would taste you as well. Please."

More than happy to oblige, Diego repositioned himself so his knees straddled Finn's head. Anyone might see them in their shaded, grassy spot, but for once, he could not have cared any less. Long fingers pulled the buttons open on his jeans and peeled the denim down to mid-thigh, letting his cock spring free, already hard and aching.

Finn's incredible tongue wrapped around his head and halfway round again and Diego moaned with the dizzy rush of pleasure. Unable to speak, mouth full of Finn, he showed him how much he appreciated the attention by tonguing at Finn's little slit and plunging down his length again.

Growls and whimpers of ecstasy replaced any coherent speech or thought for a good while after that as they devoured each other. Diego cupped Finn's balls, rolling them gently, pleased when the skin tightened under his thumb. Finn's sounds became more desperate, his hips rolling faster, and Diego pressed two fingers to the sensitive stretch of skin just behind his sac.

The reaction was spectacular. Finn arched up off the ground with a strangled cry, his fingers digging hard into Diego's thighs. The first splash of his sweet and salty seed hit Diego's tongue and he felt his own balls draw up tight. With two deep thrusts into Finn's eager mouth, Diego came in hard pulses, his muffled cries of pleasure sending Finn into twitching aftershocks.

There might have been something in the universe more pleasurable, but as Diego lay panting with his head on Finn's thigh, he was hard-pressed to think of one. "Better?"

"Yes, my hero. Thank you," Finn gasped out.

Diego flopped down beside him and settled Finn's head on his shoulder. "*De nada, corazón*. Now, I have the bad feeling I won't be able to talk you out of going, and honestly, I can't think of another solution. So talk to me. How will you get there?"

Finn raised his head and blinked at him in honest confusion. "Through the Veil."

"Yes, but when I opened it the last time, the door or gate or whatever led to our house. How would you get to New York from there?"

"Why would—" Finn's brow furrowed, then smoothed as understanding dawned. "Ah. I see the confusion. You choose the spot, my heart. Or that was how it always was before. You most likely had been thinking of home, and that was where you opened the Veil. If you wish to open it in the city, you must consciously choose to."

"Simple as that?"

Finn shrugged. "Must everything be complicated?"

Diego pulled him back down with a chuckle. "No, certainly not. I'll take simple, now and then." He stroked Finn's hair, silent for a moment. "Okay. So if I open the Veil, say, in the little park two blocks down from my old apartment, would you remember how to get to Tia Carmen's?"

"You wound me. Perhaps I did not like the city, but that does not mean I shut my eyes the entire time I dwelt there. Besides, the scent of her cooking would lead me if I became lost."

"You're joking, right? In the thousands of smells there, you can pick that out?"

"How do you think I found my way back to you the first time I ran away from you, my hero?"

"Oh… This might work, after all. What do you plan to look like when you step through?"

"Myself."

"*Querido*, think. What would happen if a naked pooka suddenly stepped out of thin air in the middle of a public park?"

Finn traced circles on Diego's chest. "I suppose you are suggesting the pooka in question might be detained by the authorities. I'll go as a dog. Humans like dogs."

"Better, but maybe a little conspicuous. Someone might want to find out who such a beautiful dog belongs to."

"Crow?"

"Perfect. Just don't go tangling with anyone named T-Bird."

"Pardon?"

"Movie reference. We'll watch it sometime when we get home." He sighed as Finn snuggled closer. *Home.* He hoped the day would come when they would have a homecoming, though he had the feeling the world had changed irrevocably for them both.

* * * *

Finn shivered in the evening breeze. The cold rarely troubled him, but this was an inner chill. The thought of leaving Diego's side again sent spears of ice down his spine, a sensation he could never quite pin down as either premonition or mere anxiety. He had promised he would do this, though, and there were dozens of reasons he would not fail Diego.

"Send someone else," Morrigan had told Diego quite bluntly.

While Diego had defended him in his calm, reasonable way, Finn hadn't spoken a word on his own behalf. She was right. He was a coward and had no sense of honor in the way other fae did. Even now, waiting for the Veil to open, he wanted to run and hide in the river, terrified of facing the noise and confusion of the poisoned city again.

He closed his eyes and breathed deeply of the clean air while he could. Running now would prove her right on all counts and bear out her assertion that he was, indeed, unworthy of Diego's love. He had heard a hundred times about true courage being the ability to carry on despite fear but he did not feel the truth of it in his bones. Fear was simply fear. If one acted despite it and through it, one was simply stubborn or stupid.

Perhaps both.

"All right, I think I have it," Diego said with a nod. "Finn? *Mi vida*, are you ready?"

Finn conjured a smile from somewhere and searched his recent memory for something to ease the tension in Diego's jaw. "Let's rock and roll." It worked — Diego's beautiful laugh sluiced over him like soft rain.

"You're certain you'll be all right? That the smog won't keep you from shifting or lay you out flat?" Diego leaned over to kiss his jaw.

"I will not breathe the poisoned air long enough, love. An hour or two, no more."

A touch on his arm startled him.

"Be careful, Fionnachd," Nathair whispered. "Hurry back."

So many reasons not to fail… He gave Nathair a quick hug, then went to stand by Diego.

"I don't know how long I'll be able to hold it open, *querido*." Diego gave him a quick kiss. "So if you come back to the spot where you crossed and the door's closed, wait there. Somehow I'll get it open again to retrieve you, okay?"

"Fair enough."

"Do nothing rash, Fionnachd. Be visible as little as you can," Eithne cautioned softly. The implication hung in the air. Humans were savage and brutal, and destroyed the things they did not understand, but no one knew this better than Finn did.

"I have lived in this city, beautiful one. I know what I'm about."

Diego shot him a raised eyebrow, but apparently chose not to contradict him. With Eithne's hand on his right shoulder and Morrigan's on his left, he closed his eyes and spread his arms, palms up. The gesture was so like the first Taliesin, Finn's heart lurched. But then,

Diego *was* the first Taliesin and all the subsequent ones, just an older soul now and less innocent. The first Taliesin had learned to work the world's magic because he had been untouched by the weight of centuries, undamaged. He'd simply opened his heart and let the flows lead him. Diego, though, wounded and barricaded, had learned by raw courage and snatched up bits of instinct. He forced the flows to come to him.

The fine hairs at the back of Finn's neck stood on end as Diego pulled the magic to him, a huge reservoir of power. With more time, someone here could have taught him finesse and control, but time was not in abundance.

The spark leaped to Diego's hand, his brow furrowed in fierce concentration. Finn shifted to crow in preparation, the view from less than knee height a bit odd as the opening in the Veil appeared. A wooden bench, a tree, and a street lamp resolved on the other side.

"Is it the right place, my hero?" Crow-Finn called out.

"Yes." Diego got out between clenched teeth. "I know that tree. Go, *querido*. Hurry. I don't think I can hold this long."

With a rush of wings, Finn leaped into the air and hurtled through, a midnight-black missile on a fae-born wind. The dense, unclean air hit him with brutal force, and he fought to stay aloft. Exhaust from a thousand vehicles competed with the stench of rot and unwashed human, cold iron and sharp, sulfurous fumes. At least the park was relatively quiet, empty of humans save one, a man who ran with that peculiar gait they called *jogging*. Not running for the joy of it or because he was pursued, but because if he did not, he would grow fat and unhealthy. Strange way to live.

"*Mi vida?*" Diego's thoughts interrupted his. "*Are you there? Have you found the way?*"

"*Just on my way now. I have it.*" Storm and thunder, he had let himself get distracted already. He flew to the edge of the park, and the street did look familiar. With two false starts, he managed to find the right direction, then despaired when he found Diego's old apartment building. All the windows stared at him with empty eyes, all the same. He had no notion which one was hers.

A passerby startled as he landed atop a newspaper box on the corner, but he ignored the man's curses. He cocked his avian head to the side and tried to recall how far up Tia Carmen's apartment would be. Six sets of stairs? Eight? Ten? Why, by all the world's waters, couldn't he remember?

Wait... A scent reached him through all the other odors, a complex, heady mix of spices, chilies and cocoa — *mole* sauce. Finn let out a triumphant caw and soared toward the eighth floor, straight to the window from whence the heavenly scent wafted. White hair gleaming in the lamplight, Tia Carmen worked at her stove, stirring the pot of sauce Finn loved so much. By all the gods, she was a beautiful sight.

He let out a sharp, corvus call, but she didn't hear, so he resorted to banging on the window with his thick beak. Her head came up, a frown on her face, then her white brows shot up when she spotted him on the window ledge.

With slow, deliberate movements, she took the spoon from the sauce, covered the pot, turned down the fire and came to open the window.

"*Buenas noches, Señor Corneja,*" she said politely. "Are you hungry? Is that why you knock?"

"It's me, dear lady, it's Finn."

"*Ay dios! Dulce*, what are you doing here? Where is Diego?"

He hopped inside and shifted to his own bipedal form on her kitchen floor, and nothing would do but she had to fetch blankets to cover him and tea to warm him while he explained as quickly as he could where Diego was and why he had come.

"So *las hadas*, they are dying?"

"It would appear so."

Her eyes lost focus a moment as she pondered. "I must go then. This cannot be. Must not be." She took Finn's arm, pressed him down into one of the kitchen chairs and plunked a plate of enchiladas in front of him. "Eat, *querido*. You are too thin again. Too worn. I need to get some things."

She brought a green tapestry bag from the closet and bustled about the kitchen gathering this and that while Finn happily tucked into his impromptu dinner.

"*Finn? Did you find her? Are you coming?*" Diego's thoughts sounded thin and harried.

"*I'm here with her, my heart.*"

There was a long pause, followed by a trickle of irritation. "*You're eating? I'm struggling like hell to keep this damned door open and you're stuffing your face?*"

"*She is not ready, love. I merely wait for her.*"

"*Carajo…Finn…please ask her to hurry.*"

"Tia Carmen? Diego says—"

"I hear him, *dulcito*. Tell him he does not need to shout so loud."

Finn hid a smile behind a mouthful of mole-smothered chicken. He had always known she was more than the kind, grandmotherly face she showed the world, but she did surprise even him from time to time.

"*Entonces*, I am ready," she said finally, her bag looped over her arm. "Where do we need to go?"

"Not far, dear lady. To the park down the street."

She sighed. "He could not pick somewhere an old lady could walk safely at night? I wish you could walk beside me, but I have no clothes for you, so I guess you need to be a crow again."

Finn held up a hand and shifted to a more suitable form. He looked up at her, letting his tongue hang out in a doggy grin. "I will be your guard dog."

"Perfect. And such a pretty dog." She stroked the black fur of his thick ruff. "*Bueno*. I will be safe with my fierce protector."

They went down the steps, Finn racing ahead and racing back in his anxiety to move her faster, but her legs would only move at one pace. All his jumping and prancing from one step to another only served to make him more and more anxious.

Half a block from the park, Diego's thoughts pierced his, laced with regret. "Cariño, *I can't hold…*"

"*Let it go, bucko.*" Finn sent back. "*Gather your strength again. We'll wait, as you said.*"

"*I don't know how long.*"

"*Never fear, my hero. I have faith in you.*"

The door in the Veil shut with an audible snap, like a limb breaking. "*Or someone's heart.*"

Finn relayed the message, though he suspected Tia Carmen had heard the gist of it. When they reached the spot where the door had been, she sat down on the bench to wait, and he curled up at her feet.

"I wish you had come just to visit," she said on a gusty exhalation. "But it is good to see you. I've missed you both."

Finn picked his furred head up and leaned against her shin. "We have missed you as well, dear lady. Perhaps we could persuade you to move to Montana with us?"

She laughed. "Me, in the middle of the forest? I have lived all my life in cities, *querido*. I would not know how to live, and my family is here. You wouldn't want to take me from my grandchildren, eh?"

The last, he suspected, was the real reason. "Very well. But you can't blame me for asking."

"We still talk on the phone."

Quite true. Finn called her almost every week. She was the top, right-hand button on Diego's phones. "It's not the same as seeing you. Being with you."

"Maybe Diego can talk me into visiting."

They talked of small things to hide their anxious thoughts. *Good thing the park is deserted.* People often talked to their dogs but passing humans most likely would not take it well when the dog answered back.

Perhaps twenty minutes had gone by, or perhaps several centuries, when the fur at Finn's nape bristled.

"Someone watches us," he told Tia Carmen. "And I do not think it is simple curiosity."

She clutched her bag tighter, a determined set to her features. "Diego needs to hurry up. This is no place for an old lady after dark."

The sharp crackle of dry leaves heralded someone approaching at speed through the shrubbery behind them. Finn leaped to his feet, snarling, as a figure broke through the screen of bushes and rushed down on them. The man made a grab for Tia Carmen's bag, but she held firm, glaring at him.

Finn growled and barked, trying to sound as threatening as possible. The man ignored him and yanked something out of his jacket. He had watched enough television to recognize a gun.

"Gimme the fucking bag, you wrinkled old bitch!" the would-be thief yelled, waving the gun in her face.

Four things happened then in lightning succession. Finn leaped for the man, jaws closing on his left arm. The gun went off. With a roar of displaced air, the Veil reopened. Startled, the man's grip loosened and Tia Carmen sprayed something in his face.

"*Finn!*" Diego's anguished cry sounded thin and exhausted.

The thief rolled on the ground, hands clawing at his face. Finn thought his view of the scene rather odd until he realized he also lay on the ground.

"*Dulcito*? Can you get up? We don't need to go far," Tia Carmen urged, her hand on his shoulder.

He dragged himself up, limbs shaking. His back leg refused to hold him. Only when it crumpled the second time did the pain register. "The churl shot me," he murmured in shock.

"Yes, he did. Though I think you will survive. Come now, just a few steps. Diego is hysterical and needs to see you are well."

"I wouldn't go so far as 'well'," Finn grumbled as he limped forward, dragging his hind leg.

They stepped through the doorway, the man still screaming behind them.

"What did you do to him? Was it some spell?" Finn asked with a last look over his shoulder.

"Pepper spray."

The door snapped shut, leaving behind the screams and the vile stench of the city.

Diego fell to his knees between his supporters. "Finn! *Gracias a Dios*...you're alive. I heard the shot..."

Finn crawled to him and placed his shaggy head in Diego's lap. "I'll heal, my heart. It's not so bad. You may want to lie down, though. You're about—"

He cut off as Diego's eyes rolled back and his limbs stiffened. Too late, he realized Diego hadn't had any of his seizure medicine in nearly two weeks. He should have asked Tia Carmen if she had some of it to bring.

While Diego twitched and jerked on the ground, Tia Carmen took stock of her surroundings.

"It is beautiful here. Just as I always imagined," she said with a nod.

"You are the wise woman?" Eithne asked, a matter of formality rather than an actual question.

"*Una bruja*, yes. Finn thinks I might be able to help."

"Astounding that he retrieved you at all," Morrigan snapped out. "You couldn't even keep one old human safe, Fionnachd?"

Tia Carmen clicked her tongue in exasperation. "No wonder you need me, if all *las hadas* do is stand around and argue." She pointed a finger at Eithne. "You, *Señora Gata*, can you carry Diego?" She waited until Eithne nodded. "Good. He must not lie on the cold, damp ground." Then she turned to Nathair. "And can you carry Finn, *Señor Culebra*? Good, thank you."

She waited for them to do as she asked, bag clutched primly in both hands. "So. Someone lead the way. I have patients to see."

Chapter Thirteen

Mediator

Diego woke to an argument in progress, fierce whispers shooting back and forth over his head.

"...must let me see!"

He struggled to place the velvet soft voice, unable to recall where he was.

"No!" That voice he knew, Finn's growl unmistakable. "Too many times has he woken alone after these fits. I will not desert him."

"It is hardly desertion, putting him down for a moment to let us see to your leg." That one...the voice had a name...Nathair. Yes.

"If the musket ball is iron, it will poison you. Please, Fionnachd." The purring voice again...Eithne.

He opened his eyes to the three faces hovering above him, the world rushing back with all the nausea and pain of post-seizure. The Otherworld, Fomorian caverns, the need to bring Tia Carmen through all flooded back. She sat with the ill fae, Easóg curled in a ball with his head in her lap while she fed something to

Faolchú and spoke softly to Lugh. Angus sat up against a pillar with Sionnach propped against his chest while Scath nestled content in Croi's arms, all of them sipping mugs of tea and giving Tia Carmen their full attention.

Diego reached up with trembling fingers to touch Finn's face. "Let them look, *cariño*. Don't be so stubborn," he got out in a hoarse whisper.

"You're awake." Finn smiled down at him. "Though I hope I don't offend you if I say you've looked better."

"That's okay. I know I look like death on toast." Diego let his head rest against Finn's chest, the strong beat of his heart comforting. "Put me down, *mi vida*."

"No one uses musket balls anymore," Finn grumbled.

"True, but the bullet probably had a steel tip, at least. Is it still in your leg?"

Finn twisted to look at the wound. "I don't...believe so. By rights it would hurt more then."

Diego used Finn's shoulder to sit up, and would have kept insisting if a commotion hadn't interrupted.

"No, no and no!" Balor roared from the other side of the Great Hall. "I have allowed two humans in my kingdom, and my benighted, cursed grandson, but not *her*!"

The *her* in question stood calmly in the entrance, one delicate green brow arched, lips pursed in disapproval. "You have my people here," Danu replied evenly. "*My* grandson. My herald. My Taliesin—"

"*Your* Taliesin! You arrogant, high-handed bi—"

He cut off, startled, when Tia Carmen placed a palm on his chest. Diego had to smile, despite how much he ached. Balor was four times her size, by far the most intimidating being Diego had ever met, and yet Tia Carmen had no fear, gazing up into his tusked face and speaking softly to him.

Diego rose on trembling legs, shaking off Finn's attempt to drag him back down. "*Majestad.*" He motioned to Danu. "I think it's time the four of us had a conversation. Somewhere quiet."

"The four of us?" she asked, her expression caught between concern and amusement.

"Yes, you and I, Balor and Tia Carmen."

"You are hardly able to stand."

Diego leaned his shoulder against the nearest column, scrubbing at his face. "I won't argue that, so I hoped we could sit down somewhere."

"Balor!" Danu called over. "Taliesin calls council."

"The poor boy's barely conscious," Balor growled. He leaned down to hear something Tia Carmen whispered to him. "Ah. The wise woman agrees." Balor straightened, jaw jutting aggressively. "For her and for Taliesin, I agree to this. Not for you."

"I did not suggest otherwise," Danu said with a chill smile.

Balor strode over, scooped Diego up in one huge, hairy arm then quite deliberately turned his back on Danu as he stalked out of the Hall. Diego bit back a sigh. For all their age, the fae could be quite childish.

The Fomorian king wound his way down several corridors and finally stopped in a large chamber with a fire roaring in a central pit. He eased Diego down onto a bed of furs near the fire, and the warmth from the sand floor seeped up to soothe Diego's aching limbs.

"I have nothing to say to him." Danu nodded to Balor as she settled nearby.

Balor merely snorted.

"That's fine, *majestads*. You don't need to say a word to each other," Diego reassured them while Tia Carmen wrapped the furs around him. "What we need to talk about is this illness afflicting your people." He smiled at his old landlady, one of his oldest friends. "It's good to see you, Tia Carmen. I don't suppose you have any aspirin?"

"*Por supuesto, mijo.* You think I would pack a bag without it?" She patted his arm and produced both a bottle of aspirin and a bottle of water from her bag.

"Ah, *gracias.* I don't know why I doubted." He downed the pills and half the water before he tried to speak again, his voice shaking slightly less than his hands. "So what do you think? Is it a virus? Something they're eating?"

She folded her legs beside her and arranged her skirts carefully. For a few moments, she stared into the fire, her expression guarded. "I have spoken to them all. They have told me how it begins, how it feels. The little one with the furred head, he told me of the prophecy."

"Did it make sense to you?" Diego levered himself up on one elbow.

She poked at the fire with a stick, sending up sparks. "They are dying, *mijo.* It will be a slow, painful death. The illness takes those who are most sensitive, like the little butterflies, and those who bear the burden of responsibility for their people. The Champions, who fight for them. The Heralds, who speak for them. The Seers, who look into the dark places no one else dares. In the end, it will take all of them. These two" — she pointed with her chin to the two rulers — "will be the last."

"Why them?"

"They are the eldest, the fountainhead. With them it began, and with them it will end."

"You said the Seers would be among the first, but Morrigan isn't sick yet." Diego managed to sit up, his head in his hands.

"No. She is not male."

"Which has what to do with anything?"

Tia Carmen shared a look with Danu. "*Las mujeres*, women of any race...we carry the world within us. A piece of that magic inside us. It will keep them well longer."

"My head hurts too much, I think. I don't follow you at all."

"For the fae to live, they need magic as we need air. But without the world in which we were all born, they have only half of what they need. They must have both, the magic here—the fae magic—and the magic of our world—the earth magic." Tia Carmen pointed with her stick to Danu. "She knows. When she closed the way between, she knew what would happen."

An ominous rumble shook the chamber. Balor surged to his feet. "You *knew*? You purposefully slaughter your own kind and kin? You heartless, unnatural *bitch*!"

"What choice was left to me?" Danu said in a weary voice, apparently unconcerned that Balor loomed over her with clenched fists. "The humans poisoned the outer world. You wished to kill them to stop them. All of them. We could have had endless war and a slow death by poison in the outer world, or a quieter one on our own terms here."

"You chose certain death for us and gave us no say in the matter!"

"I chose not to watch the slaughter of innocents, you mange-ridden, bloodthirsty brute!"

"My surviving children will die in agony!"

"My son is already dead because of you!" Danu roared as she leaped to her feet.

Ah, finally, to the heart of the matter. Diego had heard the story from Finn, how Danu's son Cian had mated with Eithne, without permission from either court. Eithne's family had insisted she was forced. Cian's family had been furious that he had taken a Fomorian as his life mate. Balor's sons had come after Cian, and in the ensuing fight, killed him. Balor blamed Cian, Danu blamed Balor. There were rumors of trickery and deceit, but to Diego, it had sounded like young, hotheaded males acting without thinking.

Eithne had disappeared for many years afterward, no one knew where. When she'd returned, Lugh had been by her side, fully grown and a master in all the arts both material and martial. Some said he was raised among the *bane sidhe*, the strange nocturnal fae who lived in barrow mounds. Others said he had been fostered by dragons. Eithne would never say.

"For two people who have nothing to say to each other, you certainly don't seem at a loss for words," Diego said dryly into a break in the argument.

They both whirled on him, eyes glowing with red flame.

He went on in a more gentle tone. "*Majestads*, you have both lost sons. I am sorry for your loss and for your terrible pain. A parent should never have to face the agony of losing a child. It is something you share, though, as you share this world and the responsibility for the people in it. You do not have to like each other, but maybe it's time to put old injuries aside."

"And what would you have us do, Taliesin?" Danu asked with an uncharacteristic crack in her voice.

"I'm not that first Taliesin, Light of the World." He used her formal title and got a raised brow. Good. She was thinking again instead of reacting. "He died over two thousand years ago."

"So. Diego, then," Balor rumbled and leaned back against the wall. "We are at an impasse."

"If you look at the problem as having only two choices, then, yes, you are in an impossible situation. Danu won't let you go through to take the world back by force, and you won't accept her decision to let your people die in peace."

"The sun will freeze first."

"But if there's another way, would you listen?" Diego looked from one to the other, waiting until he had two nods. "What if I told you there are places still in the world which are not spoiled? True, they're not perfect like here, but clean enough."

"After so many years, there are such places?" Danu took a step closer.

"Finn was poisoned when I found him. One of these places made him well again. We live in another one now."

"They must be small places. Dangerous," Balor rumbled. "The humans would find us and hunt us again."

"The witch hunts are over, Heart of the Earth. The inquisitors long gone. Modern humans no longer believe in real magic and so only see what they think they should. If it's simply a matter of having a haven, somewhere the fae could come and stand on the ground of the outer world to get better again, I think we could arrange it." Diego shivered and pulled the furs closer around him. "Though I'm not sure how many times I can hold a door in the Veil open before I'm comatose."

Danu settled back on the sand beside him. "A door could be built, little one. A door you needn't struggle to keep open."

"You said it was impossible!" Balor snapped.

She shrugged. "And so it was, before Diego came to us. The door needs four corners. A human sorcerer must be one of them. A human for the fire, one of the *sidhe* for the air, a Fomorian for the earth and one of the water folk." She turned to the mouth of the chamber. "Fionnachd, you may as well join us, since you have eavesdropped on all the rest."

Finn's head appeared around the wall. He gnawed on his thumbnail. "It was not my intent, Light of the World. I simply—"

"Yes, yes, you were worried for your love and found the conversation too fascinating to interrupt," Danu said with a hint of a smile. "Come in, dearheart. It is good to see you."

"And you, most lovely of the *sidhe*." The rest of Finn followed, limping in with a blanket clutched around his shoulders, a sure sign he wasn't feeling well.

"How's the leg, *mi vida*?"

"It will heal. There was no bullet in the wound."

"You do know my heart stopped when that gun went off."

"I'm sorry I worried you, my hero." Finn settled by him and let Diego lean against him. "I seem to do more than a bit of that."

Diego patted his arm, less exposed with Finn beside him.

"The blasted bitch knew all along," Balor muttered, still wallowing in bitterness.

"As if you had not guessed," Danu shot back.

"Please, *majestads*, your people are the priority now. They can't die." Diego clutched at Finn's arm, suddenly dizzy. "The magic will fade...the worlds will fail..."

"We have the four of us with Fionnachd. We open the door at once!" Balor struck the wall with his fist.

Tia Carmen shook her head. "Let Diego regain his strength first. He can barely hold his own head up and you want him to build magical doorways?"

Balor grunted, subsiding. "He may rest here, then. Fionnachd may stay with him. Fionnachd, you stay by your Diego. He has sense. Listen to his council and not the poisonous words of she-bears."

"I will think on this solution." Danu bent to kiss Finn's cheek. "Comfort him, keep him warm. You were always welcome in the Grove."

The room pitched and spun, the only solid point Finn's heart beating against Diego's ear. He wanted to say something to comfort Finn, he seemed so subdued and anxious, but he couldn't find his voice and couldn't concentrate enough to reach out to Finn's mind.

"Finn—"

"Shh, my heart. You have driven yourself too hard. Please rest." Finn rocked him gently, humming to him.

Diego smiled when he realized it was a Natalie Merchant song.

* * * *

Finn sat with Diego's sleeping form across his lap for more than an hour, watching Balor's magic fire, which only required a single log a day to keep it roaring. He tried to pretend it was their fireplace at home, but it was no use. Echoes from other chambers kept interrupting his attempts at fantasy, reminders of where they were and what surrounded them.

At least he understood now why he had been able to help the ailing fae. He had been in the outer world, had absorbed the magic there that they had been missing. It was not, as Nathair suggested, any special quality about Finn. He was simply a carrier of magic residue.

"*Querido*, go walk," Tia Carmen said when she came back from checking on her patients. "Your leg will stiffen. I will stay by him."

He nodded and rose carefully, only satisfied when Diego had been tucked under the furs and his breathing had evened out in deep sleep again.

"You were very brave today," she whispered to him.

"I was foolish. You saved us," Finn murmured, chewing on his bottom lip while he gazed down at Diego's handsome face.

"Finn…" A catch in Tia Carmen's voice made him look up. "Whatever someone has said to you, whatever thoughts were planted, he loves you. Never doubt that."

He managed a little grin for her. "Never, dear lady. Not even if the sun freezes."

When he wandered out to the Great Hall, he found it nearly deserted except for the ill fae and Danu, who approached them with a sharp look toward the throne. It stood deserted though, Balor nowhere in sight.

Angus tried to rise to greet her and fell to his hands and knees, gasping. She crouched down to help him back into his blankets and to dry Sionnach's tears. Then she knelt by Lugh to speak to him, stroking his hair. Scath received a gentle hug, Easóg a pat. Finn thought his jaw might unhinge at what she did next. She stretched out next to Faolchú, kissing his muzzle and nuzzling at his ear. Perhaps Faolchú truly had made love to every fae he had ever seen.

After a few moments, she rose and walked out. Driven by an odd mix of curiosity and concern, Finn followed and caught up with her near the entrance to the caverns, tears glistening on her lovely face as she turned her gaze to the moon.

"Danu? Why do you weep?"

She shook her head and swiped impatiently at her face. "Ach, Fionnachd. It is hard to see him suffering so. These are the nights Faolchú loved, with the full moon and the fog rising. He has always been so strong."

"Yes." Finn took her hand. "But there is still hope."

"So it would seem. But I cannot see what lies ahead, and Morrigan's orb has gone dark. What if we do this, we open a stable doorway, and it is the wrong thing? What if the humans hunt us as Balor says, with these new, terrible weapons?"

"There are many compassionate humans." Finn stepped closer to wrap his arms around her. "You love Diego and you see Tia Carmen. I have seen them through Diego's eyes, and there are many I have come to cherish."

"But are there enough?" She leaned into his embrace, and a frisson of sudden desire raced over his skin. Her touch had that effect on most males. "Do we go from death to death, one worse than the other? We gave them everything, Fionnachd. When they were naked starvelings, we pitied them. Showed them how to hunt and to fish and to plant. Why have they forgotten us?"

"Human lives are so short, Light of the World. And their memories often die with them. I think in the times when we weren't ever-present, they forgot. I don't say we should reveal ourselves to them, go on the evening news and shout 'here we are' — "

"Evening news?"

"Humans use it to tell them important things, like if it will rain the next day."

"They could simply look out the window in the morning."

"Yes, well, true enough, but what I meant to say was I have been living safely in the human world. I think it can be done."

She placed a soft kiss on his lips and his knees threatened to buckle. "You are different, Fionnachd. I am not certain yet it is a good thing."

With that, she vanished on the wind, leaving his arms empty and his mind spinning.

Chapter Fourteen

The Home for Convalescent Fae

By the next evening, Diego was back on his feet.

"We can't wait any longer," he insisted when Finn protested he wasn't strong enough. "Faolchú's barely breathing and Scath is just about comatose. Whatever we were doing for them before isn't enough anymore, *mi vida*."

Eyes downcast, Finn nodded. He turned to walk off when Diego seized his arm.

"Have I done something? Not done something? Said something wrong?"

Finn patted his hand. "No, my heart. I am...unsettled. Uncertain."

"About?"

"Everything and nothing. Pay me no heed. My leg aches, and I have had little rest in the past weeks. I need a good swim, a good nap in the sun, and a good screw."

Diego pulled him into a hard embrace. "Let's get this done, and you can have all that. And ice cream, too."

"Oh, yes, that would be lovely. The kind with the nuts and little swirls and things?"

"Rocky Road and Moose Tracks and whatever else you want, *caro*. I'll buy you gallons, and you can pig out."

"Hmm, I'll have to think on the order of things. It might be nice to have the swim first, though that might be better after mating, and the ice cream might be useful *during*..." Finn wandered off to find Danu, muttering to himself.

When the four necessary elements had been assembled, Diego cleared his throat. His next request could well cause the uneasy truce to shatter again. "If this works, I'd like to take Faolchú through first. He's the one in dire straits, and I think we should see how it goes before we bring everyone else through."

Balor drew himself up, eyes hard and glinting as he glared at Danu, apparently ready for an argument. She ignored him. "Of course," she said in a calm, even tone. "Faolchú will be first."

"What in blazes is that supposed to mean?" Balor growled. "What are you playing at?"

"Your champion is near death," she answered, though she still refused to look at him. "If this is the right thing, then Diego will have saved him. If it is not..." She ended with a shrug.

"Bitch," Balor muttered. "Using our Faolchú as a test."

"I don't think he has much time, *majestad*," Diego interjected before things could turn truly ugly again. "For him, I think it's this or nothing, now or never."

Balor gave him a friendly clap on the shoulder that nearly knocked him flat. "Right you are, boy. No matter *her* reasons, we have to save him."

"My heart," Finn spoke softly in his ear. "You truly want me as the fourth here? Perhaps someone more powerful...?"

"*Dios*, Finn, who could we have water-wise more powerful than you?" Diego reached up to smooth a stray wisp of hair from Finn's cheek. "Who else do you know who survived two lightning strikes?"

"That has nothing to do—"

"Yes, it does. You're a survivor, *mi vida*. There's enormous power in that. And it's *your* strength that's always guided me before."

Diego rolled his shoulders, willing himself to relax as he turned back to Danu. The moon sent fingers of silver light through the trees, glinting off the islands of rising fog and Danu's pale skin. He shivered, struck by a creeping alienation. He was the oddity here, the stranger in a land that had never seen a human birth.

Diego drew a deep breath. "Okay, so I make the opening, then you three make the doorway? Is that how this works?"

"It is your spell, your working," Danu told him. "You must direct the flows. We are the notes in your song."

"Great, wonderful." *Too bad I can't sing.* "All right, then. Let's see how it goes."

No matter how many times he managed it, the initial effort of reaching for the flows made bulldozer-sized butterflies lurch around in his stomach. First, his own barriers needed to come down, an act he had come to think of as lowering the drawbridge and raising the portcullis. Not in a literal sense, but the visualization helped him open his mind and body to the magic all around him.

In the human world, he had never bared himself to the flows while in physical form. The rush of power danced over his nerves like frozen lightning, racing through his blood in mad whirlwinds that stole his breath. He stood still, arms spread, finding his balance, pulling the flows to him from every rock and tree and blade of grass in the vicinity. For a moment, with the magic potential pouring into him, using his body as its vessel, he succumbed to the dangerous illusion of omnipotence, strange thoughts of what could be done in this state careening about in his head.

He channeled the energies toward his fingertips and the madness passed, his mind becoming his own again as he concentrated on the task at hand. He narrowed his focus until he could push against the Veil, the cool, impermeable membrane like mental silicon. Sparks leaped from his fingers while he gathered the lightning into a baseball-sized globe on his palm. He chewed on his lower lip as he condensed the hissing, spitting sphere, smaller and smaller.

Camel through the eye of a needle.

With his house in Montana embedded at the forefront of his thoughts, he hurled the tiny nova ball of lightning at the Veil, breath held when it made contact. It crackled, spreading blue light out in questing vines through the fabric of the Veil. The wind whipped up to a roar, and the Veil ripped open with a deafening thunderclap.

Thrown to his knees, Diego fought to keep the opening stable. There, through the ragged tear, appeared the back garden of the house he shared with Finn. The wheelbarrow still sat where he had left it by the patio, before his trip to New York. Finn had promised to put it away and had obviously forgotten, a thing so much like Finn that Diego was nearly overcome with longing for their quiet, simple life together.

All right, it's open. Now what?

Instincts, Lugh had said. *You have them all still, several lifetimes worth, though you have hidden them from yourself...*

His instincts told him to do...what? Building a doorway, a frame, what the hell did he know about building anything? Except...every structure needed a solid foundation.

"Balor!" he called out, his voice harsh in his ears as he shouted over the wind. "I need you first! Lay a line of force down across the bottom! Our Earth, on which to stand!"

The Fomorian king nodded, apparently having no trouble understanding what Diego meant, even though he hardly knew himself. Balor raised his huge, hairy arms, an earthquake-deep rumbling in his chest. While no visible magic flew from his fingers, the gathering of energy was no less formidable than Diego's. The ground beneath their feet rippled and sighed as a loam-dark line swept across the bottom edge of the tear to hold it steady. Diego felt it meld with his magic, cleave to it until he held the earth spell within his own.

He allowed himself a breath, then called out, "Danu, the top! Sky above! The firmament that keeps the heavens from crashing on our heads!"

She stepped forward and with a simple flick of her wrist, drew a line of white light along the top, healing the ragged edges there. Her magic fought Diego, less willing to fold into his, but he held his ground and coaxed it gently into place. The wind settled to a murmur.

"*Corazón*, you're next," Diego encouraged Finn. "Your water to my fire so I don't burn the doorway down."

Head flung back, feet planted, Finn spread his arms over his head, the air shimmering blue around his long, lean body. Whispers of moisture caressed Diego's face as Finn called the water vapor to him out of the fog and the clouds. Finn's lips parted, the look of ecstasy on his face so like his expression during orgasm, Diego's cock twitched.

So beautiful, my river god, my love...

Finn swept his arm up from his hip and a shining line of cerulean crept up the left side to join Balor's dark line to Danu's white. Such familiar, beloved magic...Diego had been enveloped in it, shored up by it in times of greatest need. It was an easy thing to embrace the water magic and blend it into the whole.

Now Diego reached into his own magic again, the fires burning in his human soul, those same fires that attracted the fae to humans again and again like moths to bug zappers. His side of the doorway blazed red-orange for a moment until he could add his line of magic to the rest of the spell. The four sides flared brighter, then settled into a soft, silver glow, an echo of the moonlight that disappeared if the viewer turned or took half a step sideways.

Lungs aching as if he had run twenty flights of stairs, Diego knelt with his arms wrapped tightly around his ribs, trying to catch his breath.

"It appears, my hero, you have again done what could not be done." Finn stroked his back gently, soothing his labored breathing.

"Up, help me up," Diego panted out, grateful for Finn's strong hands under his arms as he gained his feet. "Let me make sure the coast is clear, okay?"

"Coast?" Balor asked with a frown. "I see only woods."

"An expression, *majestad*. Let me make certain no one's around who shouldn't be."

"Why didn't you say that, then? Go on, boy. Don't dally."

Diego made his way through the doorway on unsteady legs. He braced for a shock when he crossed, but though the magic shivered over his skin, crossing the threshold proved painless. The house stood staring with blind eyes, the garden silent except for the crickets and small night creatures scurrying on important business.

"Ah, home." Finn's long arms wrapped around him from behind.

"Didn't I tell everyone to wait?"

"Surely not me." Finn stepped around him. "I just wanted to fetch some jeans from the bedroom."

"Right. You just want to make sure there aren't any more nasty surprises for me in the house."

"The thought had occurred."

Diego took a quick turn around the outside of the house while Finn checked inside. Everything appeared normal, the truck where he left it, nothing out of place. Finn returned in his favorite pair of black jeans.

"There's naught amiss in there. All quiet," he said as he bent to kiss Diego's cheek.

Which meant the rescued girl was gone and all her things with her. "Thank you, *caro*. You left the wheelbarrow out."

Finn cocked his head to one side. "I thought it looked rather nice where it was."

"Putting it away slipped your mind."

"Yes."

Diego chuckled and slipped an arm around Finn's waist. "The world's only senile fae. Let's go get our first guest."

"Our guests." A soft smile crept onto Finn's face. "Yes, I suppose they will be that." He kissed the top of Diego's head as they crossed back into the Otherworld. "You are much steadier this time, love."

"I'm not fighting to keep the door open while someone stops for dinner."

"Ah. Yes. I would apologize, but it truly was not my fault."

"Teasing, *mi amor*, just teasing."

When they returned to the little group gathered at the doorway, Balor already cradled Faolchú in his arms, Nathair hovering at his elbow.

"Please, I must go with him," Nathair requested, a tremor in his voice.

"Of course." Diego took one long, green hand in his. "Wouldn't dream of separating you. It's all clear. No humans around but me."

Nathair took a shaky breath and accompanied him back through, the rest trooping after. Diego wanted Faolchú placed on the chaise on the patio, but Nathair insisted the bare ground would be better and chose a spot at the back of the garden under an ancient oak. The only sign Faolchú still lived was an occasional rattling breath, and Nathair's eyes shone with tears as he knelt and held out his arms to receive his dying lover.

As soon as his body touched the grass, though, Faolchú's eyes shot open. A weak moan caught in his chest as his body stiffened and trembled violently. Nathair tried to soothe him, stroking his head, and murmuring. Faolchú was beyond hearing, and with a sharp cry, began to convulse.

"I'm here, love, I'm here—" Nathair cut off with a yelp when Faolchú abruptly vanished.

"No...no," Diego whispered, shaking his head. "What just happened? Damn it..." He seized Finn's arm as Nathair burst into tears. "What have we done?"

A huge hand fell on his shoulder. "It's all right, boy. All will be well," Balor rumbled.

"How can it be? We killed him!"

Finn cleared his throat. "No, my hero. He's found his way into the Dreaming to heal."

"How can you be sure? *Dios*, that's not how it looks when you do it!"

"You would feel it, my boy." Balor patted his shoulder. "When one of the fae dies, the very earth wails. We all reach the Dreaming in our own ways."

"Oh." Diego drew in a slow breath, willing the ache in his chest away. He knelt with Nathair to hold him. "Then why is Nathair sobbing?"

Finn answered in a single word. "Relief."

Silent until that moment, staring out into the woods as if she had no interest in the events, Danu finally spoke. "This is a fitting place, Diego. There are humans near, but not many, and not too near. You may bring Lugh next."

"Scath, next, I think, *majestad*." Diego's face heated when she arched a delicate, green brow at him. "At least Lugh still wakes up when you talk to him. Poor little Scath's fading fast." *Your little messenger boy, he's good enough to use when you need him but not good enough to save?* Too open to the world still, Diego realized his angry thoughts had reached her, at least in part, when both her eyebrows crept up further.

"Have a care, my Taliesin," she said too softly. "You were never a fawning flatterer, and so I trust you. But do not question my motives."

"I'm sorry. I just —"

She held up a hand. "I will indulge you, since you have toiled so hard to save us. Scath may come across next."

"Generous," Balor muttered. "Gods-be-damned —"

"Thank you, *majestad*," Diego spoke to drown out the growled epithets.

Finn went to fetch Scath while Diego tried to calm Nathair's hiccoughing sobs. "You stay with us as long as you need," Diego reassured him. "As long as it takes. When he feels better, there's good hunting in the woods, lots of deer, rabbits, pheasants and turkeys."

"Turkeys?" Nathair got out on a huge sniff.

"Great, big, delicious birds, lots of meat on them, not good fliers. Faolchú will love them."

"Good." Nathair nodded, wiping at this eyes. "He'll need plenty. He's become so thin."

Humming, Finn returned carrying Scath, Croi plastered to his side. The *féileacán* were a sad sight, wings drooping, their brilliant colors reduced to gray. Scath's head lolled against Finn's shoulder, his normally lively features still as death.

Diego's heart lurched, thinking they might be too late, but of course the little fae lived still, or Croi would not be up and walking.

The hammock by the house soon held both *féileacán*. Croi gathered her other half's limp body close and began to sing in her clear, trilling voice. A blue-green glow blossomed from her and soon enveloped them both, taking form as a sphere and growing slowly opaque until it hid them from view. The cyan bubble encapsulating them rose to hover two feet above the hammock, emitting a low hum.

"Any idea what that's all about?" Diego pointed with his chin.

"The *féileacán* do not go into the Dreaming," Finn answered with a soft smile. "This is their healing place, their, ah, infirmary, if you like. She will nurse him back to health inside there."

"Croi really is a she, then?"

Finn's forehead creased. "She is…the feminine half of their whole. To call her female might be misleading."

"Thanks. That's a big help."

"Always a pleasure to be of service." Finn took his hand and bowed over it to plant a kiss on Diego's palm. "Especially to such a handsome man."

That simple touch sent desire ricocheting through Diego's body, leaving him dizzy as blood simultaneously rushed to his face and his groin. "Flattery will get you all sorts of places."

"Into your bed? In the next few minutes?" Finn licked at the pulse point on his wrist, the bulge in his jeans reiterating his wishes.

"Soon, *mi vida*. Right now isn't really a good time."

With a pitiful sigh, Finn straightened and settled for a soft kiss.

"Where's Danu?"

Before Finn had a chance to answer, the *sidhe* Queen in question stepped back into sight, through the doorway. She directed a small army of litter bearers, and Diego was pleased to see she had thought to bring all the sick fae rather than only her own. Of course, the choice might have been thrust upon her. The way

Sionnach had wrapped himself around Angus, baring his sharp teeth if anyone's hand got too close, it had probably been impossible to separate them.

They set Easóg down next to Nathair, who helped him from the litter onto the grass and held him until he disappeared, fading rather than blinking out as Faolchú had. Angus, tossing in the grip of fever, levitated a foot off the ground before he winked out, while Sionnach, on hands and knees, turned three times round his tail, settled in a little ball and slowly vanished behind a curtain of light.

Only Lugh remained, listless and unresisting as they lifted him from his litter. Diego hurried to him, determined to make certain his crossing was easier than Faolchú's.

Arms empty once again, Finn could only watch as Diego scurried over to Lugh's side. The terrible pain returned around his heart, along with Morrigan's words, as Diego stroked the *sidhe* champion's hair and murmured to him. Lugh took his hand and said something to make Diego smile. The blood pounded so hard in Finn's head, he was certain it would erupt from his scalp in great geysers.

Jealous. Gods, yes, he was jealous.

He simply couldn't fathom *why*. Several centuries before, when he and Taliesin and the world had been much younger, he had gone off for a year to explore. Apparently, the Taliesin of that lifetime had pined terribly for him and had taken comfort in Lugh's arms. When he'd found them together in a thicket, Finn had simply climbed in beside them, and they had shared Taliesin between them, an afternoon they had all very much enjoyed.

Now the thought of sharing Diego made him want to bite someone, and not in a loving, playful way. That and the doubt that crept up on him as he watched Diego soothe and ease Lugh into the Dreaming put him in a dreadful mood. Not that he thought Diego would fall into another male's arms, not while he felt himself attached to Finn.

But is this attachment the best for him? Gods help me...I don't know.

A few hours later, Sionnach and Easóg returned from the Dreaming, and Finn forgot his uncomfortable thoughts as Diego had him fetching blankets and cushions, water and socks for Easóg's feet since Tia Carmen, who had followed the fae back through, declared the little pine marten was too cold.

The fussing and bustling continued when Angus reappeared soon after, still weak and aching, but free of fever. The garden began to resemble human Emergency Rooms Finn had seen on the picture box, or...no, there was a better comparison.

When another *féileacán* pair, a red and yellow couple, stepped through the doorway, she supporting his faltering steps, Finn spread his arms and smiled to reassure them.

"Welcome to Sandoval's Home for Convalescent Fae."

Chapter Fifteen

Glamours and Agate

Recovering fae proved finicky eaters. Tia Carmen made huge batches of scrambled eggs and bacon the next morning, which Finn devoured without complaint, but while Sionnach and Easóg consumed the eggs with evident relish, they wouldn't touch the bacon.

"Burned meat," Sionnach had sniffed in distaste.

Angus happily crunched the bacon, but paled at the sight of eggs. Lugh, who had returned from the Dreaming early that morning, turned his head away from both with a pained moan.

"I have had my breakfast, thank you, kind lady," Nathair insisted when she offered him a plate. From the little tufts of fur at the oak's base, Diego surmised 'breakfast' had consisted of small rodents, which made sense. Nathair was, after all, a garden snake.

He mentioned this back in the kitchen and Tia Carmen smacked her forehead. "*Por supuesto*, I am growing old and slow. It is their animal natures. Poor Lugh. *Un toro* and I offer him dead pig."

Nothing would do but she had to make a huge pot of oatmeal, with apples and raisins, which Lugh tolerated much more readily. Finn was more than pleased to help with the remainder since there was little he would *not* eat.

"Missed home cooking, did you?" Diego asked in amusement while Finn wolfed down his third helping of everything.

He received only a deep, satisfied growl in response, since Finn was too busy stuffing his face to talk.

"*Bien, mi amor*, I won't tease you." Diego kissed the top of Finn's head. "You obviously need it."

Finn's hand shot out to grab his wrist. He finished his mouthful before he looked up at Diego, eyes pleading. "Now?"

The wistful expression on that handsome face and the need in those black eyes almost made Diego relent. They had slept on the back porch the night before, in case anyone might need them, sharing a sleeping bag for warmth. Finn had begged quite persuasively for sex then, but Diego had been exhausted and falling asleep under Finn's soft caresses. Not to mention the fact that several people with exceptional hearing and night vision slept only a few feet away.

"I need to take Tia Carmen shopping, *querido*. I'm sorry. But she didn't exactly bring luggage with her, and she says we're out of everything."

"Ah. Of course, of course. It will keep."

Finn's carefully painted-on smile didn't fool Diego one bit, though. The hurt and disappointment rode behind his eyes.

"I'll just tell Nathair I'm going." Diego walked to the back door. "In case he... *Dios ayudame*, what the hell?"

A huge man stood in the back garden, easily seven feet tall, with shoulders so broad, he would have to turn sideways to fit through the door. He loomed there, in nothing but a black kilt, arms crossed over his chiseled chest, looking like he owned the place. Something about the stance, the defiant lift of chin, the serious scowl...

Diego went out and approached slowly. "Balor?"

The tusks were missing, but the snort couldn't have been anyone else's. "Yes, boy, it's me. I thought this would be better in full daylight. In case humans were about."

"But...I thought Fomorians didn't shift?"

"We don't. Open your eyes, dunderhead. It's naught but a glamour."

Diego reached out with more than sight and, yes, Balor was still the same under the illusion. "Oh. Um...*majestad*, if you're trying not to draw attention to yourself, you may want to rethink the glamour and add clothes?"

Balor let out a speculative rumble. "Like yours?"

"Well, yes. You're magnificent as a human, but your size is unusual enough. If one of the rangers comes by to check on us and sees you like that, they're likely to faint."

"Out of fear?"

"Perhaps partly." Diego gave him a glance up and down. "One of them is female, single and very much looking. The male prefers other men and adores big ones."

"Hmph." Balor's illusion flickered, the kilt replaced by jeans and a skin-tight T-shirt, both black. "Better?"

"Still jaw-dropping, but better. *Majestad*, I need to go out for a while for some supplies. Will you be here?"

"I will watch over them."

Not really what I was asking, but oh, well. "Good, thank you. If any humans do show up, would you please let Finn deal with them? He's been living in this century a little longer, and the locals all know him."

Balor's brows drew down. "They *know* him? So he was not telling tales and truly *has* been living among them?"

"In a limited sense, yes. They don't think of him as anything but human. Most of them even like him."

"Dangerous game," Balor grumbled. "It will turn and bite him someday."

Diego laughed. "I don't think so, *majestad*. It took him quite some time to convince *me* he wasn't human, and he honestly tried his best. If he told anyone out here that he's a fairy, they would simply pat his arm and say, 'Oh, it's okay, we know you're gay'."

"Pardon?"

"Never mind. I'll be back in a few hours."

In the truck on the way into town, Tia Carmen sat silent and pensive, staring out of the window.

With the little main street in sight, Diego finally asked the question he'd held onto the entire drive, "Do you know what's wrong with Finn?"

She startled out of her thoughts to blink at him. "Besides being underfed?"

"Yes, underfed, overtired and recently shot, besides that." Diego shook his head. "He's been so…moody. So tense."

"He doubts, Santiago. It eats at him."

"Doubts? Doubts what? That I love him?"

"No, *mijo*, I think he knows that. But somewhere he has picked up a thought. Whether it was something said to him or something that happened, I don't know. But I have seen him watching you, too serious and worried. He wonders if he is what you need, I think. Wonders if he is good enough for you."

"He...what? Where the hell would he get such an idea? He's the best thing that ever happened to me, the most wonderful thing." Diego parked in front of the Dry Goods and yanked up the hand brake in frustration. "Damn it."

"Maybe he needs to hear these things from you."

"I've told him. It has to be more than that." Diego scrubbed a hand back through his hair. Then a thought hit him. "Maybe I need to make sure he understands there's no one else for me. Maybe saying it isn't enough with all he's been through."

"*Quizás*, it's possible. Just don't forget him in the confusion of everything else you are busy with."

The girl behind the counter in the Dry Goods glanced up from her magazine when they walked in, her face breaking into a brilliant smile. "Hey, Mr. Sandoval! What can we do for you?"

"Hi, Molly." Diego waved to her. "This is my Aunt Carmen from New York. Could you help her find some clothes?"

"Oh, sure. Stupid airline lost your luggage, huh?"

Tia Carmen shrugged with a little smile. "Eh, it happens."

"So where's Finn?" Molly asked as she came around the counter.

"Back at the house entertaining. Some of his friends from back home are visiting."

"Oh, how cool! More hot guys from Ireland? Wow, you gotta bring them into town, Mr. Sandoval. I mean, I know they're probably all, you know, but it's just such a hoot to hear Finn's cute accent. And a whole group of them?" Molly fanned herself.

"We'll see." Diego laughed. "They're kind of a rowdy bunch."

"Even better." Molly grinned. "You need anything for Finn?"

"If you have any jeans his size, add it to the pile, please. He's managed to lose a pair somewhere."

Tia Carmen flapped a hand at Diego. "Go do your other shopping, *mijo*. I don't think you want to be here to watch us look at old lady underpants."

Diego laughed and wandered down the street to the little grocery to fill Tia Carmen's requests and procure what he had promised for Finn. Two coolers full of meat, eggs, butter and ice cream later, he had only one other stop in mind. At the end of the little row of shops sat a dusty antique store. He had often wondered how the crotchety old man stayed in business. His only customers seemed to be the summer tourists, and the displays never changed.

He took a deep breath of clean air and stepped into the musty interior, the bell over the door jangling loud enough to wake the most peaceful dead. The glass eyes of a fox stole glared at him from an ancient hat rack. *Not a good place to bring Sionnach.*

"Good morning, Mr. Peters." Diego nodded politely to the stout, elderly gentleman on his high stool, hunched over his paper.

Mr. Peters glanced up with a sour expression and returned to his reading.

Fine. Old coot. Unlike the majority of this friendly little town, Mr. Peters had never given him the time of day. Diego hadn't been able to figure out if it was because he was gay or because he was Latino or from New York or just not someone with a 'real' job. Hands clasped behind his back in a non-threatening, perusing-without-touching sort of way, Diego meandered over to the jewelry case. As he had hoped, this case hadn't changed any more than the rest of the shop.

In the left-hand corner on the top shelf, the ring had a fine film of dust on it, as if it hadn't been handled in years. Set in a band of gold filigree, the yellow agate had the most beautiful tree-shaped intrusions, as if nature had been painting a miniature landscape.

"Excuse me, Mr. Peters? How much for the dendritic agate ring?"

Mr. Peters peered over his spectacles. "You can't afford it."

"Please — it's perfect. Name a price. I'll manage."

"It's not for sale."

"Then why is it in the case?"

"Because it's for sale, just not to you."

"Oh." Unhappy in any confrontation, under other circumstances he might have walked out. This, however, was too important. "Mr. Peters, what in the world do you have against me? Have I ever been rude to you?"

The old antique dealer stared at him for a long, uncomfortable moment. "You New York artsy types. You think you own the world. That everything has a price tag. You don't know the real value of anything. I sell you that ring, you'll probably end up losing it at some orgy or in some drug-infested club."

"It's not for me, Mr. Peters," Diego told him. "It's for someone I love more than life. Someone I'd give the world to if I could. But, as you say, the world is not for sale."

Mr. Peters paused, bushy white brows drawn into a frown. He folded his paper and crossed his arms over his chest. "It's an engagement ring, then?"

"Yes, sir."

"For that tall Irishman you run around with?"

"Yes, sir. At least I hope it to be."

Mr. Peters slid off his stool, his movements as ponderous as any walrus, and retrieved his keys from a hook on the wall. "Now, this isn't like a diamond that you can bang about. It's delicate. Something rare."

"I understand, sir. Finn would, too. He's been fascinated by them for many years."

"Twelve hundred dollars."

Diego hid a grin. *Let the haggling begin.*

Eight hundred dollars later, he walked out of the shop with a velvet box, a lighter heart and his first smile from Mr. Peters.

When he returned home with Tia Carmen, the back garden thrummed with excitement. Croi's bubble had disappeared, and Scath made tentative attempts at short flights from the porch to the edge of the woods and back. Lugh, standing rock-solid again, caught Scath when he faltered near the vegetable patch. Best of all, Faolchú had returned, lounging comfortably on the grass with his head in Nathair's lap, sucking gently on his lover's long fingers.

To his dismay, Diego realized the garden and woods crawled with fae. Twinkling *féileacán* lights danced in the branches. Elusive, graceful shapes chased each other through the woods. Couples occupied the chairs, the hammock and a good portion of the grass. When Faolchú turned with a little growl, nudged Nathair onto his back, and settled between his thighs, Diego's face flushed forge-hot. *God, he's going to screw him right there, in front of everyone.*

From the erotic sounds drifting out of the woods and the movements of the various couples in his garden, Diego realized belatedly Faolchú wasn't the only one. Sionnach let out little fox-bark yelps as Angus pulled him onto his lap and thrust up into him. Even the pair of wildcats under the yew bush, who were most likely *sidhe*, mated in a hissing, clawing ball.

Diego made a hasty retreat inside. He leaned against the back door and cleared his throat. "*Oye,* Tia Carmen...you may want to stay away from the windows for now."

Naturally, she stopped putting away groceries at that announcement and peered out of the window. Instead of being scandalized, though, as an old lady should be, she smiled. "They celebrate. They feel the life catch fire again."

"Um, okay. But couldn't they at least wait until dark?"

She swatted his arm. "You are such a prude, Santiago."

Still, he was going to have to speak to Danu and Balor about everyone staggering their visits. Such a thick concentration of fae would eventually draw unwanted attention.

"He is a prude." Lugh's rich, deep voice sounded behind him. His hand fell on Diego's shoulder to turn him. "But a devastatingly handsome one."

Diego took the teasing as it was meant, though he did back up a step. The fae, Lugh especially, had a poorly developed sense of personal space. Lugh smoothed a curl from his cheek, making Diego all too aware of his earthy musk.

"I'm so glad you're feeling better," Diego forced out and cleared his throat against the unintended husk in it.

"So am I, little man." Lugh threw an arm around his shoulders, heedless of his discomfort, and turned to Tia Carmen. "Scath would like to know if you have any of that lovely tea. He's feeling chilled."

"Of course." She nodded. "I can make some quickly."

"Chilled? Poor little guy." Diego moved out of Lugh's impromptu embrace. "I'll go get the electric blanket. Even if he doesn't want it over his wings, it should help."

Diego had taken three steps down the hall when a figure surged out of the shadows and shoved him face-first against the wall. A lean-muscled frame pressed hard against him, grinding against his ass. A long hand trapped both his wrists above his head.

"Now," Finn growled low in his ear.

"Finn? What the hell?"

"I want you. I *need* you." Finn fumbled at Diego's jeans, undoing the fly. "Now."

Diego forced calm into his voice. "You're hurting me."

"I can't stand it anymore. You won't deny me again."

"What are you going to do, *querido*?" Diego fought both a rising panic and a lump in his throat. "Force yourself on me if I say no?"

The hand fumbling at his crotch stilled. The pressure on his back vanished. He turned to see Finn with his face buried in his hands, shoulders slumped.

"My love...forgive me." Finn's voice broke and cracked. "I—"

When he turned to flee, Diego was ready for it and lunged for him. "Oh, no, you don't. You do *not* do that to me and just run off."

Finn fought to get loose, Diego took a firmer hold and they tumbled to the carpet in a heap of flailing limbs. Finn no longer sought to hold him, though, and didn't aim a single blow his way, all his efforts channeled into clawing at the carpet, trying to get away.

"*Mi vida, mi amor,*" Diego murmured, nuzzling under his ear. "Ease down. Relax. I won't hurt you."

Finn whimpered, curled into a ball and shook with silent tears. At least that was a more familiar reaction than turning into a lust-crazed beast.

"I don't mind when you get fierce and demanding." Diego stroked his hair. "It's a huge turn-on sometimes, but that was definitely over the top. Want to tell me what this is all about?"

"Please let me be," Finn whispered. "I'm a monster."

Diego sighed and took Finn in his arms. "No, you're not. You stopped before things got out of hand. But you're obviously all off-balance."

"He touched you." Finn uncoiled far enough to lay his head on Diego's shoulder. "He touched you so tenderly, and something exploded inside my head. Did I truly hurt you?"

"No, *querido*, don't worry. I'm fine. You're jealous. It's something most people have to deal with. You're just not used to it."

Finn shuddered. "It's a horrible feeling. It claws at my insides like a badger trying to dig out."

"Lovely image." Diego tilted Finn's face up to plant a soft kiss on his lips. "I'm yours, *caro*, only yours. Do you want to go upstairs?"

Finn closed his eyes on a hitching breath. "I don't think I could…at the moment."

"We don't have to do anything. Cuddling works for me."

"Perhaps later." There was that dejected tone again, that downcast stare. "I think I might do with a swim, though."

Diego nodded. "Good. You need one. Get yourself a nice, fresh fish while you're out there. I love *you*. Only you. Don't forget that." He took Finn's hands and pulled him up. His original plan had been to make his proposal as soon as he could get Finn alone, watch his eyes light up when he pulled out the ring, but he didn't want to do it with Finn in such a state. He wanted him steady and calm, so he could understand what was being asked of him.

He walked Finn out through the kitchen, arm around his waist, past Tia Carmen and Lugh. At the door, he took Finn's head between his hands and pulled him down for what he meant to be a tender kiss. Finn tried to pull away, but when their mouths met, he melted against Diego, his lips parting on a soft moan, inviting Diego in. Little sparks crackled from Diego's fingers when he combed them through Finn's thick, black hair, and the kiss turned searing. The world faded away except for Finn's tongue stroking his, Finn's strong hands caressing his back.

Tia Carmen clearing her throat brought Diego back to reality.

He pulled away with a soft kiss to Finn's cheek. "Take whatever time you need, *mi amor*. I'll be waiting for you."

Finn gave him a bone-creaking hug and walked out, leaving Diego with the aching feeling that he had handled things badly ever since he'd come home from New York.

"*La medida del amor es amar sin medida*," Tia Carmen murmured.

"Please, no wise proverbs right now." Diego scrubbed his hands through his hair. He couldn't bring himself to turn around, to see the worry, or worse, pity in her eyes. After Finn shifted into a huge black eagle and flew off to the river, Diego stalked out of the house as well, determined to find the fae monarchs and plead for a little sense regarding the use of the doorway.

By evening, he had accomplished what was needed. Danu and Balor had defied expectations, agreeing readily to Diego's terms while remaining cool but civil with each other. The fae would try to limit their visits to after dark, and those who came and went during daylight hours would adopt human forms and manners to the best of their ability.

Cool and civil did not apply to Miriam, though, when Diego called her. She had left several messages while he was away in the Otherworld, each one increasingly caustic and belligerent. He held the phone away from his ear when she recognized his voice on the other end.

"Sandoval! Where in motherfucking hells have you been? You've got some great, big, brass balls, fucking around like this!" Miriam bellowed. She continued at full blast for a good three minutes, and Diego wondered what other people in her building thought of these tirades.

When she took a breath, he asked dryly, "Do you want an answer, or would you rather keep shredding me?"

"Yes, I want an answer, you little shit!"

"I'm very sorry. I didn't mean to be out of touch for so long. Some of Finn's friends ran into a little trouble, and we had to help. I couldn't get a signal from there, and we've been a little busy."

The creak of her chair as she shifted carried over the phone. "Finn's friends, huh?" Her voice was still a growl but no longer ear shattering. "Immigration trouble?"

"Something like that, and some of them were really sick."

"Next time you find a land line and you check your goddamn messages, got it?"

"Yes, ma'am."

Lecture out of the way, Miriam calmed. "Everyone all right? Your handsome beefcake okay?"

"Everyone's much better, thanks. You said you had news?"

"Damn straight. We're getting movie offers."

Diego's jaw dropped. He had to clear his throat twice and still squeaked when he asked, "Really? For *Dragon Rites*?"

"No, for your life story." He could practically see Miriam roll her eyes. "Of course for *Dragon Rites*, kiddo. I emailed you the offers. Take a look. Tell me what you think."

"But...wait. Doesn't the publisher have movie rights?"

She snorted. "Do you *read* your contracts?"

"Not the whole text. They're so long. That's why I have you."

"Freaking lucky thing you do, too, or these sharks would eat you alive. I withheld movie rights and the publisher agreed since so few fantasy novels ever go to film. They didn't feel like it was worth fighting me over."

"Oh. Thank you." Diego flopped down on the sofa in his den. He had a garden full of supernatural creatures and now he had to force himself to think like a modern human again. It wasn't fair to his overloaded brain. "I'm so sorry I worried you, Miriam."

"Please. I wasn't worried. I was pissed."

At that, he had to smile. If she hadn't been worried, she wouldn't have been so angry.

A few hours later, he had read through the proposals, had picked the one he thought looked most sympathetic to the story and the characters and realized it had grown dark. Finn would probably stay out for the night. It wasn't the first time. Hunting was good in the early fall and being alone in the wilds was, after all, Finn's natural state. Knowing those things didn't ease the ache around Diego's heart one damn bit.

He wandered out to the kitchen around eight for coffee and a sandwich and found Lugh leaning against the counter.

"Could I speak with you, little man?"

"Of course. Everything all right?"

Lugh hooked an arm around his shoulders and led him outside. "I'm going home, Diego, to sleep in my own bower."

"Oh." Diego heard an unspoken subtext in those words. "You know you're welcome here as long as you like. Anytime. And you've been doing such a good job riding herd on all these party boys and girls."

"Thank you, but I fear I must be going." Lugh cupped Diego's face in his huge hand, thumb brushing softly over his lips. "It tears at me, to watch you with him. Kissing him. Touching him so tenderly. Knowing I can have none of it."

"I'm sorry," Diego murmured. "I never meant to hurt you."

"*Ach*, I know, little one. It's not as if…before, in other lifetimes, I loved you, but it was not the same. You were not the same. Less careful, less mindful, you were not so cautious with your heart. Now…perhaps it is because I cannot have you that I want you more. Perhaps it is because you shine so much brighter than you ever have."

"I can't parcel out love…"

Lugh held up a hand. "I know. You are a good man, an honorable one, which is why I must go for a time. Throw myself into creation, think of other things." He laced their fingers together. "But I am, as I have always been, your friend. If you are ever in peril or in need, simply open your mind and call. I will be by your side in an instant."

Diego nodded. "I'll remember. Thank you. Will you be all right?"

With a soft sigh, Lugh leaned in close and brushed a snow-soft kiss over his lips, the brief contact sparking with his banked desire. "I will manage, never fear."

Lugh stepped back and smiled, then turned and disappeared through the doorway.

On the porch rail, a tiny black songbird let out a mournful cheep and flew off into the night on a sudden flutter of wings.

Chapter Sixteen

Boys' Night Out

An honorable man...

Yes, Diego was that and so much more. Finn sat on a sandspur with his knees pulled up under his chin, downstream from some of the river's most spectacular rapids. The Flathead crashed and sang, music that should have made his heart leap, but it wasn't his beloved Shannon back in Ireland, and it wasn't even the Pointe Wolf where he had first courted Diego. Beautiful as it was, this river only made the lonely hole in his heart grow to a chasm.

The memory of Lugh with Diego tormented him, the words between them and the easy friendship. When Lugh had kissed Diego, Finn had half expected him to haul back and wallop the *sidhe* warrior, but he had not. Diego had stood stunned, rubbing at his lower lip as if savoring the sensation.

Not that Finn blamed him. Lugh was handsome enough to make anyone's knees weak and his kisses held such careful fire, as if he might consume his lovers if he let his unbridled passion loose. Worse still, he had a hero's heart, something Finn would always lack.

"Diego deserves a hero," Finn murmured to the dragonfly sharing his sandbar. "Someone who makes things right instead of making them worse."

The dragonfly paid no attention, whispering dragonfly thoughts, intent on catching its dinner.

"You're right, of course." He heaved a shaky sigh. "Dinner must still be caught, no matter how sorry certain pookas feel for themselves."

He waded out into the rushing water, the pull of any river beyond him to resist for long. The soft blue of his own personal magic danced over him as his body condensed and his arms shortened, shining scales rushing to replace skin. Soon a huge salmon leaped upstream, fighting for every inch of gained ground against the whitewater onslaught.

* * * *

Diego stared out of the window, steam from his coffee caressing his face. Finn hadn't come home the night before, hadn't appeared for breakfast, and now Tia Carmen was announcing she had booked a flight home.

"You don't need me here anymore, Santiago," she told him briskly as she washed dishes. "You have everything settled."

He turned to her with a crooked smile. "Settled? With all these *loco* fae coming and going?" He held up a hand when one of her white eyebrows arched at him. "I understand. I do. You need to get home. We've kept you too long, and with the snows coming soon, the flights out get a little spotty."

"I promise to come back for a real visit. In the summer, though."

"Thank you for everything you've done. For putting the puzzle pieces together." Diego's brow furrowed. "How long has it been that way?"

"What way, *mijo*?"

"That you knew you could feel things, see things other people couldn't."

She shrugged. "I have always seen different things. Heard things no one else heard. *Mi abuela*, she was a witch. She saw it in me and taught me. To heal, to comfort, to soothe, to help things grow. Little magics, not grand, dangerous things like yours."

"How long have you known about me?" he asked softly, turning his gaze out of the window again.

"From the first time I met you." She laughed. "Why else would I let a deadbeat writer with a credit report full of holes move into one of my apartments?"

Outside, a lean, compact man curled up on one of the Adirondack chairs, his bald head gleaming in the sun. Dressed in the jeans and T-shirt the fae males had adopted as their 'human' uniform, the man had tattoos of green scales running up the backs of his arms from his wrists to disappear under his shirtsleeves. The only visitor who remained entirely in the garden, Nathair seemed content to putter about and sleep in the sun, waiting for Faolchú to recover his strength. The tomatoes and peppers, sad, scraggly things under Diego's care, groaned under a surplus of ripening abundance since Nathair had begun to sing to them.

A much taller man shambled out of the trees, his careful gait indicating residual pain. Thick salt-and-pepper hair tumbled past broad shoulders and huge hands clutched a bloody fur bundle. Faolchú crouched on his heels in the center of the garden and tore into the rabbit with his teeth, a bright red stream trickling down his chin.

Good to see him hunting on his own, disturbing to watch him eat. Diego pulled his gaze away. "What time's your flight?"

"Two-thirty," Tia Carmen said in a too-serene voice.

"Two-*what*?" Diego shot a glance at the clock. "*Ay, Dios.* We need to go now. Are you packed?"

"Almost."

"Okay, give me just a sec." He leaned out of the back door. "Nathair?"

Nathair cracked open one golden eye.

"I'll be back in a few hours. Try to keep a handle on things for me?"

"I shall," Nathair said on a yawn as he sat up. "Faolchú, love, what a mess…"

While the garden-snake in human form took a damp cloth to the bloody ruin on Faolchú's jaws and neck, Diego reached out toward the river. "*Finn? Mi vida? I need to take Tia Carmen to the airport.*"

The reply came back, distant and distracted. "*Tell her farewell for me, love.*"

"*Will you be home when I get back?*"

"*Soon. I'll come soon.*"

At least Finn had answered this time instead of pretending not to hear.

With some creative driving and a few traffic laws bent, Diego managed to get Tia Carmen to the terminal in time. Many tearful goodbyes and promises of phone calls later, he made his way home again.

No Finn still on his return, though Angus and Sionnach had taken over his living room. The *sidhe* herald knelt by the powered-up stereo, a look of intense

Diego

concentration on his face as he eased the tuning knob through the frequencies, listening to the voices, the music, and the static in-between, all with equal fascination. Sionnach was sprawled on his stomach on the floor, leafing through catalogs of men's clothing, his illusory clothes changing every few pages as he 'tried on' what he saw on the glossy pages.

"Do you like this one?" Sionnach asked, his feet swinging above the perfect, firm mounds of his ass, now encased in white PVC micro shorts. A sleeveless mesh shirt clung to his torso, showing off every lean line of muscle.

Angus turned his head, nostrils flared. "You will not wear that for anyone but me, do you hear, little fox?"

"So possessive suddenly," Sionnach snorted, but a little smile tugged at his lips as he ducked his head back to the catalog. The glamour shimmered again, the scandalous clubbing outfit replaced by a black silk button-down and fitted slacks. "This one?"

"Better," Angus growled.

"The black shirt's a little severe for you. Maybe green?" Diego chuckled when the midnight silk shifted to a rich emerald. "Very nice. You boys seem more comfortable with the human world than some of the others."

Sionnach shrugged. An expensive pair of boots joined his ensemble when he turned the page. "I missed humans."

"Missed tormenting them, you mean," Angus muttered. He turned off the stereo and rose to join Diego by the sofa. "Heralds have always spent more time out in the world. There was a time when messages went back and forth between the fae and human courts."

"I guess that was long ago."

"Diego, are you well?" Angus gripped his shoulder.

"I'm okay, really. I just wish Finn would come home."

Angus shook his head, golden hair sparking in the late afternoon sun. "Fionnachd has always done as he pleases, when he pleases. Better to try to command the sea to cease its assault on the shore than to think to command a pooka."

"Hush. You do not comfort him, Far-seer," Sionnach said. "He will return. He loves you."

By the next morning, though, Finn's side of the bed still sat cold and empty. He was nowhere to be found in the house or the garden.

"I could track him for you, Light-wielder."

Faolchú's rough growl startled him and Diego whirled to find the wolf-warrior in his kitchen. *How does such a huge being move so quietly?*

"Thank you, no. You need your rest and, really, I can track him myself."

"And you have not done so because..." Faolchú crossed his arms over his chest. The bones still stood out too prominently at his ribs and collarbone, but the mass he had regained in such a short space of time was nothing short of miraculous.

"I know...where he is. I feel him." Diego pulled a slow breath in through his nose. "I'd hoped he would work things out in his head and come back to me on his own."

One of Faolchú's grey ears twitched. "Perhaps he believes his offense too great and he waits for your forgiveness first."

"Maybe."

"Listen to me, little one." Faolchú's hands gripped Diego's forearms, claws digging into his skin. "You cannot be hesitant with Fionnachd. He needs strength, needs someone to seize him by the nape and shake him."

Odd, how everyone wanted to tell him how to handle Finn all of a sudden. Though Faolchú was right about one thing. It was time to go out to the river.

"Right. Um, did you need me for something?"

Faolchú's teeth bared in a lupine grin. "Nathair tells me you have sweet cream which has been frozen. He raves over the virtues of it so. I yearn to try it myself."

What is it about predators and high milk-fat food? Still, the calories could only do him good. Diego reached into the freezer and picked the peach ice cream out from behind the cartons of Rocky Road. While Finn loved chocolate, there was a good chance Faolchú's body would have a canine toxic reaction to it. He handed the carton off with two spoons and received a wet-nosed nuzzle to his ear as a thank you.

Outside, the wolf head and paws vanished again under the human glamour. Faolchú made a handsome man, with a strong jaw, Husky-blue eyes, and that arresting mane of thick hair that looked so finger-burying soft. He settled Nathair on his lap and allowed himself to be fed by the spoonful when Nathair discouraged him from going face down in the carton.

From everything Diego had heard, Faolchú had been a screw-everything-with-a-heartbeat kind of male, alpha to the extreme, stalking his conquests until they surrendered. Now, though affectionate with his friends, he showed no interest in anyone but his beautiful garden snake. If their relationship could work, blending the wild and the domestic so successfully, surely there was hope with Finn.

Diego loaded his backpack with food, blankets and a few other necessities, laced up his hiking boots and ventured out into the woods. Finn had been wary of the Flathead at first, saying it was an arrogant river with a high opinion of itself, but he had eventually warmed up to it, and Diego knew all his favorite fishing and sunning spots along the three-mile stretch near the house.

A strange, harried quality lurked in Finn's thoughts when he reached out for him — the glimpses Diego caught were chaotic and scattered. From this, he was certain where Finn would be. The huge, black fish he spotted leaping upstream against the rapids confirmed his suspicions. He spread the blanket out on the sandspur and settled in.

"Finn, I'm here. I can see you from where I'm sitting, mi amor. *Come out of the river and talk to me, please."*

At first, only the jumbled images of rapids and rocks reached him. Diego persisted, calling again and again. Finally, Finn's thoughts took shape.

"You're here? In the river?"

"No, on the bank. Come out to me. You sound exhausted."

Silence, then a sleek, black shape arrowed toward the bank, shifting from fish to otter as it knifed through the water. The otter crawled up onto the sand, collapsed in an untidy heap, and shifted to Finn, who lay panting, eyes staring into the distance.

"You were a fish too long, weren't you?" Diego said gently as he covered Finn with a second blanket. "Is this what you've been doing for two days? Fighting class-four rapids?"

"Diego..." The whisper was weak and raw, as if Finn's vocal chords had been flayed.

"All right, it's all right." Diego shoved him up so Finn could lean against him.

With a third blanket, he ruffled Finn's hair dry. The pack then gave up a hairbrush and a stack of chicken sandwiches. After devouring three out of five sandwiches, Finn was steady enough to sit up on his own so Diego could brush out the tangle of his waist-length, blue-black hair.

"Now, then," Diego began in what he hoped was his sternest voice. "I don't care what anyone's told you, and I don't care what nonsense you've told yourself. We belong together, you and I. Do you hear me?"

"Yes," Finn whispered miserably. "Are you angry with me?"

"No, *caro*, I'm not angry with you."

"You should be."

"Why, because you let your hormones override your brain for a couple of minutes?"

"I could have caused you harm."

"You didn't."

"I ran away when I should have stayed with you."

"You need solitude sometimes. I know that."

"Diego?" Finn turned to face him. "I wish I could be more for you."

"I don't want more." Diego smoothed his fingertips over Finn's cheek where a dark bruise, probably from a rock, had formed. "I don't want anything else. Anything different. I don't want anything but you."

Finn put his head on Diego's shoulder, his breaths hitching.

"Don't you dare cry," Diego said in a mock growl. "Or I'll knock your silly head into next week."

The beginning of a sob turned into a strangled snicker, since they both knew he would never do any such thing. Soon they were both howling with laughter, rolling in each other's arms on the blanket in a release more necessary than sex.

When they quieted, Diego stroked the wild hair away from Finn's eyes. "I've missed you, *mi vida*. Our bed's been cold."

"Forgive me, my hero." Finn's long fingers stole over Diego's collarbone, sending a shiver through him. "I have not...been myself."

Diego nipped the end of his nose. "Then who are you?"

"I hardly know some days."

"We are, all of us, a hard kernel of self at our core." Diego rose up on his knees, determined the moment would not pass again. He crossed his arms, grabbed the hem of his shirt, and yanked it off over his head. "But we find our definition in relation to others. How we perceive them, how we act toward them, how they perceive us." He undid the button on his jeans and unzipped the fly slowly, feeling the heat of Finn's gaze like miniature suns. "You are my Finn. My brave Finn who fought for me against a monster, who was my light in my greatest despair, who was willing to face a seasoned magical warrior to try to find his way home to me."

"But I didn't—"

"It doesn't matter what happened. It matters that you tried. My Finn. *Te amo, te quiero.*" He stood to yank off his boots and peel out of his jeans and briefs. "Take me. I need you so."

For a moment, Diego wondered if Finn's brain was still stuck on fish as he sat with his mouth opening and closing, gaze running up and down Diego's naked body. He finally moved, easing toward Diego as if he might startle. Still on his knees, Finn curled forward to kiss Diego's anklebones. He uncurled bit by bit as he licked a warm, wet line up the back of one calf, stopping to suck on the sensitive skin behind the knee.

Diego let his head fall back on a soft moan as Finn continued his sensual climb up his body, peppering kisses over his thighs. Finn lifted his head, his eyes an adorable mix of lust and confusion.

"You're certain you want such a beast to take you?"

"Yes." Diego cupped Finn's face in his hands. "Take me like a beast. On all fours."

Finn cringed. "I'll hurt you. I've nothing to ease—"

"Backpack. Front pocket."

"Ah." Finn managed a little smile as he fished the lube out. "You seem to have come prepared, my love."

"I had high hopes."

Finn took him by the hips, turned him and hugged him from behind. A hard rush of desire slammed through Diego when Finn's cool erection nestled between his cheeks. He leaned back into Finn's arms, needing the support.

"We are out in the open." Finn's breath stole over his ear. "You do not fear being seen?"

"A little. *Dios*." Diego held tight when Finn sucked on the back of his neck. "I don't care so much right now."

"You could hide us. Obscure us with magic."

Long hands traveled up Diego's torso, fingers pinching his nipples to hard peaks. "I don't think I could concentrate on magic."

"Then I will." Finn lifted a hand and fog rolled down the bank, a thick, unnatural blanket settling all around the sandbar. "There, my heart. Safe from prying eyes."

Finn tightened his grip and pulled Diego down to kneel on the blanket with him. Diego leaned forward on his hands when Finn pressed a hand between his shoulder blades. Shivers of need danced over his skin and a soft moan escaped as Finn caressed his backside.

"Down on your elbows, love. Easier to balance," Finn whispered against the small of Diego's back. "And it will be more pleasurable for you."

Head spinning, Diego complied. No one had ever done this to him before. He had never felt comfortable enough with anyone to take up such a vulnerable position, not until this moment. He gasped as two well-lubed fingers breached him and he rocked back, silently pleading for more, but Finn would only invade so far, gently, slowly.

"*Caro*, please," Diego grated out. "Don't be so damn careful. I asked you to take me, so do it."

Finn stilled, shivering against Diego's back, and for a moment he worried he had pushed him too hard. Then with a shaky breath, Finn withdrew his fingers and a wave of heated relief swept over Diego when the smooth, slippery head of Finn's cock replaced them.

"Ready, love?" Finn murmured against his shoulder.

"Damn it, Finn, just—" Diego's words cut off in a sharp cry as Finn plunged inside. He panted through the initial pain, then as Finn caressed that sweet spot deep inside with each deep stroke, the pain melted, firefly sparks of intense pleasure dancing through him. Finn filled him so completely, stretched him so perfectly, as if they had been made just for each other.

Diego gripped the blanket with both hands, shoving back to meet Finn, encouraging him deeper, faster, moaning when their balls slapped together with each hard thrust.

"My heart, my light," Finn panted out. "So beautiful. So...gods..."

Diego felt the stutter in his rhythm and knew Finn was close. He reached back and grasped one of Finn's hands to guide to his aching cock. Finn took the hint, fingers closing around him to pump in time with their bodies. The pressure in Diego's groin became unbearable. His balls drew up tight in a sudden rush.

"I'm coming… Finn…oh, God," he got out before his climax slammed up through him, stealing conscious thought. Short, sharp cries leaped out as the pulses shot through him one after another. Finn's arms wrapped around him tight and his teeth fastened on Diego's shoulder as his body bucked and jerked, his bellows muffled against Diego's skin as he came.

When Diego could think again, he found himself on his side with Finn still nestled inside him, pressed up against his back, breathing hard. *My Finn…*

"Did you miss me?" he whispered with a little smile.

"Sweet Mother, yes," Finn mumbled against his neck. "More than words can say."

Diego stroked his arm with two fingers. "Then don't stay away so long next time."

Finn's only answer was to pull him in even tighter, nuzzling at his shoulder.

With the magic fog dissipating, Diego decided it was time to go. He pulled out a pair of jeans for Finn, got dressed and packed up. They walked together in comfortable silence, Finn's hand gripping his, as they had not done for many days. A flight of *féileacán* flashed by, a moving rainbow of will-o-wisp lights chasing each other in a kaleidoscopic dance.

"They are so happy." Finn watched them with a soft smile.

Are you happy? Diego kept the uneasy thought shuttered and instead said, "I thought we'd take the boys out to dinner tonight. You and I, Sionnach and Angus, Nathair and Faolchú."

"To Annie's?" Finn's eyes lit up.

"Yes, to Annie's. Would you like that?"

"Oh, I would lie down and kiss her feet for one of her steaks. But you think it wise? All of us out in plain sight?"

Diego squeezed Finn's hand. "I've already told people you have friends visiting from Ireland. Americans expect foreigners to be a little odd, and everyone has the glamour thing worked out so it's convincing. Not that Angus needs to do much more than hide his ears and his eyes."

The old wariness lurked in Finn's eyes for a moment, but Annie's steaks won out. "Very well. You know these people best."

Two hours later, everyone piled into the 4x4 for the trip to town. Faolchú had to sit up front with Diego, his bulk simply too much for the back seats. Finn explaining how to work the seat belts for the safety of everyone involved was just too surreal, but they managed the trip without any major incidents. To protect Finn from the steel frame, the truck's interior had been lined with silk, a request the auto upholsterer had found bizarre but had accepted once he'd found out Diego was a writer. Apparently, writers were allowed to be strange.

Annie's Restaurant occupied the old train station, a charming nineteenth-century building she had renovated a decade previously, though she had kept the old ticket windows so customers could have a glimpse of the kitchen in the back. Annie's was the only real restaurant in town, and since the other two establishments serving food were bars, several customers always occupied the ten-table dining room, even in the slow season. Annie, herself, manned the front that evening. Her broad face broke into a bright smile when she caught sight of Diego.

"Hey, stranger! Where the heck have you been keeping yourself?" She bustled over, her gaze running up and down the bodies to Diego's left and right. "You definitely need to come more often if you're going to bring so many handsome men. From Ireland, I think I heard?"

Diego chuckled. Something said to one person in town eventually got around to everyone. "Hi, Annie. Good to see you. Yes, this is Sean." He put a hand on Sionnach's shoulder, then pointed around the group. "Angus, Nathan and Falco. Of course, you know the good-looking troublemaker in the back."

"Evening, Annie," Finn said with a little waggle of his fingers.

"I do, and I see you haven't been feeding him properly again." Annie shook her head with a mock-scowl. She took Finn by the arm to lead him to the round table at the back. "That's all right, sweetheart. We'll take care of you since Diego doesn't know how."

"Shameful how he mistreats me." Finn put the back of one hand to his forehead. "I am fortunate, indeed, that you are here to rescue me."

"We'll get you fed up, don't worry." Annie patted his arm and waited until they were settled. "Are you boys all artists like Finn?"

The fae shifted uncomfortably, casting glances around the table to see who should answer. Diego came to their aid. "No. Sean and Angus are in…communications. Nate's a horticulturist, and Falco's a fighter."

"Oh, sure, I can see that." Annie nodded, letting her eyes run up and down Faolchú's hard body in a brazen fashion. "Though he looks like you've been starving him, too."

Faolchú raised his head to give her a devastating smile. "I have been quite ill, beautiful lady. Diego has been nursing me back to health."

Her flirting melted into maternal concern. "Oh, hon, did these boys drag you out of bed too soon? Are you warm enough?"

"I'm well on the road to recovery, never fear." Faolchú caught her hand and brushed his lips over her knuckles.

Annie blushed, and Diego helped her cover up her flustered state by ordering for them all, steaks, rare, for the three big men, and roast chicken for himself and the little ones.

"You're a dreadful flirt," Nathair murmured when Annie hurried off to the kitchen.

"She likes me." Faolchú smiled and licked his teeth. "She smells delicious."

Diego, on his left, leaned over to whisper, "You wouldn't…would you?"

"What?" Faolchú turned puzzled blue eyes to him, and wrinkled his nose. "Devour her? Ugh, no. Humans taste foul. The cooking smells, I meant."

A waitress brought beer and bread, and they chatted quietly, since Diego had instilled in them the need to use their 'inside voices'. When dinner arrived, Sionnach and Nathair picked at the chicken daintily with fingers and forks, humming and growling in delight at the flavor. Angus possessed a basic grasp of knife and fork, though he speared the cut pieces with his knife and ate off the tip. Faolchú appeared completely flummoxed, and would have picked up the entire steak in both hands if Diego hadn't leaned over to cut it up for him.

For the first time in weeks, Diego felt truly relaxed. Back home, among friends who were now safe and well, he ate and drank and enjoyed the company.

* * * *

Finn had learned not to lick the plate when they were out in public, though it was sorely tempting with all the lovely juices still pooled there. Instead, he excused himself to find the pretty young waitress to beg another basket of bread.

He had thought she had gone into the kitchen, but when he poked his head in, only Annie and her cooks were there. Annie handed him the bread for the price of a kiss on the cheek and shooed him out. As he sauntered back down the short hallway to the dining room, a snatch of conversation made his steps falter.

"That group over there," a smooth baritone inquired. "Are they from around here?"

A young woman giggled, the little waitress. "Oh, no. I mean, Mr. Sandoval, he lives here. He's like our resident writer, right? And his boyfriend, Finn, the tall, cute one. Guess he went to the men's room or something. The rest are visiting Finn from Ireland. Isn't that cool?"

"Yes, very." The man's voice seemed friendly but Finn sensed something underneath that stirred the hairs on the back of his neck. Some hidden intent lurked beneath the innocent questions. "Are they all paired off?"

"Sure seems that way." Now Finn heard the frown in the girl's voice. "You have a problem with gay guys, mister?"

The man laughed. "I think my husband back home would have a problem with that."

A liar by nature, Finn knew one when he heard one. The waitress laughed, though, evidently relieved. "Well, okay, then. Guess there's no harm in looking, though, huh?"

Finn breezed out of the hallway as if he had been walking at a brisk pace all along. He winked at the waitress and stole a quick glance at the man. Dark suit, close-cropped dark hair, clean-shaven, well-kept, something about him struck Finn as off, as if the suit and the urbane expression were a uniform.

He tried to still his shaking hands as he put the basket down and resumed his seat. Diego wasn't fooled one bit.

"*Mi vida*? Everything all right?"

Finn tore off a hunk of bread and casually began to sop up the meat juices. "The man at the front table is asking questions about us. He gives me the…what's the expression? The creeps."

Diego's expression tightened but he was too smart to turn around and stare. "Probably just a businessman passing through, *caro*. Man has a right to be curious if he wants."

Every fiber of Finn's being screamed that the man was dangerous, but he nodded, unwilling to spoil the evening for Diego, and made a good show of finishing his meal in contented silence. During dessert, a dizzy wave of relief sluiced over Finn when the man left.

They all thanked Annie profusely as they took their leave, promising to return again soon. Most fae were wary of humans, but because Annie was Diego's friend, they accepted her readily. Emotion swelled in Finn's chest as he watched Diego saying goodbye to everyone in the dining room, no one able to resist that earnest face and beautiful smile.

Gods, I love this man.

Later that night, when the moon had set and the night's quiet settled in every corner and crevice of the house, Finn lay awake in bed, staring at the ceiling. Diego lay in his arms, leg flung across Finn's, his head nestled on Finn's shoulder, his chest rising and falling slowly in deep, peaceful sleep.

Finn kissed the top of his dark, curly hair. *I wish I could be more for you.* Something was coming, something bad, and his heart sped with terror thinking he might not be able to protect his love from the storm.

Chapter Seventeen

The IER

Tendrils of cool fog crept over the back porch steps the next morning. Diego padded out to perch on the rail with his coffee. He had left Finn in bed, burrowed under the covers, his face so angelic in sleep Diego couldn't bear to disturb him.

The fog shrouded the doorway to the Otherworld, rendering it entirely invisible. Even in the brightest light, the opening remained elusive unless one felt the magic pulsing there or one stood directly in front of it and realized the landscape no longer matched.

"Probably should find a way to hide it altogether," Diego muttered to the garden.

"Hide what, love?" Finn stood in the doorway in nothing but a pair of black silk boxers, a glorious sight as he stretched, long, lean muscles rippling.

"Good morning." Diego chuckled and pointed with his mug. "The doorway. This is a relatively safe place back here on private property, but I don't want someone stumbling on it by chance."

Finn wrapped his arms around Diego from behind, kissing a soft line down Diego's jaw to his shoulder. "Hmm, yes, I suppose there are ways. Humans always had trouble finding them before, since most humans are quite head-blind and don't see such things."

"True." Diego hummed in pleasure and tangled his fingers in Finn's hair when soft lips fastened on the side of his throat. His voice gone husky, he asked, "Are you hungry, *mi amor*?"

"Always," Finn whispered, his sharp teeth grazing Diego's skin.

Diego turned to cup the side of Finn's face. "Then why don't you go grab your shower, and I'll make you breakfast."

"I like showers much more when they include you."

"But you like your breakfast ready when you come out, too. I can't do both."

Finn heaved a tragic sigh, and Diego's heart stuttered at the way his pecs moved on the long inhalation. "Very well, as you wish. I must reek dreadfully this morning, if you push me away so quickly."

"You smell fantastic," Diego murmured, burying his face against Finn's chest. "And you look amazing. But I want you sitting down and serious and not distracted. I have something I want to talk to you about."

"Have I done something wrong again?" Finn asked in a small voice.

"No, no, *cariño*, don't worry. I just—"

A figure barreling out of the fog interrupted his thoughts. Faolchú bounded through the garden and ignored the porch steps in favor of an impressive vault over the rail. "Fionnachd! There are herds of summer-fattened deer in the forest! Come hunt with me. There could not be a more perfect morn for it."

Nathair appeared on the bottom step as if he had materialized from water vapor. "My light, perhaps Diego wished Fionnachd's company this morning."

Faolchú stopped bouncing on the balls of his feet. "Ah. I... Your pardon. Did I interrupt?"

"It's all right," Diego reassured him on a helpless laugh. The excitement thrummed from both would-be hunters, and it seemed cruel to deny them. "Go on, you two miscreants. What I need Finn for will keep."

"You are certain?" Finn asked.

When Diego nodded, he found himself swept into Finn's strong arms and bent backward for a fierce kiss. Finn's lips, firm and demanding, urged him to open. Diego parted his lips with a moan, their tongues dueling for supremacy for one breathtaking moment. Then Finn released him with a grin and a wink, leaving Diego panting and dizzy as he and Nathair watched the hunters lope off toward the woods. Blue light flickered around Finn as he ran, his body melting and condensing until black wolf-dog Finn ran beside Faolchú.

"It is tempting to go watch the hunt." Nathair slipped an arm around Diego's waist and laid his head on his shoulder. "They are wonderful to see together."

"Hmm, yes, to a point. I don't think I'd be able to watch them pull down a deer and tear it to pieces."

"They would make a clean kill, swift and sure. A hard blow to the head —"

"Honestly, hon, I don't want to know," Diego said with a squeeze to Nathair's shoulder. "Where's our fox and eagle this morning?"

"Court duties called them away. They said they would return soon, most likely carrying messages."

Diego laughed. "I got so used to having them here, I forgot you all have a life outside my garden." A howl drifted to them from the depths of the forest, the half-mournful song of the pack hunt. Diego shivered. "How in the world did you two get together? I can't see you running in the hunt with him, and I don't see him hanging out with you to pull weeds."

"We have known each other for so long, but never saw each other clearly." Nathair's voice held an aching tenderness. "Then shortly after Danu closed the Veil, I was out gathering mushrooms for soup. A deer in flight crashed through the thicket beside me, and Faolchú crashed into me. He lay atop me, apologizing and asking if he had hurt me. I looked up into those winter-blue eyes and suddenly never wanted him to get up."

"He felt the same right away?"

Nathair laughed. "No. Or, rather, he tried to deny it and kept pursuing everything but me. But he kept coming to me for little favors. 'Nathair, do you have any bread?' 'Nathair, there's a thorn between my pads I can't get out.' 'Nathair, do you have something for an aching head?' Until one day in my garden, he knelt at my feet and said, 'If I can't have you, I will die. Please don't refuse me.' When a hero comes and pleads on his knees, how can you refuse?"

"Not that you wanted to."

"Not even for an instant."

"So, did you eat, or can I tempt you into having some eggs with me?"

The morning passed in relative quiet. An attempt to get some work done followed breakfast with Nathair, though Scath and Croi decided to visit Diego, chatting about this and that, insisting on perching on the arm of his chair or in his lap. Distracting didn't begin to cover it. By the time they decided to fly off into the woods to play, Sionnach and Angus caught him in the kitchen, bearing messages that gave Diego a headache.

"A second doorway in Ireland?" Diego rubbed at his temples.

"That is the request from Himself," Sionnach confirmed.

"And Danu says what in response?"

Angus shrugged. "Much what one would expect. She declares it too dangerous and will allow no such thing."

"So, they want me to do what about this?"

"To mediate, oh, wise Druid-Bard." Sionnach flashed his most charming smile.

Diego sighed, irritated that the two rulers could not hold simple negotiations on their own. He needed to talk to Finn, damn it, to give him the ring, and would if they could get a moment's peace. "Could it at least wait until tomorrow?"

"At your leisure, Light-wielder," Angus intoned with a courtly bow.

"Well...good." Diego blinked at the unexpected realization that he had a choice. "Good. You boys can stay for lunch, then. Sionnach looks ready to pass out, and you don't look too much better."

Sionnach sank into the nearest chair. "The Voice takes a good deal of effort."

"And leaves one drained." Angus swayed where he stood, and Diego pushed him into the next chair over.

"They should both be ashamed, using you like this when you've both been so ill." Diego put the kettle on, then dug in the cabinets for the tea Tia Carmen had left. "I know, sacred duty and all that, but they could have a little sense."

Sionnach crawled into Angus' lap and used a broad shoulder to pillow his head. Diego could only imagine the torture of the past hundred years for them—the separation, the stolen moments. They certainly were making up for lost time, unable to keep their hands off each other for more than a few minutes at a time.

Suddenly, Sionnach's head jerked up. "Someone is coming. Vehicles like yours, Diego, driving up the road to your house."

"I better go have a look." Diego shot them a reassuring smile, Sionnach looked so anxious. "Don't worry. Probably just the rangers. You'll like them."

When Diego opened the front door, though, he found something other than park service trucks pulling up outside. Four gunmetal-gray panel vans skidded to a precision choreographed halt on the gravel drive. Not park service, but they appeared to be from some government agency if the official emblems on their sides were any indication—a picture of Earth twined round a banner with the letters 'IER'. *Feds? Environmental agency?*

A man dressed in coveralls climbed from the passenger seat of the lead van. He stopped at the bottom of the front porch steps, glanced down at his clipboard then up at Diego. "Mr. Santiago Sandoval y Romero?"

The use of his full given name pulled him up short. No one had addressed him that way for years. "Yes? Can I help you?"

"You're Mr. Sandoval, the owner of this property?"

"Yes, I am. What can I do for you?"

More men emerged from the vans, some of them in midnight blue coveralls, others in what appeared to be full biohazard suits. Diego's surprise ratcheted up to full-scale alarm.

"Sir, for your own safety, we need you to come with us."

"For my—has there been some kind of toxic spill? Chlorine gas accident?" Diego still stood in the doorway, one hand motioning behind him to keep Sionnach and Angus out of sight. Both fae wore their human glamours, but the situation made the hairs on Diego's arms prickle. *Who are these people, and what the hell do they know that they've come here? Did someone see something in the woods? Report it to some agency? Dios, what the hell do I do now?*

"Something like that, sir." The man with the clipboard held his position, the other men fanned out around the house. "We need you to come with us now, Mr. Sandoval. For your own protection. We're evacuating the area."

"I need a better explanation than that, I'm afraid." Diego tried to keep his voice friendly and calm. "If there's been an accident, I have friends hiking out in the woods. I can't just leave them here."

"Leave that to us, sir. We'll get everyone out, don't worry." The man spoke to him, but his head swiveled this way and that as he checked to one side of the house and the other, glanced toward the garage and the roof.

Something was terribly wrong here. These might be legitimate government agents or they might not, but the evasiveness was a bad sign.

Sionnach flattened himself against the wall inside the front door, out of sight. "Who are they, Diego? Are these enemies? They smell sharp and dangerous."

Diego leaned inside where the man couldn't see him. "I'm not sure, but I need you and Angus to grab

Nathair and run. Get through the doorway where you'll be safe."

Angus let out an offended snort and came to stand by Diego in the doorway. "We shall not run like hunted mice when you are in danger. If there's to be a fight, we'll stand by you."

"I don't want there to be a fight," Diego whispered desperately. "I don't know what they want, and I don't want you involved. Go!"

"*Diego!*" Nathair's panicked cry came from the side of the house, followed by anguished screams.

"Fuck." Diego didn't hesitate. He leaped down the front steps and tore around the house, while clipboard man shouted at him to stop.

Two of the anonymous figures in hazmat suits held a wildly struggling Nathair between them, his hands cuffed behind his back, agony contorting his handsome features. *Steel cuffs, damn it.*

"Get those cuffs off him!" Diego bellowed. "I don't know who you people think you are, but I want you the fuck off my property, now!"

"Positive ID, I repeat, positive ID," came a voice from one of the hazmat helmets.

"Sedate and go to full restraints," clipboard man called out.

"*Carajo!* Hold on one damn minute, you bastards!" Diego dove for Nathair, not certain what he intended, only to find himself hauled up short when two men, each the size of a Grizzly, seized his arms.

Diego fought and kicked, certain his struggles were futile but too furious to stop. Nathair had passed out from the iron-induced pain so the sedate they injected seemed overkill.

Events spiraled out of control at a whirlwind pace. Sionnach, his glamour abandoned, leaped for one of the men. He sank his teeth into the man's arm and scrabbled at his abdomen with his sharp back claws. A sharp pop went off on Diego's left and Sionnach went limp with a dart in the back of his neck.

Angus shifted to eagle and dove at the man with the clipboard, talons aimed at his eyes. Curses and shouts went up as rifles aimed his way. Several darts missed him as he wheeled and dodged.

"Angus, go! Get away! Get help!" Diego shouted. Too late, Angus tumbled to the ground with a dart lodged under his right wing, golden pinions trapped awkwardly under him as he fell. The men gathered up the limp bundle of feathers, calm as could be, as if people shifted into screaming golden eagles and half-foxes every day. *Why the hell don't they even look surprised?*

"Diego? What's happened?" Finn's thoughts reached Diego, full of anxiety and rising anger.

"*Dios*, no..." Diego whispered and closed his eyes to try to speak rationally, mind to mind. Difficult since he was being shoved face first to the ground, his arms dragged behind his back, and handcuffs fastened tight around his wrists. "Mi vida, *don't come to the house. There are men here who want to catch you, like an animal.*"

"They have you? Diego! No! Not again! I won't let this happen again!"

"It's not like that time!" Diego sent the frantic thought, knowing Finn's memory had fastened on the Inquisition and the witch burnings. *"Finn, no! We need help!"*

Again, his plea came too late. In a thunder of hooves, Finn burst from the trees, the black pooka horse exuding menace with his flame-red eyes and wind-whipped mane. Worse yet, he wasn't alone. Faolchú roared out of the woods on his heels, blood on his chest and muzzle from his recent kill.

They bore down on the men, bowling them over, tossing them aside as if they were no more than sofa cushions. Faolchú took a dart to the shoulder and fought on, slowing, staggering, but too stubborn to go down. Another dart hit Finn's right foreleg. He reared, screaming, and shifted to dragon.

"Holy hells!" one of the men bellowed. "What the fuck is *that*?"

They scattered and took cover, finally registering the shock they should have from the beginning. To Diego's horror, some of the men threw down their tranquilizer rifles and pulled out handguns. He kicked out, taking the one in front of him out at the knees, but it wasn't enough. Another one behind the lead van took aim. The shot popped and Faolchú staggered back, clutching his chest. Another shot spun him to the left, blood spraying from his shoulder as he went down.

"Stop it! Stop! You don't know what you're doing!" Diego screamed. "Finn, don't! God, no! They'll—"

Several sharp cracks sounded in quick succession. Finn's graceful dragon form twisted in the air, then plummeted to the earth with an ear-splitting shriek, a rivulet of blood trickling from the corner of his jaw.

"Finn? Finn!" Pain threatened to crush Diego's chest. He had done this, had brought them here and killed them all. *"Dios ayudame...Finn!"* The carrion stench filled his nostrils. Nausea rose up his throat. He was going to seize. Damn it not now, not *now*.

Someone flipped him on his back, spoke to him, asked him about medical conditions, but he could no longer respond. Two soft lights danced above the porch roof, one blue and one green. With his last conscious thought, he stretched out in desperation. *"Lugh! Help me..."*

He had no way of knowing whether Lugh had heard from the other side of the Veil as the world exploded into a million falling slivers of glass.

Chapter Eighteen

A Matter of National Security

"Pulse at over two hundred."

"Pressure's dropping fast, eighty over sixty…seventy over forty…"

"I need that epi now, folks! Let's move like you've got a purpose in life!"

The voices reached Finn over a vast distance, a long, dark tunnel separating him from the world. Bright lights flashed in and out of his vision, sickening jolts of movement lurched through the haze. All the rest was pain, so much sharp, agonizing pain, enveloping him, stealing thought and sense. The urge to scream stabbed at him constantly. He might have been screaming all along but he couldn't recall and could no longer discern if he was.

One thought remained to torment him as a counterpoint to the agony. *My light, my hero, I have failed you. Again.*

* * * *

So thirsty. Blinding headache. *Why won't someone turn off that damn light?*

Diego moaned when he tried to roll over. Sheets, blanket, pillow, he was waking up in a bed, at least. He cracked an eye open and found his vision filled by a metal rail. Hospital bed, somehow he'd ended up back in a hospital.

But which hospital and what the hell had happened?

Seizure, men from the government, weapons firing...

"Finn!"

He surged up halfway before the nausea and the heated iron spike through his skull slammed him back to the mattress, writhing and tossing. Monitoring equipment chirped and beeped alarms. Hurried footsteps dashed to his bedside.

"Mr. Sandoval? Can you hear me? You need to lie still...that's it."

Someone dimmed the lights and shut off the alarms, slid an arm under his shoulders, and held a straw to his lips. The gentle hands and soothing voice belonged to a broad-shouldered man with close-cropped blond hair.

"Doctor?" Diego croaked out.

"No, sir, I'm your nurse, Sergeant Morrison. Doc's on her way."

Sergeant... Dios, *I'm in a military hospital.* Diego managed a weak nod and allowed himself to be lowered back to the pillows.

"Well, hello, there." Another face joined the sergeant's hovering over him, this one attached to a young woman with a heart-shaped face and a glorious fall of auburn hair. "Was starting to wonder if you were ever going to join us."

"Who..." Diego grimaced and swallowed against a raw throat.

"I'm Dr. Brennan. You just relax, Mr. Sandoval. Zack's going to get you settled and give you something for the pain, and I'll be back in a few for a chat."

Diego fought against panic. Two things kept him from blurting out questions—the fact he could barely speak and the uncertainty of his situation. The military presence could mean he was in the hands of any one of dozens of government agencies, though the little operation on his front lawn suggested the CIA or NSA first and foremost. If that were the case, information would be the key commodity, which he would part with sparingly and only when he could think straight.

His nurse, a rather handsome one he had to admit, elevated the head of his bed, helped him with aspirin and water, and brought him another blanket, careful of Diego's left ankle, wrapped tight with an elastic bandage.

"Here's the direct line to me, Mr. Sandoval." Sergeant Morrison put the call button by his right hand. "You need anything, you feel sick or dizzy, you ring for me, okay?"

I need Finn. Diego nodded, eyes closed. Damn it, where was Finn? Had he survived? He tried to reach out, to find the bright spark of Finn's mind, but something pressed in on him, stifling the world's magic and truncating his reach and negating the power he had become so accustomed to having at his fingertips, as if his limbs had all been amputated at once. A boulder-sized lump rose in his throat along with the helpless despair. Even knowing a good deal of his emotional turmoil was post-seizure depression didn't help. How could he bear to go through this again, separated from Finn, not knowing?

God help me, I can't do this. Tears stung the backs of his eyes.

A chair scraped next to the bed. "Do you need a moment, Mr. Sandoval?" Dr. Brennan sat beside him, a clipboard in one hand, and a box of tissues in the other.

"No." Diego sniffed and shook his head, gulping air in an attempt to prevent sobs. "Just…"

"Hits a lot of folks that way, don't worry. You take a few minutes." Dr. Brennan's bright green eyes held every sign of real compassion. Her friendly sincerity only made Diego more suspicious.

"Where…?"

"Okay, I guess I need to say this right off the bat. I'm not at liberty to discuss anything but your medical condition. Not location, not whys and hows, and not the, ah, incident."

"Is that what we're calling it?" Diego rasped out. "Strangers invade my property and shoot people I care about, and it's an 'incident'?"

"There are a lot of things that aren't in my power to do for you or answer for you." She leaned her head on her hand. "So how about you let me do my job and accomplish the things I can for you?"

He struggled with that for a moment, wanting to shake her and demand information. With a soft sigh, he finally whispered, "Diego."

"Excuse me?"

"Please call me Diego. Or I'll keep looking around for my father."

She laughed at that. The evidence of a sense of humor gave him some hope. "All right, Diego. Have you had seizures previously?"

"Yes. About three years."

"Taking anything for them?"

He waved a hand toward his feet. "What happened to my ankle?"

"You were restrained when you seized. It's sprained. Painful, but nothing broken. Meds? You didn't have any on you."

"Carbamazepine. They didn't exactly give me a chance to get the bottle out of the medicine chest," he said in a dry tone.

"I'll write a scrip for you and send Zack down to the dispensary. Allergies? History of fainting? Dizzy spells?"

The familiar questions went on and on, a list countless doctors had run through with him, so he was able to answer in a civil, mechanical fashion, falling back on the automatic expectations of a doctor-patient relationship. She truly seemed competent and friendly, but Diego still resented that this doctor had been thrust upon him in such horrible circumstances.

When she left, Sergeant Morrison returned with the meds and some dry toast. Since no time elapsed between her going and him coming in, Diego surmised the room was monitored, everything he said overheard and most likely watched.

"Been in the service long?" Diego asked, since it seemed odd not to speak to a man who had probably seen him naked.

"Only forever, sir." The big sergeant chuckled.

"Can't be that long. You're, what, twenty-two?"

"Twenty-five, sir. Military family, Dad, Granddad, Mom, so it seems like always." He picked up Diego's wrist to take his pulse. "How about you, Mr. Sandoval, you ever enlist?"

"No. They wouldn't have me now, I suppose, with the medical problems. But mostly the 'don't ask, don't tell' issue kept me away."

"Yessir, that can be tough." Morrison's eyes tightened. A muscle in his jaw twitched. Direct hit. "But lots of soldiers manage, and it's better than the old days when it was automatic dishonorable."

"True." Diego stayed quiet for a few minutes, letting Morrison do his work. "Sergeant? I know you probably have orders, but could you tell me one thing?"

"Depends on the one thing, sir."

"Was there anyone brought in with me? Are they…were there casualties?"

Morrison's gaze twitched up and to the left. Ah, there the tiny camera perched. "Couldn't say, sir. I'm assigned to take care of you. That's all I know."

Bullshit. "I understand, Sergeant. Not fair to badger you."

"No harm, no foul, sir."

After another long silence, the Sergeant settled in the bedside chair to fill out paperwork. "I'm reading your book," he murmured without looking up, a shy smile tugging at his mouth.

That was unexpected. "You are? The Dragon one?"

"Yessir." The little smile grew more uncertain. "Don't suppose you'd tell me if Trae buys it? I mean…it'd be kind of harsh if you killed him off."

Diego stared at him. "You really think that's a good question to be asking me right now?"

"Sorry." The smile disappeared as a flush rose up the Sergeant's neck.

Damn. Good job, alienating my one possible ally. "I didn't mean to snarl. I'm sorry. Just look at it from where I'm standing, ah, lying. I can't figure out how to get answers to things that might be life and death right now. All you have to do to get yours is finish the book."

"Right." Morrison ran a hand back through his short hair with a little laugh. "Look, Mr. Sandoval, I wish I could help you. But this is a strictly need-to-know operation. I only know what I need to do my job."

Diego searched his face a moment—an honest one with long-lashed, gray eyes that didn't seem capable of hiding even a white lie. "And even if you did know, I can't jeopardize your career and expect you to tell me things you've been told not to. So, I won't ask you, and you read the rest of the damn book. Deal?"

Morrison grinned, showing perfect white teeth. "Deal. You get some rest, Mr. Sandoval. I'll be back later."

Sleep crept up slowly, dragging Diego under by degrees. He dozed, twitched awake with his heart pounding then dozed off again several times before he drifted deeper where dreams lurk.

He walked a stark landscape full of dust and harsh light. No shadow fell in front or behind him. An outcropping of jagged rock rose before him, its bright sandstone gleam somehow forbidding. He climbed, because he knew he must, every inch of ground gained a torment to his bleeding hands and feet.

Halfway up the fall of stone, the narrow way opened to reveal a flat, inclined table of rock where Finn lay spread-eagle, short chains holding him fast. He opened his eyes — sightless, hollow pits — at Diego's approach. "My love," he whispered. "You must not tarry here."

"I can't leave you like this." Diego stroked the matted hair back from Finn's missing eyes.

"Go. Find a way out. Save yourself this time."

"No! Not without you."

A huge, misshapen bird with a hooked iron beak landed and tore into Finn's side, devouring strips of flesh. Finn gasped, but seemed to lack the strength to cry out.

"Shift to something else! Slip the chains, come with me," Diego pleaded as he tried to shove the monstrous bird away.

A single tear slid from Finn's eye. "Iron... I cannot. Don't be a fool, my hero. You are the only hope for the fae. All the fae. You must live this time. If they execute you, the door will fail. Without both halves, the fae die."

Diego jerked awake, trembling. Dream...it was only a dream, wasn't it? And why in the world had his dream cast Finn as Prometheus? Drying sweat cooled on his body. He shivered, then cried out when the door to his room opened.

"Just me, Mr. Sandoval." Sergeant Morrison came in pushing a wheelchair with a pile of cloth on the seat. A frown creased his forehead. "Sorry to wake you up, but you've got a meeting I need to get you to."

"What sort of meeting?" Diego winced at how breathless he sounded.

"Dunno, sir. 'Get him dressed and wheeled down to the conference room'. That's what I was told. I know you're probably not feeling up to it yet, sir, and I'm sorry about that."

"But orders are orders," Diego murmured.

The sergeant lowered the bedrail so he could help Diego sit up on the edge of the bed. Together, they exchanged the hospital gown for a pair of blue scrubs identical to the ones Sergeant Morrison wore, and a pair of disposable slippers. With more gentleness than expected from such large hands, he eased Diego over into the chair and tucked a blanket around his lower half.

"You ready?"

Shaky from the effort of moving even that little bit, Diego nodded.

"Look, Mr. Sandoval, if you feel like you're gonna keel over, you need to say so now. I can tell them you're just not strong enough yet."

"No." Diego gulped a breath. "Let's go. Maybe these people I'm going to see have some answers for me."

"Might have a lot of questions," Sergeant Morrison said softly.

"Right. That, too. Zack?" Diego looked up into the worried face of his would-be protector. "It'll be all right."

The sergeant said nothing to that, just patted his shoulder and wheeled him out of the room. The unbroken, uniform gray of institutional corridors dashed Diego's hopes of finding some clue of his whereabouts. No windows interrupted the blank walls, no artwork or even printed memos decorated the stark, naked expanses. They passed door after door, each room identified only by a four-digit number.

Finally, Sergeant Morrison knocked on door 5558. It opened, he wheeled Diego in, and went to parade rest at his left. A long conference table took up most of the room, its five occupants sitting on the side opposite the door. Two were military, in desert camouflage, one wore a black suit and smug expression that screamed government agent, while the remaining two older gentlemen wore lab coats.

The white-haired lab coat in the center looked up briefly from his papers. "Thank you, Sergeant. That will be all."

"Sir—"

"Dismissed, Sergeant!" the military man on the left barked out.

Sergeant Morrison snapped to attention, saluted and executed a perfect about-face without further argument. The door shut with a sharp click behind him.

For a few uncomfortable minutes, they all sat in silence, the black-suited man staring fixedly at Diego while the others read through their papers. The intimidation tactics irritated him and struck him as childish. These people had invaded his home, abducted him without explanation…but a show of temper would undoubtedly be counterproductive.

Heart pounding, Diego managed a steady tone when he finally asked, "Gentlemen, am I being detained here?"

The central figure lifted his head with a frown, white eyebrows drawn together. "Currently, you are under medical observation."

"But that, Mr. Sandoval, is subject to change," Black Suit said with a bland smile.

Diego had to fight against a nervous laugh. The way the man said his name sounded far too much like Hugo Weaving saying '*Mister* Anderson'. He wondered how many times he had watched *The Matrix* to get the inflection just right. "And what, exactly, is that supposed to mean?"

Black Suit laced his hands together atop the table and leaned forward. "You're Cuban, Mr. Sandoval?"

"My parents emigrated from Cuba. I was born in Miami."

"Communist sympathizers?"

"No, they weren't. They would hardly have fled to the States then." The line of questioning aggravated Diego more than the cold-war melodrama. *Leave my parents out of this.* "What in God's name is this all about?"

"We have some questions, Mr. Sandoval," the quieter military man said.

"So do I. Starting with where are we, and why did you drag me here?"

"You're hardly in a position to make demands." Black Suit's soft voice dripped with menace.

"Maybe not, but the last time I checked, I'm still a US citizen, which comes with certain inalienable rights. I haven't been granted a phone call. My attorney isn't present. I haven't been charged with anything. Therefore, I'm under no obligation to answer a damn thing."

Black Suit gave him a chill smile. "These rights can be set aside, Mr. Sandoval, when it becomes a matter of national security."

"A matter of... Am I being accused of something or not?"

The younger lab-coated man, stork-thin and balding, cleared his throat. "No one is making accusations. We just have some questions."

"I respectfully refuse to answer anything until I get some answers myself. You can't just keep me here, at any rate. If I disappear, my family, my publisher, the public — people will ask questions."

"Like when you disappeared for over two weeks this past month?" The military man on the left barked out. "Let's start with that, Sandoval. Where the hell were you?"

Diego fought to unclench his jaw. "I haven't done anything illegal or unethical. Nor have I jeopardized the safety of my country in any way. I refuse to answer any questions until I've been allowed to speak to my attorney."

"Your attorney?" Black Suit chuckled. "There aren't any laws to cover what you're mixed up in. I'm not even certain you understand how serious this is." He motioned to someone behind Diego. "Don't worry. You will."

The wheelchair spun back around to the door. Diego twisted his head to find a uniformed man with a sidearm pushing him back out into the hall. Two more flanked them on either side. *Oh, hell, what now?*

They escorted him to another featureless door. This one opened up to a completely empty room, about eight by eight. *Not a room, a cell,* mierda. Visions of waterboarding and beatings raced across Diego's thoughts, the threat of torture more real by the second when his guards yanked him from his chair and stripped him.

"What are you going to do?" He tried to catch one of the guards' arms but the man pulled away.

Instead of answering or commencing the beating Diego expected, the three guards gathered up his blanket, scrubs and wheelchair and left the room. The unmistakable sound of a bolt slamming home destroyed any illusions of getting out into the hall to find help. Diego sat naked in his stark new space, head buried in his hands. Every muscle ached from one of the worst seizures in months and his ankle stabbed at him every time he moved. He had no place to lie down but the concrete floor, no place to relieve himself but a small grate in the corner and nowhere to hide from the cameras that certainly monitored him.

Dios, what have I done? Why didn't I hide them better? The door still stood open in his backyard. What if government agents had already gone through and slaughtered countless fae? He should have been more cautious, thought it through, and kept them better hidden. Not that they should have hidden. It was their damn world, too—they had every right to be there.

The room gradually grew warm, then uncomfortably hot. Diego lay down on the cool concrete, sweat prickling his skin, seeking some relief. Just when he thought he might pass out from the heat, fans kicked on to dry the sweat and revive him. Wonderful if it had stopped there, but the temperature plummeted until he lay curled in a tight ball, shivering hard enough to rattle his teeth. When the fog of his breath began to leave ice crystals on the floor, the fans shut off and the cycle repeated, from one extreme to the other, on and on for what might have been several hours.

I deserve everything they throw at me. I've probably killed my love and my friends and doomed every magical being to extinction.

He tried again to reach for the flows of magic, for some trickle that might help him summon enough lightning to take out the door, but again he came up against that strange, gray pressure blotting out the magic.

Eventually, exhausted, he tried to drop into a twilight sleep. As soon as his eyes slid shut, though, a Sousa march blared from hidden speakers, loud enough that the bass notes vibrated through the floor. The room lights flickered off and on at random intervals, the music came and went, and so it continued, stifling to frigid to stifling again, with the strobe effect of his room light and the cacophonous intrusions from the March King, until Diego's body finally had enough and seized again.

Chapter Nineteen

Necessary Experiments

The voice Finn had come to hate with all his heart drifted into his half-waking state.

"Three-inch abdominal incision, fully closed, minimal residual redness along incision site. Auto-closure time four hours, twenty-two minutes. Ten percent drop in healing efficiency. Amputation site stable. Bleeding negligible. Otherwise no closure of site apparent after...five hours, twelve minutes."

Of course not, you bloody fool! I need my hand back! Finn wanted to scream but the leather contraption they had shoved between his teeth prevented speech. He seemed to recall it had arrived shortly after he had bitten someone, most likely while they sliced his hand from his wrist.

He growled, the only sound he could manage, and closed his eyes to call to his hand, which they had crammed in a jar across the room. Calling a part of himself back should have been as easy as drawing breath. Something besides the iron in the room dulled the edges of his magic, muted it, keeping the flows thin and distant. He clenched his teeth on the leather, concentrating as hard as his dizzy brain could manage.

The brittle shatter of glass warmed his heart.

"Fuck!" The voice was younger than the hated one. "Sorry, sir, but... Damn. The hand's crawling *back*."

"Are we recording? Are we getting this? Fantastic. Utterly fantastic. No, no, let it go. Let's see what happens."

Finn's breath caught and he nearly sobbed in relief when his hand climbed the table he lay on and nestled next to his wrist again. *Goddesses of all the waters, that was too hard.*

"Spontaneous reattachment begun at seventeen thirty-two." The sallow face belonging to the hated voice hove into Finn's vision. "Subject is conscious again. Increase that drip, keep him twilighted. Once we have full attachment, I want the amputation performed again."

Again? Finn yanked on his restraints, a pitifully weak effort. His eyes roamed the room in a wild attempt to find some sympathetic face, but no one looked at him as anything but an object.

"We have to see if the phenomenon is repeatable."

Bloody hell.

* * * *

"...ever do anything like that to a patient of mine without clearing it with me first!"

Dr. Brennan was shouting at someone nearby. Diego's heart slammed against his ribs. *Stimulant? Damn it, damn it, how much more can things possibly hurt?* Lights slipped by overhead. He lay on his back on a gurney, rolling down the corridor. He twisted his head to see who pushed the gurney, oddly comforted to see Zack Morrison there, even with his mouth set in such a grim line.

"You're overreacting, Doctor." Black Suit's smooth voice was not nearly so comforting.

"Am I, Gerry? He could have stroked out while you were playing Guantanamo. How much good is he to you if he's dead or brain-damaged?"

"He didn't, and he's not," Black-suit, Gerry, answered.

Dr. Brennan made a disgusted sound. "Men are such idiots."

"Thanks, Doc," Morrison said with a dry snort.

"Not you, Zack."

They returned to the familiar hospital style room where another nurse helped Morrison lift Diego from the gurney to the bed.

"I think he's awake, Doc."

"No thanks to some people," Dr. Brennan muttered. "Diego? You with us?"

"Tea," Diego rasped out through chattering teeth. "Please."

"I'm on it, ma'am. Be right back," Morrison said as he hurried out again.

Dr. Brennan shook her head while she checked Diego over. "They nearly kill you, and you still find time to say 'please'. You're a rare find."

"Still alive." Diego grabbed her sleeve. "Dr. Brennan…need to know. Is Finn alive? They kill him?"

"Easy, there. Who's Finn?"

It occurred to him in a fuzzy, belated way that she might be there to soothe information from him, since he had been uncooperative in the face of threats. A friendly face, someone he was supposed to trust instinctively, maybe she was the good cop to their bad. "Never mind. Sorry."

She patted his shoulder with a worried frown and replaced his arm under the blankets.

While he drank the decaf tea and came down from the stimulant careening around in his bloodstream, Dr. Brennan told him what had happened. Diego's seizure had apparently scared the living hell out of the techs monitoring his room. Inexperienced and anxious, they'd failed to find a pulse when they'd burst into the room to check on him. One of them had had the bright idea to pull out the med kit, which happened to contain adrenaline injections.

"Watching too many movies. Damn kids," Dr. Brennan concluded.

"So what now? You make sure I'm better so they can torment me some more?" Diego asked. The pained look on Dr. Brennan's face made him wish he'd kept his mouth shut.

"I'm going to do the best I can for you, Diego. Though I'm afraid it might not be much."

The rest of the day passed much like a normal hospital stay, Sergeant Morrison coming and going with meds, vitals checks and trays of food he tried to coax Diego into eating. In between, Diego slept, his exhausted body not giving him much choice.

Early in what he assumed to be morning, since there had been several hours with the lights off, Sergeant Morrison returned with the wheelchair.

"Mr. Sandoval, I'm so damn sorry…"

Diego held up a hand to stop his apologies. "They want another meeting. It's not your fault, Zack. I just hope I can stay awake."

"Now, there's a defense they don't teach in training," Morrison said with a crooked grin.

"What's that?"

"When you're interrogated, go narcoleptic."

Once again, Diego suffered through being helped to dress and eased into the wheelchair. His weakness frightened him, the way the simplest movements made his hands shake. He supposed he had never noticed it before because he had always been allowed to rest after a severe seizure.

Sergeant Morrison put one hand on his shoulder as he wheeled him out.

"What's this for?" Diego patted his hand.

"You pass out on me, sir, I'd rather you didn't take a header onto the linoleum."

"Got it." Diego leaned back and tried to calm his shaking, more grateful for that warm, comforting hand than he cared to admit.

Several alterations signaled an abrupt change in tactics for this second meeting. A smaller, more intimate conference room housed an oval table where Diego was granted a place rather than being isolated hearing-style. Only four other men graced the table, the bulldog military man conspicuously absent. A pitcher of water and a glass stood near his right hand, and a flat screen hung on the far wall.

"Sir," Morrison clipped out from his place behind Diego's chair. "Dr. Brennan's left orders for me to stay with the patient."

After some shuffling and murmuring, the senior lab coated gentleman nodded. "You may remain, Sergeant. In case Mr. Sandoval has another episode."

"They normally occur only during moments of extreme stress," Diego said mildly, wishing his voice were steadier.

"Yes. Regrettable. Some of our colleagues are less…patient than others."

The remaining military officer spoke up. A general, perhaps. Diego had never learned which insignia meant what rank. "Mr. Sandoval, we're aware of your record of public service. We know you're a compassionate, civic-minded citizen. And this is why some of us are willing to give you the benefit of the doubt. I, for one, believe you have no idea what you've stumbled into."

"I don't have any idea where the hell I am, for a start," Diego said. By the little furtive looks around the table, he knew this wasn't what the general meant. Frustration warred with exhaustion and he wrapped his arms around himself, willing his trembling to slow.

"Mr. Sandoval, we'd like to show you something," Gerry said with a chill half-smile.

He pointed a remote at the screen. Images began to play that sent a prickling rivulet of anger up Diego's spine. The first image was of his house in Montana. Diego watched himself climb out of his truck with groceries. The front door burst open and a beautiful black dog bounded out, feathered tail waving wildly. Diego's heart lurched when the dog spoke. "You're home, my hero! At last! Did you bring the cream?"

Diego glared at the agent. "How long have you been watching my house?"

"For a while now," was the bland reply. "We've been investigating you ever since the CDC sent us a very odd blood sample from a certain clinic in Brooklyn."

My Finn... For a moment, Diego could only stare mutely, an ache lodged in his chest as more short clips of his beloved pooka graced the screen, Finn's smile, his laugh, his voice, all caught in snippets by a stranger's spying camera. *Everything I've done, everything I tried to do to help you since the day we met...it all put you in jeopardy.*

More images followed of Sionnach and Nathair, in their glamoured forms and in their natural states, caught by night-vision cameras. Fairy lights in the forest flittered across the screen. Lugh stepped through the doorway from the Otherworld into Diego's backyard, though it was a side view, which made it appear as if he had stepped from thin air.

The elderly scientist spoke again, "We've theorized that much of their devices utilize nano-technology, since no hardware is apparent even under the highest magnification."

"You see, Mr. Sandoval." The general leaned forward, his hands clasped atop the table. "We believe these few caught on camera are an advance force and that you, as the only human at the epicenter of this alien invasion, may hold the key to saving the human race."

Diego stared from one to the other, his tired brain struggling with what sounded like nonsense words. Finally, he latched on to the key phrases. A harsh laugh born of frustration and disbelief leaped from him. Once begun, the hysterical laughter ran away from him until he ran out of breath, his head on the table as he gasped helplessly.

"Mr. Sandoval?" Morrison's hand landed gently on his shoulder. "You okay there?"

Diego raised his head, his chest still heaving. "Oh, God, you must be kidding me."

"We couldn't be more serious," the general went on. "The Institute for Extraterrestrial Research was built in the event of first contact. You're in a secure base, Mr. Sandoval, hidden inside a mountain, surrounded three hundred and sixty degrees by layers of lead and concrete. This place could withstand Armageddon."

Scenes from the day the vans had invaded Diego's front yard played on the screen. The ache in his chest grew to a wrecking ball.

"These are formidable adversaries." The younger scientist stood, stoop-shouldered and long-limbed. He used his pen to point to an image of Sionnach leaping at one of the men, back paws poised to eviscerate. "With a dangerous and varied arsenal." He pointed to the sky and Angus in his eagle form preparing to swoop. "Natural physical weapons. The ability to morph."

Diego held his breath when Finn and Faolchú broke from the woods. While he knew how this would end, more or less, he hoped beyond hope that he might be able to tell if they all still lived.

"The ability to utilize the natural surroundings as offensive weaponry." The scientist pointed to Faolchú flinging up rocks at the attackers with flicks of his fingers.

Faolchú went down. Blood spattered the grass. Dragon-Finn soon followed, his wing broken under him and a gaping hole torn in his chest. Diego bit back a cry of anguish. On screen, Finn shifted back to his own form, dragging himself toward Diego's convulsing body. Five tranquilizer darts later, he finally lay still.

"Instantaneous transport." The scientist pointed to where Faolchú suddenly disappeared. "Though we have yet to discover the location of the ship that must be in close orbit."

Gracias a dios, *Faolchú made it into the Dreaming*. Diego bit down on his bottom lip to keep the tears back.

"Even a weapon resembling ball lightning."

Diego watched in horror as his convulsions intensified on the screen. A blue sphere formed above him, though to the uninformed observer it could easily have been forming over Finn or Nathair who lay beside him. The lightning ball hovered, flashing, then split into hundreds of blinding forks, most of which drove harmlessly into the ground. One hit the house, setting the porch steps on fire, while another hit one of the gray vans. The van windows exploded in a shower of shards.

He continued to watch the screen in agonized silence as his image and those of the four remaining fae were loaded onto stretchers and into the vans. The man with the clipboard waved at the house and ordered the fire put out and the area gassed, apparently to discourage any more 'instantaneous transport' at the site.

"Are they here?" Diego heard the raw, ragged whisper, shocked that it came from his own throat. "Are they alive?"

"The injured men all survived, though two are still in the infir—"

"No! *Dios*…what is *wrong* with you people?" Diego scrubbed his hands over his face. "The people who were with me. At my house. The four you kidnapped."

Gerry drummed his fingers on the table, an unreadable look on his face. "All four subjects have been secured here."

"The aliens have been quarantined, since they are quite dangerous," the younger scientist said as he turned from the screen. "We are grateful for the opportunity to run necessary experiments, though."

Diego squeezed his eyes shut on a long shudder even as his heart thumped a hard staccato against his sternum. *He's alive...thank God, he's alive...* "What sorts of 'necessary experiments'?"

"What we're hoping is that since you were in close contact with the aliens, you might have some knowledge that could help," the general went on as if Diego hadn't spoken. "If we're going to be prepared for the upcoming invasion, any kernel might prove vital."

"Invasion. I see." Diego stared at the screen where the vans prepared to drive away from the house. The whole thing was just too damned surreal. He had considered the possibility that someone might discover the fae, sooner or later, but not that a paranoid government would be convinced that they were some sort of *War of the Worlds* landing party.

He blinked at the image onscreen. He thought he saw a tiny blue light hover over the van in the rear, shimmering. As the line of government vehicles drove away, a green twinkle joined it, both lights zipping after the retreating vans. He couldn't be entirely certain, but he couldn't very well ask them to replay the last scene so he could be sure.

He tucked away the possibility they had been followed and concentrated on the present. His keepers apparently believed rough treatment might kill him. Good. They wanted what he knew in the worst way, so he had some leverage.

"I'll tell you what I know," he said softly. "I guess it's a little late not to. I'm not sure you'll believe me, but I'll try. But I'm not giving you anything until you let me see them. The, um, aliens. Speak to them."

"Out of the question," snapped the elder scientist. "I won't have ongoing experiments compromised."

"They're far too deadly," the younger one insisted. "We couldn't allow it."

Gerry's fingers ceased their drumming. His voice was silken cream as he said, "Oh, I don't think there's any harm in him *seeing* them. Through the viewing windows. And maybe he could speak to the control subject. That one seems docile enough."

What spun through that man's mind was a mystery to Diego, and he wasn't sure he wanted to know. He had to jump at any opportunity to see where they were being held in case a chance came along to get them out.

I can't even walk, and I'm trying to puzzle out an escape plan? Cart, meet horse, not sure who goes where...

He had to see Finn.

"I have to agree, Doctor." The general nodded in a way that said there would be no more argument. "Observation won't compromise your work."

Diego leaned back in his chair as he was wheeled out again, with a glance up to make sure who had the handles. "Don't leave me, Zack," he murmured.

"Not if I can help it," Morrison whispered back.

The whole group stuck in a tight knot down the hall and into an elevator at the end. The younger scientist pressed the floor button. Seven, Diego noticed, though they descended as the floor numbers increased rather than the other way around, into the depths of the earth.

From Hell's heart I stab at thee... Not a good time to be channeling Captain Ahab.

Wide corridors lined with interior windows greeted them when the elevator doors opened. The windows looked in to workspaces of various sizes with counters and high stools, lab equipment and incomprehensible machines. They stopped at a shuttered window. Gerry flicked a switch and the shutter rose silently to show a bare room no larger than an average prison cell. In the center of this room, knees drawn up to his chest, rocking, sat Angus.

"The glass is one-way. He can't see us," the younger scientist declared.

Diego swallowed hard. While Angus seemed in reasonable physical condition, he stared, wild-eyed, his beautiful, golden hair a disheveled mass of snarls. To see the proud herald reduced to this hit him like a fist to the gut.

"You're...experimenting on him?" Diego couldn't manage more than a hoarse whisper.

"Yes. We should see it in a moment."

A siren shriek split the air, muted outside the cell, most likely deafening inside. Red and white strobe lights flashed. Angus leaped up and pressed himself against the back wall. His chest heaved as his wild eyes searched the floor. Electric sparks spit and hissed along a black grid lining the concrete, seemingly at random. Angus clawed at the wall as if he could escape up it, agile enough to avoid most of the electric shocks. A few bit at his feet, though, strong enough that he cried out in pain, and when the siren stopped, he sank back to the floor, sobbing.

For a moment, Diego lost the ability to speak, as if the demonstration had stolen the air from the corridor. He fought for a breath and snapped out, "What the hell was that supposed to prove? That electric shocks hurt?"

The elder scientist gave him an indulgent smile. "Of course it does. The negative stimulus is designed to engender a false sense of peril, to encourage him to morph into his winged form so we can film and study the transformation."

"And has he done it for you?"

This made the man frown. "No. We've increased to voltage three times and still no success."

Calm, calm, shrieking like a drama queen won't help him. "Has anyone suggested that maybe he can't?" His own trouble reaching the flows of magic occurred to him. "Maybe the space is too small or there's something blocking his abilities?"

"Yes, several variables may be factors." The scientist nodded, completely undisturbed. "A larger space is being prepared for a new trial tomorrow if this one continues to prove unsuccessful."

"It's obviously not working," Diego persisted. "Maybe give him a break until then? Give him a blanket, at least, let him rest?"

He was studiously ignored as the group moved on down the hall. A few rooms down, they stopped again, this time in front of a window looking into a hospital-style room with a single bed and a collection of monitors and equipment. A small, hairless figure lay curled in a tight ball on the bed, shivering. Diego stared, horror creeping through him as he realized what he saw. They had shaved off all Sionnach's hair, his glorious auburn waves shorn off, his beautiful, bushy tail reduced to a rat's naked string, his legs and dainty fox-feet devoid of fur.

"And what's this supposed to be?" he choked out.

"Pharmaceutical and toxicity trials," the older scientist answered as he took down the chart from the wall and leafed through it. "Oxycontin, I believe was scheduled this morning. Ah, yes, that's it."

On the bed, Sionnach twitched and curled tighter around his stomach.

"Their bodies don't always react like ours," Diego began.

"Oh, yes, we've seen that."

"And his hair? Why did you have to take his hair and fur?" Diego fought against tightening his hands into fists. The little fox fae would feel the humiliation as strongly as any pain.

"For hygienic purposes initially," the younger scientist answered. "But it has an astounding rate of re-growth. We're monitoring the effects of various substances on the growth rate as well."

"Could I speak to him?" *Comfort him, let him know he's not alone and that his love still lives.*

"I'm sorry, but no. Access to this room is strictly controlled."

"Sionnach, do you hear me?" No answer came back, though, with Sionnach either too far under the drugs or too hampered by whatever blocked the flows of magic. On down the hall they trooped to the next stop, no better than the last two. A sign beside the door read 'control subject', which should have implied that the person inside had been spared any injury or indignity. This was not the case.

Nathair knelt in the far corner of the room, his back to the window, one arm shackled to the wall. He had stretched to the limit of his joints and the chain as if he might pull free by sheer will alone. A cot hung from the wall, but this, too, he avoided as far as he could.

"Madre de dios," Diego spat out. "You idiots. Let me in there. Now, damn it!"

Gerry made a little gesture toward the general, who gave a terse nod. "Let Mr. Sandoval in to see the subject, gentlemen. Sergeant, you stay out here."

"But —"

"Stand down, Sergeant!" the general barked out.

With the door opened, Diego pushed against his wheels and made his slow way into the room, his arms shaking by the time he reached his friend. Nathair cried out when Diego touched his shoulder, yanking desperately on his chain.

"It's me. Shh, hush. Let me see." Diego's eyes blurred with tears at the deep burns on Nathair's wrist from the steel cuff. "God, how stupid can they be?"

With shaking hands, he tore a strip from his blanket and tucked it between the metal and Nathair's skin. Panting, Nathair turned to watch him with dazed, red-rimmed eyes. His shining green scales reduced to a dull gray, his face drawn with pain, he pulled his lips back from his teeth in a weak snarl.

"Nathair…it's me," Diego murmured, stroking his shoulder.

"Diego?" Nathair whispered, his soft, fluid voice hoarse and ragged. "Are we leaving?"

"I'm sorry, hon, I wish we were. I'm being held here, too. For now. But maybe I can help you a little. And I have something you need to hear." Diego slid out of the chair to sit on the floor. He took Nathair in his arms to whisper in his ear. "Faolchú lives. I saw him slip into the Dreaming."

Nathair's eyes snapped open wide and he leaned against Diego with a whimper.

"You need to hang on. We'll get you out somehow. And back to him." Diego turned his head toward the door and shouted. "You have to switch out this cuff! It's an iron allergy. It's killing him. Aluminum, plastic, anything but steel."

Two of the uniformed security troops appeared in the doorway. They strode forward, picked Diego up as if he weighed no more than a bit of lint, and deposited him back in his chair.

"Please listen to me! Just this one thing!" he protested as they shoved him toward the door.

"Thank you, Mr. Sandoval. We'll take care of it," the general said with a gesture to the two men.

They threw Nathair face down on the floor, the larger one with his knee planted firmly in the center of his back.

"Diego! Help me!"

His weak, terrified cry had Diego out of his chair. He clutched the doorframe for support, his trembling legs threatening to pitch him to the floor. "Stop it! Let him up! He's not a threat to you — he's a *gardener* for Christ's sake!"

"You're getting overwrought, Mr. Sandoval," the elder scientist said with what could have been real concern. "Maybe the sergeant should get you back to bed."

But the goons had the cuff off now and Nathair had passed out, perhaps from relief.

"No, please. I'm sorry. I just…" He sank back into his chair like a good patient. "There should be one more?"

"Yes," Gerry answered with an unreadable expression. "There's one more."

They turned down another corridor where a shift occurred in the atmosphere. Guards stood watch at every heavy, steel door. The equipment, the expressions of the staff hurrying by, all had a more solid, serious appearance. A cold hand gripped Diego's heart. He needed to see Finn, but the fear of what they had done to him nearly cost him his nerve.

The reality turned out to be so much worse than anything he could have imagined.

They stopped in front of a long observation window that opened into one of the larger labs. Several figures in white coats and surgical masks worked around an exam table. At first, they obscured all but the long, elegant feet at the end of the table. Finn's feet, without a doubt. Then one of them moved away, giving Diego a clear view. He clapped his hand over his mouth to silence his cry of horror.

Leather straps secured Finn to the table without a sheet for modesty or a blanket for warmth. A leather...bit, for want of a better word, had been shoved between Finn's teeth. Bruises mottled his pale skin, several open gashes bled sluggishly, but the worst of it — dear God — Finn's right arm ended in a ragged, bleeding stump.

A terrible, anguished sound came from somewhere. Diego only realized he was the source when Morrison's hand landed on his shoulder.

"Mr. Sandoval?"

"I don't...*carajo*..." Diego glanced from one face to the next in utter disbelief. Any attempt at logical, persuasive speech died a horrible death at the sight of Finn's tortured, wasted condition. "You monsters! What the *fuck* have you done?"

The elder scientist seemed unruffled by this outburst. "The subject exhibits astounding regenerative abilities. These are being thoroughly documented."

Diego slammed his fist against the glass. "No! Tell them to get away from him! Set him loose and give him to me!"

"Mr. Sandoval, you're hardly in any position to make demands." Gerry's soft voice held a hint of ice.

With a howl of rage, Diego launched himself at the agent. He tangled both fists in the man's jacket and slammed him up against the wall. "You motherfucker! Watching us for months! Stalking us! Did it get you off to see us together? Did you have a camera in our bedroom?"

Gerry's expression only changed far enough that the corner of his mouth twitched into a bitter half-smile. "You poor, deluded little man. After everything you've seen here, you still have no idea how grave this situation is."

"It's only 'grave' because you're killing them! They're not aliens, you morons! They come from Earth. They've always lived here. Longer than humans. Maybe longer than dinosaurs, I don't know! They *belong* here!"

The agent's expression softened. "That's what they told you?" His right hand came up to cover Diego's, as if to comfort him. "Mr. Sandoval, they're not human. You are. I understand that you've become attached to them. That you've even taken one as a...lover, God help you. I'm sorry about that and I'm sorry this hurts, but you need to search your heart now, and realize what's important beyond your selfish desires.

"This is the first time we've had a chance to study these beings. The aliens at Area 51 were a hoax. A myth. It never happened. These aliens are real. And we believe their intentions may not be peaceful. Their scouts arrived in secret, attempting to infiltrate human society. A peaceful mission would contact Earth's governments directly. They have shown themselves to be aggressive, with deadly weaponry. Please understand, Mr. Sandoval, the fate of humanity rests here, with us, and we take our responsibility very seriously. Now you have to decide where your loyalties are. To your country, your planet, your family, the whole human race or to an alien being who has fed you lies and toyed with your emotions in the most unscrupulous ways?"

Inside the lab, Finn's head thrashed from side to side as the white coats prodded at one of his wounds.

Diego tightened his grip, pounding Gerry against the wall with each word, "He's. Not. An. Alien!"

"Hey, hey, Mr. Sandoval." Big, gentle hands covered Diego's, prying his fingers from the wool suit jacket. "You're upset. We get that. But this isn't the way to handle it."

Sergeant Morrison slid an arm around his waist and pulled him away. To his utter shame, he turned into the embrace, hiding his face against that broad chest, letting the sergeant support him back to his chair.

"Finn..." Diego's anguished whisper barely got past his throat as his nurse turned his chair away from the window. "*Dios*...no...my *Finn*..."

The lights slipped by overhead as Diego slid into numb, helpless despair.

Chapter Twenty

Suspending Disbelief

Diego? Through the red haze, Finn felt the brush of his beloved's mind, a brief, fleeting touch, enough to know his Diego was in agony. Somewhere in the back of his thoughts, he had known Diego was held captive as well, but what had these monsters done to him to cause him such pain?

Oh, my love…a stronger male would shred these bonds and charge to your rescue. But I'm fading. Failing. Sweet goddesses help us, we need a hero, and it's bloody certain that's not me…

* * * *

"Mr. Sandoval?"

Diego turned his head, too weary to lift it from the pillow, to meet worried gray eyes. "Please stop calling me that," he whispered.

A flicker of surprise ran through him when Sergeant Morrison blushed. "I can't call you by your first name, sir."

"Because I'm a civilian? A prisoner?"

Morrison sank into the chair by the bed, staring at his feet. "Well, you're right there. It is protocol to call civilians 'mister'. But it's more 'cause you're, you know…" He made a circular motion with his hand as if he needed to pull the word out of the air. "Famous."

The bitter laugh leaped from Diego's chest before he could stifle it. "I wrote a couple of mildly successful books. That's hardly famous. And even if I were, it wouldn't do me a lot of good now, would it?"

The blush had reached all the way to the sergeant's ears. "You're in the paper sometimes and there's websites about you. Websites other people've made. Fans. I'd say that makes you famous."

"Where are you going with this?"

"I think you're a good guy, Mr. Sandoval. You put your heart into the things you write. And it's a good heart. And I hate seeing you like this. So if you wanna tell someone about it, I'm here. About the…not-so-aliens and Finn."

"Because they won't believe me and you will?"

"Yeah. You know, what do they call it? Willing suspension of disbelief."

"That's for fiction. When you suspend disbelief for a time so you can enjoy the story."

"Could work for real life, too, sometimes, don't you think, sir?"

Diego opened his mouth to disagree and shut it again. The man had a point. "They're not aliens."

"Yessir, you said that."

"They're not from some distant planetary system. There's no ship — mother, scout or otherwise — orbiting the Earth."

Morrison nodded. "Got that much, sir. So what are they? Mutants or something? Like Wolverine?"

"They're fairies."

A frown creased Morrison's handsome forehead. "I'm trying to help here, sir. Not nice to get all sarcastic."

"I'm completely —" Diego broke off when he understood. "Oh. No, sorry. Not that kind of fairy. I mean the kind you find in fairytales. Magical beings who've lived alongside humans since the beginning."

"But they're, um, big. None of these guys would fit on a flower. And they don't have wings." A look of horror spread across Morrison's face. "Did we take their wings?"

Diego heaved a slow breath. He wanted the sergeant to go away and leave him in peace, wanted to spend all his energy trying to reach Finn. But if one soul believed, there was hope others might, and the more people who did, the better their chances of getting out alive.

"No one took their wings. There are lots of different kinds of fae. Some of them have wings. The four held captive here don't. Not in their current forms."

"So what kind do we have here?"

"You have one *sidhe*, two Fomorians…and Finn."

"And Finn is…"

"A pooka."

Morrison scrubbed his hands back through his short, blond hair. "Maybe you should start at square one for me, Mr. Sandoval. Tell me how you met Finn."

Diego settled with his hands laced over his stomach. The camera in the corner recorded every word and they both knew it. Maybe this was the sergeant's way of sparing him a longer, grueling interview if he voluntarily told his story first. *Fair enough.*

"I was driving home one night over the Brooklyn Bridge when I spotted a naked man on the rail. There weren't any first responders on the scene, so I figured I'd better try to talk him down…"

He related the whole first few weeks with Finn, how sick he had been, how Diego had assumed he was delusional, how his assumptions had been shattered when Finn had sat him down and run through a rapid series of shifts from one animal form to another, on and on, until he'd had no choice but to believe. He skipped the part where they had gone to Canada and Finn had inadvertently woken the wendigo. No need to give his listeners any more ammunition if he admitted that, yes, magical creatures could also be malevolent. But he did tell the rest. About his seizures and the lightning in his head, as Finn put it, about the Veil and the Otherworld, how the fae had been failing and what they needed to be whole again.

"Okay, so what you're saying," Morrison said with a little frown, "is that if our world and their world are cut off from each other, if the magic, um, currents don't have a place to flow back and forth, they kinda…stagnate? Like a pond without a fresh water source? And the fairies get poisoned by the stagnant magic?"

"Not a bad way to think of it." Diego nodded. "The two worlds are separate. The magic in them is different flavors, if you like. But they can't be cut off completely from each other. They're two halves of the same Earth. It was certainly about to be the death of the fae, and I think it would have had terrible consequences for humans eventually as well."

"And you were using your house as a fairy ER. Got it. So how do they get back and forth?"

"That, my friend, is not something I'm going to tell you with half the base probably listening."

"Oh. Right." Morrison stood and puttered about the room a few minutes, cleaning up supplies, taking Diego's vitals. Finally, he asked so softly the monitoring devices might have missed it, "You love him, don't you?"

Diego squeezed his eyes shut against the hard thud of his heart in his chest. "Yes."

"G'night, Mr. Sandoval. I'm off shift. You try and get some rest." Morrison gave his shoulder a last pat before he walked out, his brow still furrowed in a troubled expression.

Diego's few minutes of peace were cut short when Dr. Brennan came to see him. She took the chair Morrison had vacated and pinned him with her gaze. "Your story has holes, Sandoval."

"Was everyone listening?"

"Those involved, yes."

"Of course there are holes. I can't have entire populations of fae put at risk."

She tapped her pencil on her knee. "No, I mean, it's really hard to believe the things you *did* say. You claim you can feel their magic. That you can manipulate it yourself. So why don't you? Why can't you just poof out of here? Why don't they?"

"Because there's something blocking the magic here, something…" Diego trailed off as a sudden realization slammed into him. "The lead. The lead shielding around the base. That has to be it. All the steel would hamper *their* abilities but iron doesn't bother me." He sat up, rubbing a weary hand over his face. "Of course...of course..."

"Rather convenient explanation, don't you think?"

"Honestly, Dr. Brennan, I don't care whether you believe me or not. That is, I do care but there's not a hell of a lot I can do about it." He reached out and gripped her forearm. "Go see Finn. Take the damn gag out of his mouth and talk to him. Give him his hand back. Then you'll see magic."

"You think I'm an idiot? That subject bit three staff members before they muzzled him. Nearly tore one person's finger off."

"He's not a 'subject'," Diego said. "He's a person who thinks and feels, who will listen, if approached with calm compassion. Just...think about it."

She tore her arm free and stalked out, leaving Diego with the sinking feeling that he had gained one ally only to lose another.

Short of some miracle of diplomacy, he couldn't imagine how he was going to get his friends, much less himself, to safety. He eased out of bed, wondering if they'd even locked him in, and nearly fell flat on his face when his ankle shot fire-lances of pain up his leg. Teeth gritted, he hopped on his good foot to the door. The knob turned, he eased his head out, and encountered the broad backs of the two armed guards stationed in the hall.

I guess that was asking too much.

He made his way back to bed and flopped down, panting. Ridiculous. If he couldn't even get across the room and back without exhausting himself, how did he expect to mount an escape? Even in perfect health, on the off chance the door might be unguarded at some point and assuming he could make his way undetected to the experimental rooms, how in the world would he manage to break four disabled, ailing fae out of locked rooms and drag them out of a heavily guarded base?

No, there had to be another way. If he could get a message out to Miriam, she might be able to use her government contacts, her vast network of family and friends, to influence matters here. Maybe he could send a message with Zack somehow. He didn't want to cause the sergeant any problems, but a quick 'I'm in trouble' note might work, provided he was willing and didn't think it an act of treason.

Diego slid back under his blankets to rest. Zack wouldn't be back until morning, so there was little else to do at the moment. *When did I start thinking of him as Zack? And why do I trust him when I shouldn't trust anyone?* He did, though, on a gut-instinct level. Had Diego met him in a bar or at a party a few years before, he would have dismissed him as too nice, too earnest, the kind of man who would never put up with the unstable, scattered life of an aspiring novelist for long. But as someone to have at his back in a bad situation, he struck Diego as ideal.

He drifted for a bit, in and out of troubled thoughts and anxious half-dreams, until he finally fell into a restless sleep.

* * * *

The shocking bray of an alarm siren yanked Diego awake. He sat up in bed, heart hammering, and only had time to wonder whether it was a fire alarm when his door slammed open.

A figure in battle fatigues and a Kevlar vest shot toward the bed and Diego jerked back in dismay before he realized the soldier was Zack. He had a rifle slung over one shoulder and a pair of handcuffs clutched in his fist.

"You'll be safe here, Mr. S.," he clipped out, brisk and professional. "I've gotta get you secured. I'm sorry, but it's SOP."

Before Diego had time to protest, Zack had snapped one cuff around his wrist and the other around the bedrail.

"What's happening? What the hell's going on?" Diego shouted above the alarm.

"Don't know yet. Call to stations. I've gotta go report. I'm gonna lock you in, sir. Nothing can get through that door. You stay put and you'll be safe, okay?"

"But what if it's a fire?"

"Then I'll be back double-time and carry you out myself, you hear me?"

"Yes, Sergeant," Diego said, too baffled and anxious for anything more.

Zack was up and out as swiftly as he had entered. The lock slid home, and he was gone, leaving Diego in his isolation, unable to hear anything over the sirens. There might have been running footsteps in the hallway. The lights flickered out and returned once, twice and a third time. When the sirens cut off abruptly, the utter silence was more frightening than the heart-pounding cacophony had been.

In that terrible, anticipatory stillness, Diego strained to hear some sign of life, an unreasonable dread washing over him of being left alone in this manmade cavern, his imagination turning the white walls into an antiseptic tomb.

Suddenly, he knew something was in the hallway. A presence of frightening strength whispered across his mind, something so powerful the lead shielding failed to damp it entirely. It lurked outside his door, silent, waiting.

The sharp thud against his door tore a cry from his throat. *Dios ayudame, go away, go away...* A second heavy thud slammed against the door. To Diego's horror, the steel dented. A third hard blow and the dent bowed inward.

Diego yanked on the bedrail, trying to force it loose from the frame. The last thing he wanted was to face whatever this was shackled and helpless. If he could rip the rail free, the length of metal could double as a weapon.

The door hinges buckled. He worked frantically, crying out in frustration when the rail wouldn't budge. Another blow and the thing would be in the room. *Damn it, damn it...*

With a shriek of metal, the door slammed open. A huge figure filled the doorway, backlit from the brighter light of the hall. A step brought the figure into the room to reveal a powerful body covered in shining, silver scales.

"Evening, little man," a familiar voice spoke as the figure reached up to remove his winged helmet. "Did you miss me?"

"Lugh!" Diego sagged in relief. "You scared the hell out of me. God, yes, I missed you. You don't even know."

One black brow lifted. "But you don't rush into my arms? Oh, I see...let me help you with that." Lugh strode to the bed and snapped Diego's handcuff between his fingers, the broken metal falling against the bedrail with a discordant clank.

"Show off," Diego muttered. "How did you get in here? Are you alone?"

Lugh shook his head, his braids swinging. "I am most assuredly not alone. Come. We mustn't tarry here."

"Right." Diego slid off the bed and limped the two steps to him while Lugh's dark eyes narrowed in anger.

"They've hurt you."

"It was an accident," Diego insisted. "Don't go all Alpha Champion protective on me."

"Ah. As you wish." With less effort than should have been possible, Lugh scooped him up and strode out of the broken door. He hesitated in the deserted hallway, looking up and down the corridor.

"How did you find me?" Diego felt compelled to whisper in the oppressive silence.

Lugh nodded down the hall where a soldier lay crumpled on the floor. "That young man was persuaded to show me."

"*Dios*... Did you...?"

"He's alive, m'dear, don't fret. He'll wake with a bit of a headache." Lugh must have seen the concern still on his face. He smiled. "I have offered him no harm. Merely entered his mind and planted a...suggestion. He believed I was an angel and willingly brought me here. He sleeps."

"Oh. Good."

Lugh still scanned the hall. "Now where has that blasted wolf gone?"

Heavy footsteps pounded in the corridor. With a scrabble of hard nails slipping on linoleum, an enormous figure in black careened around the corner and barreled toward them. Diego's heart lurched. The last time he had seen that armor and that horned helmet, Finn had been inside. He knew better, but still suffered a wave of disappointment when the helmet came off to reveal Faolchú's lupine head.

"Diego! You're alive!" Faolchú snatched him out of Lugh's arms and hugged him tight, nuzzling at his hair. Then the wolf head lifted to address Lugh in an agitated way. "It's nothing but a plague of doors! By the Earth's bones, how are we to find them? We can't take the time to break them all down."

"Perhaps our Diego knows," Lugh suggested.

"Where the others are?" Diego nodded, stroking Faolchú's muzzle to calm him. "I'm pretty sure I can remember the way. And I'm glad you're okay."

Faolchú snorted as Diego directed them to the elevators. "It would take more than a few musket balls to do away with me, little one. I was angry with myself, though, for acting before I could think. A simple earthquake might have ended all this before it started."

"Push that bottom round thing." Diego nodded to the 'down' button on the wall. "But how did you find this place? And where are all the soldiers?"

"As for the how." Lugh leaned against the wall while they waited for the elevator. "I heard your call for help. When I arrived, you were gone, but the blood on the ground and the noxious vapors surrounding your house spoke volumes. I summoned the winds to clear the air and Croi came to me with an odd tale of men without faces who had kidnapped the five of you."

The doors opened, Diego motioned them inside, and pointed to the button for the seventh floor, which Faolchú pressed carefully with his fore-claw.

Lugh went on as the car descended. "Scath followed the vehicles and since he and Croi cannot lose one another, no matter how far apart, we waited until he knew where you had been taken. This brute" — he nodded to Faolchú — "came back out of the Dreaming howling for blood. Grandmother pleaded for caution — for some reason the wolf listens to her — then we gathered our forces and traveled here by night."

Faolchú rolled his eyes. "They took my beloved. I was a mite upset. As for where the human warriors are at the moment, our war band keeps them busy."

"War band?" Diego's heart sank. "We need to hurry, then. Please. These people are confused, they're acting on false assumptions, but they're not evil. I don't want people to die."

"We knew you would say so," Faolchú said on a dry, barking laugh. "And so Balor and Danu have forbidden the killing of humans unless we are given no choice." The elevator door opened on the seventh floor. "Which way?"

"Down there." Diego pointed left. "We should come to Angus first."

"Stupid human caverns," Faolchú growled as he jogged down the hall. "Burrowing into the rock only to fill it with metal and *machines*. Makes my skin crawl."

"This one." Diego pointed. "The door's locked, though."

"So was yours, little man," Lugh said with a grim smile. He stepped across the hall, put his head down and charged the door, slamming into it again and again until it buckled and bent just as Diego's had. This door, thicker and heavier, took a few more blows but eventually burst open under Lugh's relentless assault.

"Sometimes it's good the bull's so damn stubborn," Faolchú muttered.

Lugh straightened with a grunt and peered inside the room. "Angus? Oh, dear gods…"

"No, no!" Angus's cry rasped and cracked, his beautiful, confident voice a ruin. "Don't tread on the black lines! The lightning will try to devour you!"

"There's no lightning now," Diego called out from his perch in Faolchú's arms. "Angus, can you stand? Can you walk? We have to hurry. We have to get Sionnach."

"Sionnach?" Blue, half-mad eyes peered out from beneath tangled golden hair. "He no longer lives. His light is gone."

God, I hope not. Diego tried again. "You can't hear him because of where we are. Take Lugh's hand and we'll go to him. You'll see."

Trembling, Angus reached up to grasp the silver-gauntleted hand offered to him. He rose, clinging to Lugh as if he might drown, and stared at the grid of electrical lines on the floor.

"Lugh, pick him up, maybe. Carry him out so he doesn't have to step on the lines."

With a nod, Lugh did just that, and though Angus gasped and squeezed his eyes shut, he went without further protest. Lugh set him down in the hallway where he managed to hobble along unassisted on his burned feet. Three doors down, Diego stopped them again.

"This is Sionnach's. Angus, maybe you shouldn't loo—"

Too late, Angus had spotted his lover through the window. He pressed his palms and forehead to the glass and wailed like a banshee.

"Storm and thunder!" Lugh lunged for him and clapped a hand over his mouth, pulling Angus into his embrace. "Hush. Quiet. He's been ill-used, but if Diego says he lives, you mustn't take on so. We need you strong, Far-seer, to get him safely away."

Angus' chest heaved, but he nodded, arms wrapped tight around his ribs. Lugh moved away to repeat his battering-ram performance, only to be halted by a metallic *snick* down the corridor.

"Thought I asked you to stay put, Mr. S." Zack's soft voice held both anger and regret as he stared down the muzzle of his rifle at the little group in the hall.

"I know. But I had some visitors and plans changed," Diego began carefully.

"He can't shoot us all," Faolchú snarled as he put Diego down.

Diego seized his arm. "Don't. Please. Zack's my friend. He doesn't want to hurt anyone." Slowly, with one hand on the wall, Diego limped toward the sergeant, whose aim never wavered but whose eyes registered uncertainty. "Zack, you know all this is wrong. You know it has to stop. They've come for their own, then they'll leave. They're not here to start a war or take over the country."

"They're attacking the base, Mr. S. That's not exactly peaceful."

"Has anyone been hurt?"

Zack's eyes darted between Diego and the fae. "Hell, I don't know. It's a mess up there. There's this huge…boar-looking thing that just looks at people and they fall over."

Diego glared at Lugh. "I thought you said Balor had agreed to restraint."

"He has." Lugh spread his hands. "He has uncovered his Bane Eye, but only by half. They are merely stunned."

Stunned would have been a good adjective for Zack as well when he turned to regard the *sidhe* champion. His eyes grew huge as they met Lugh's and traveled up and down that heavily muscled, armored body. A strangled sound caught in his throat and he lowered the rifle.

"Is that a fairy prince?" he whispered.

Diego seized on Zack's obvious fascination. "Yes. This is Lugh the Shining, grandson of the *sidhe* Queen and the Fomorian King. Lugh, this is Sergeant Zack Morrison, who has been taking care of me."

"Then you have our gratitude." Lugh swept through a graceful bow. "For looking after our bard."

"Oh. Um. You're welcome...Majesty? Highness? What do they call you?"

"Lugh, most of the time." Lugh turned on his knee-weakening smile. "Though Faolchú over there has gifted me with some other choice names from time to time."

A series of thuds pulled everyone's attention back to the window where Angus pounded desperately on the glass, tears streaming down his face. A crack appeared under his right fist, spiderwebbing outward with each blow.

The soldier in Zack disappeared suddenly in favor of the nurse. "Hey, hey, bud. Don't do that. You're gonna slice your hand open."

"That's his lover of several centuries in there," Diego said. "They made him half-crazed in that electric torture room and now he sees what they've done to his Sionnach."

Zack shot him an anguished look. "You don't play fair, Mr. S."

"I don't have time to right now," Diego said gently.

Jaw clenched tight, Zack watched a moment longer, then let out a slow breath through his nose. "Damn it. I'm gonna be in so much trouble."

He pulled a key card out of his pocket, swiped it at the security box by the window, and the door opened with a soft click. Angus rushed in with Zack close on his heels.

"Little fox? Can you hear me?" Angus whispered, his hands hovering over Sionnach's shaved, still body as if unsure where it might be safe to touch.

Calm and professional, Zack gently moved him out of the way. "It's gonna be okay, bud. Let's get these IV lines pulled and, let's see, grab a blanket for me from over in the closet there? Attaboy."

Within moments, Zack had Sionnach unhooked from the needles, tubes and monitors, wrapped in a blanket and handed into Angus' waiting arms.

"My love... He lives, he lives..." Angus whispered, rocking back and forth with his face buried against the blanket.

Diego knew exactly how he felt, but they had to keep moving. He slid his hand under Angus's chin to lift his head and pushed the tangled hair back from his eyes. "Look at me, Herald. You can fall apart all you want when he's safe, okay? For now, we need you to be the hero you are. You're stronger than this."

Summer-sky blue eyes blinked at him in confusion and Diego had an anxious moment where he was certain Angus was too far gone. Then something hardened in that anguished gaze, a spark of the proud, stubborn *sidhe* showing through. He straightened and nodded before limping back out into the hallway to join the others.

"Nathair had better be next," Faolchú growled.

"Yes, yes, we're going there," Diego muttered, trying to turn on one foot. He stifled a yelp when he was summarily scooped up again, finding himself perched in the crook of Lugh's right arm.

Zack gaped. "Wow. I thought there were explosives involved when I saw Mr. Sandoval's door. But you just knocked it down, didn't you?"

"We all use the talents we are given," Lugh said far too seriously and waved for Zack to precede him.

With the door-opening process simplified, Faolchú was able to get Nathair free of his new aluminum cuffs and carried out of his cell in less than thirty seconds. Still ashen and dazed, Nathair kept a white-knuckle grip on Faolchú's ruff.

"Little serpent, you need to talk to me," Faolchú rumbled, nuzzling at Nathair's cheek. "You have my heart hammering faster than a nuthatch after grubs."

"I—" Nathair choked on his words, swallowed hard and began again. "Beloved, I don't know how many times my heart can bear almost losing you in a single month."

"Ah, he loves me still." Faolchú shot Lugh a wolf-grin. "Even if I am a stupid brute."

"I have never called you stupid," Lugh protested. "Limited, single-minded, without imagination, but not stupid."

And now Finn… Diego only half-heard the banter, his heart leaping forward with equal parts anticipation and dread. "Querido, *do you hear me? I'm coming…*"

When they reached the section of secure labs, the eerie quiet took on an ominous taint. No research staff bustled about, no guards patrolled the hallways, no lights shone in the labs.

"Zack? Where is everyone?"

"Military personnel have been called topside to meet the incursion," Zack explained. "Non-coms are confined to quarters until the all-clear."

"Non-coms?"

"Sorry. Non-combatants."

"So why were you down here?"

Zack ducked his head. "I had a funny feeling you weren't gonna stay put. Don't ask me how. But my primary orders are to keep you safe."

"Which I've now put in direct conflict with every other order, I'll bet," Diego said with real regret. "I'm safe with these two. I don't want to get you in more trouble than you already are."

"I think I could argue refusing to follow illegal orders at this point, sir. The detention and unlawful treatment of a neutral nation's citizens."

"So you do believe."

"Disbelief's not only suspended, Mr. S." Zack shook his head on a bemused little smile. "It's completely shattered, gone MIA."

"Duly noted, Sergeant."

The lab which doubled as Finn's prison was dark like the rest. Diego squinted, trying to pierce the gloom to catch a glimpse of Finn while Zack unlocked the door. For a few eternal moments, Zack fumbled for a light switch, and the glaring overheads flicked on.

In the center of the room, covered in a clean, white sheet, Finn's table stood empty.

Diego's head swiveled around the room, searching desperately. He wriggled out of Lugh's grasp and limped the two steps to grab Zack by the shoulders, "Where is he? Goddammit, Zack, where the hell is he?"

"I don't know, Mr. S." Zack's stricken expression bore out his words. "I really don't."

"He's in the morgue," a familiar voice spoke from the doorway. Dr. Brennan stood there, her chin raised in defiance.

"*He's what*?" Diego's sight dimmed, he felt strong arms go around him.

"He's in the morgue. They think he's dead."

That single word brought him back from the brink, allowed him to breathe. "They think so," he said cautiously. "But you don't?"

"No." She edged back a step when she caught sight of Faolchú. "His heart beats about four or five times an hour. I'd say that's a deep hibernative state, not mortality."

Another thought occurred to Diego. "Why are you here, Doctor?"

Faolchú was obviously more interested in nosing at Nathair than in her, so she tore her gaze away to answer. "I took your advice and came to talk to him myself, but they'd already declared him dead. I felt terrible, since he seemed to mean so much to you. So I went to the morgue, to see if I could understand what you were trying to say. His heart beat once under my hand. I waited a few minutes and it contracted again. I was coming back up to get his hand for him." She pointed to the shelf where Finn's right hand sat in a jar.

"Thank you for that." Diego eased his hold on Zack and turned to her. "But what made you change your mind?"

She flushed and dropped her gaze to her shoes. "I... Look, this is going to sound crazy. But when I touched him, I *heard* him. In my head. And he wasn't thinking about conquest or spaceships or another planet. He was thinking of a cabin in New Brunswick. And making ice sculptures. And you."

A suspicious crack entered her voice on the last word and Diego fought the lump in his throat. He knew the memory Finn had been drifting in, the day when Finn had made him a beautiful garden of ice art and had declared, on bended knee, that he would remain faithful and true. God, it seemed so long ago.

"Grab the hand, Zack." Diego fought the quaver in his voice. "Doc, I'm not involving you in this any further, and I don't want you getting hurt. Zack can show us the way."

She hesitated, then asked, "You'll take Zack with you, won't you? Wherever you're going? They'll court-martial him. Put him away for the rest of his life, or worse."

"Zack's welcome, if that's what he wants," Diego offered.

"You stick by Mr. Sandoval, Sergeant. That's an order, hear me?" she said on a little quaver.

"Yes, ma'am, loud and clear," Zack told her. "I'll be all right, Doc. Don't worry."

"You better be."

Diego thanked her and gave her a hug before Lugh swept him up again. They increased their pace as much as Angus could tolerate, half-jogging to a stairwell where Zack took them down another flight. They entered the morgue by a simple set of swinging doors — no need to lock in the dead. Only one table held a body, covered in a white sheet.

"Finn..." Diego whispered and struggled free of Lugh's arms again. He used the tables to pull himself over and snatched the sheet back to reveal the sorry state of his beloved pooka. His skin ashen, he had dropped considerable weight — most likely from the strain of his body being forced to regenerate again and again. His expressive face was terribly still, the rise and fall of his chest undetectable. To the unsuspecting eye, he did, indeed, look dead.

"But only mostly dead," Diego whispered the reference from one of Finn's favorite movies as he reached down to stroke his tangled hair back from his forehead. *"Mi amor? Can you hear me?"*

"Beloved? You can't be here. If you've gotten away from your jailers, you must run. Please, my hero, my light, I'm finished. You must get away."

Diego slid an arm under his shoulders and held him close as he had wished to for days. *"Don't be ridiculous. Not without you."*

"Mr. S.? I'm sorry, but we gotta move."

"Give them a moment to talk," Lugh interjected.

"I don't hear anything…"

"Mind to mind, bucko. If you did hear them, I would ask you not to eavesdrop."

"We have help, querido. I think we can all make it."

"Zack, can you carry him?" Diego tamped down on the tears he wanted so badly to shed. "He's tall, but he's not heavy."

"I've got his hand." Zach shoved the jar-encased hand in one of his cargo pockets. "May as well take the rest."

Diego spoke close to Finn's ear. "Finn, love, this is my friend, Zack Morrison. He'll be as gentle as he can. Don't bite him."

"Is he handsome?"

"Very. Really nice eyes."

"Hey!" Zack protested as he shouldered his rifle and slid his arms under Finn. "No talking about me behind my mind."

Captives retrieved, it was time for an exit strategy.

"Okay, so it sounds like you came in the front, but there's no way we're getting back out that way," Zack explained as he hustled them down the hall. "Not with casualties and walking wounded. There's a side shaft, built as a fire exit. Might be hard going for Angus, up the stairs, but it's our best chance to get you out and around behind your own forces."

They hurried after Zack, his combat boots and the fae champions' feet thudding thunder-loud in the silence until they reached a door clearly marked 'fire exit' in bright, red letters. It struck Diego how absurdly easy escape would have been if one knew the way, but then Zack shifted Finn's weight in his arms to pull out his key card again. Even the fire exits were locked. Zack shoved the door open with his shoulder and leaned back against it to hold it open for the rest of them.

A metallic rattle told them they were no longer alone.

"That's as far as you go, Mr. Sandoval." The soft, ironic voice dropped Diego's heart to his feet. Gerry stood behind them, handgun drawn, flanked by two huge marines with rifles. "Put down whatever you're carrying. Hands up."

"Do what he says, guys," Diego said around the anger choking him. "I don't want anyone shot."

"Did you think the corridors weren't monitored? Did you think no one was watching?"

"Then why wait so long to stop us? Why now, when we're almost out?" Diego demanded.

"I wanted to give Sergeant Morrison a chance to do the right thing. But he's obviously turned traitor, just like you, Mr. Sandoval. Traitors to your planet and to your own kind."

"You've got it all wrong, Agent Pulaski," Zack protested. "They're not aliens, they're—"

"Yes, I've heard. Aren't you a little too old to believe in fairytales, Morrison?" Gerry sneered. "Swallowing their lies whole because you have a crush on one of your favorite novelists."

Diego risked a quick glance at Zack, whose face had flushed crimson. "Maybe, so, sir. But that's not why I believe him. You're so set on being right, you've gone blind. It's all right there on your own tapes. I mean, why the hell would an alien turn into a *dragon*, for chrissakes? What would someone from Alpha Centauri or whatever know about dragons?"

While the bitter words flew back and forth, everyone lowered their burdens to the ground or to their feet. Angus stood staring down at the blanket-wrapped bundle of Sionnach, the picture of defeat, a single tear trailing down his cheek. His lips moved but Diego couldn't make out what he said.

"The alien who transformed was living with someone who *writes* about dragons. Use your head," Gerry countered. "Lay your weapons down, Sergeant. Cooperate and I'll try to help the tribunal see that you were duped. You can still avoid execution, at least."

"You shall not take the sergeant," Lugh broke in, arms crossed over his massive chest, all bristling arrogance. "I am Lugh mac Ethnenn, prince of the *sidhe*, and he is mine now, one of my war band. You cannot touch him."

"I don't care if you think you're the god —"

Gerry's words cut off when Angus leaped at him, the *sidhe's* light, powerful body hurtling across the distance as if he had springs in his feet. "Cretinous piece of worm dung!" Angus bellowed as he came. He slammed into Gerry. They went down in a tangle of limbs. The handgun went off and all hell broke loose.

Diego went face down on the floor when something collided with his back. Lugh and Faolchú both disappeared, moving faster than the human eye could follow. Shots popped off, echoing in the hallway. Zack slammed into the wall and slid down to the floor, obviously hit. One of the Marines crumpled to his knees, his left leg torn and bleeding. Lugh reappeared behind him, Faolchú behind the other, and the Marines were dropped, out cold, each with a single blow to the head.

Angus still screamed incoherently, his long fingers wrapped around Gerry's throat, slamming his head against the floor repeatedly.

"Angus, stop." Lugh pulled him gently off his opponent. "Enough."

"He would stand and watch!" Angus wailed. "Tell them more lightning and more often. Please let me kill him." He whimpered and clutched his side, blood oozing through his fingers.

"We have promised not to kill today, Far-seer. Don't make us break oath. And you are wounded, let me see."

Diego twisted his head to find the object on his back was Nathair, panting and trembling. He sat up and moved him gently aside so he could crawl over to Zack. There was a hole in his vest, just left of center.

"Zack?" He ran a hand over the close-cropped blond hair. "Please don't die..."

Gray eyes opened to regard him seriously. "Nah. Not today, Mr. S.," Zack gasped out. "This is what the Kevlar's for."

The bullet might not have penetrated, but he was obviously hurt as he winced and grunted his way back to his feet.

Dios, *now what?* Zack would barely be able to make the stairs on his own, and Angus had taken a bullet in his side. The two champions seemed unperturbed, though. Faolchú slung Sionnach over one shoulder and Finn over the other. Lugh took Angus in his arms, motioned for Nathair to climb on his back, then waved to Diego.

"No, I'll manage. The stairs have rails. I'll swing myself up. Help Zack."

The sergeant held up a hand, leaning on his rifle. "I'm okay. I'll take rearguard so I don't slow you down. Up the steps, all the way to the top. There's a hatch up there. You just turn the wheel to the right and push it open. Let's go, folks, move like you've got a purpose in life."

Lugh led, making his way up with what Diego thought ridiculous speed considering how burdened he was. Faolchú matched him step for step, taking the stairs two and three at a time when Lugh did, as if this, too, was a competition between them. Diego fought not to roll his eyes, though he supposed it was only natural since they had been sparring opponents for so long. The result was that Diego and Zack fell farther and farther behind until they were four flights back and could no longer see their companions.

Then Diego realized he was alone. "Zack?" A hand on either rail, he swung back down the steps and found Zack sitting with his back against the wall two landings down. Diego tugged gently on his arm. "I think we're almost there. Come on."

"Ribs are broke," Zack panted, his face parchment pale. "Pretty sure. Can't do it, Mr. S. Sorry. You go on. You've gotta...get them safe. I've got your back."

A metallic clang reached them from the bottom of the stairs followed by booted footsteps. More soldiers in pursuit.

"No, Zack, come on, damn it!" Diego tugged again, trying to get Zack up and moving. "You're a Marine, right? You know better than to leave a man behind."

The sergeant made a valiant attempt only to collapse half a flight on. "You're a...stubborn man." He lifted his rifle, pointing it down the stairs. "Go. I'll...give you time."

"You have another weapon?" Diego plunked down on the step shoulder to shoulder with him.

"Handgun...right hip...holster."

Diego fumbled for it and aimed down the stairs while Zack stared at him.

"You can't...kill anyone...Diego."

"Why the hell not?"

"You're...a novelist."

While Diego tried to puzzle out that odd statement, the boots on the stairs pounded closer. *This is it, then. I'm going to die here because of a sprained ankle and not-quite-adequate body armor.*

Just as the first soldier's head came into sight around the landing, a thunderous roar shook the stairwell from above. The stairs trembled as an impossibly huge body leaped down them, entire flights at a time.

"Fuck..." Zack whispered. "It's that boar thing."

Balor roared again, the soldiers on the stairs unable to react out of shock. He lifted his hand to his emerald-encrusted eye patch.

"Don't look." Diego turned away and threw his arms around Zack's head to protect him. "Close your eyes." He knew enough of the stories to suspect what came next.

With one eye cracked, facing the oncoming soldiers, Diego watched as a dark cone swept down from above. It couldn't be called a beam, since it was the absence of light, a darkness that sucked all the surrounding light into its depths. The cone swept over the soldiers, engulfing them one by one and leaving crumpled, unconscious bodies in its wake. Balor's Bane Eye, which could kill at a glance if he uncovered it fully.

Balor's heavy tread advanced down the stairs. Shots fired at him vanished into the darkness. A panicked attempt at retreat ensued, the remaining soldiers at the top unable to shove past their comrades still advancing from below. Balor mowed them all down until silence returned to the stairwell.

"Well, boy?" Balor growled as he replaced his eye patch and turned to Diego. "Are you whole?"

"More or less, *majestad*." Diego gulped a breath, trying to calm his hammering heart.

The Fomorian King pointed a claw at Zack. "This is ours?"

"Yes, *majestad*. He's injured."

With a snort, Balor scooped Zack up in one arm. "I will have some choice words for my blasted grandson. Leaving a wounded companion behind."

"To be fair, I don't think he knew it was this bad." Diego clung to a broad shoulder as he was picked up as well.

"You lead a war band, you bloody well *know* the condition of your warriors," Balor snarled as he leaped back up the stairs that bent and creaked under his weight.

"Perhaps the scolding can wait, *majestad*," Diego urged. "I think I might need some help making a doorway."

"Just the request I would make of you. My strength is yours."

When they reached the top, Diego saw why Lugh had not come back for them himself. Most of the fae warrior band had gathered on the rock outcropping where the fire exit hatch let out. Below them lay the field of battle. Four lonely figures still held the field, retreating slowly toward them.

Danu and Lugh stood with arms outstretched, supporting a dome of magic which stopped the missiles and bullets fired at the fae. Faolchú stood beside them, and when a small tank rumbled from the cavern mouth serving as the entrance to the base, he placed both palms flat on the ground. A tremor rumbled through the earth, centered on the tank, which wobbled and toppled on its side. Morrigan, armed with only a wooden club, zipped back and forth across the field, felling any soldier foolish enough to try a flanking maneuver.

"Time to go," Diego murmured. He reached for the flows of magic and bit back a sob of relief when the currents swept over him. Like the return of his sight, or a missing limb, his body felt whole again. "Balor, I will need you to steady me."

A huge, clawed hand closed over his shoulder, unexpectedly gentle. The white sphere of magic fire gathered in Diego's palm, and he pulled mercilessly at the strength offered him and the flows around him to concentrate the magic enough to punch through. He had done this enough times now to know the exact instant, the exact pitch of magic singing along his nerves. With a sharp cry, he flung his tiny, dense sun and pierced the Veil.

There would be no building of permanent doorways here, though.

"Get them all through! Danu! Fall back! We're clear. Get to safety!"

The fae war bands, *sidhe* and Fomor, rushed past him, twenty warriors from each court, carrying the wounded and incapacitated. Balor remained by his shoulder as one by one, the last defenders reached them and crossed over, Morrigan, then Faolchú and Danu, with a nod to him, until only Diego, Lugh and Balor remained.

"Go, you ninny!" Balor roared at his grandson. "Diego holds the way open, and I hold Diego!"

"But Grandfather —"

"Don't argue with me, boy! Gods of rock and stone, you'll be the death of me!"

A rocket-launched grenade hit nearby, sending a shower of rock down from the nearby mountainside. With an anguished look, Lugh lunged through the doorway.

"*Majestad*," Diego said in a strained voice. "I just realized I can't hold it open and get through as well. You'll have to leave me."

Balor surprised him with a huge, scary grin. "Just shows how much you have to learn, m'boy."

He snagged Diego around the waist, crushed him to his massive chest and flung himself through the doorway, which snapped closed just as he rolled clear, shutting out the dust and the din of the modern battlefield so abruptly, Diego thought he had gone deaf.

"Leave me, he says," Balor said with a snort. "I wasn't going to all that trouble just to leave the prize behind."

Diego surveyed the Otherworld field where they had landed, the wounded already being seen to by fae healers. "A little warning next time, maybe?"

Zack lay on the grass nearby, his earnest gray eyes wide in childlike wonder as he took in the scenery of the Otherworld and all the fae moving around him. Eithne knelt beside him to begin working his body armor off.

"You're a...kitty," Zack blurted out.

Lugh crouched down on his other side to assist. "Careful what you say, Sergeant," he said with a little smile. "That's my mother."

"Oh." Zack gulped a breath. "Sorry, Your Highness."

"Do you need help with the pain, Sergeant?" Lugh's brows drew together in a concerned frown. "You've gone dreadfully pale."

"No. Thanks, though," Zack murmured and let his head fall back onto the grass. "It's just a lot of stuff to, you know, take in at once."

Diego rose unsteadily, found a stick to use as a cane and limped off in the direction of the trees.

"Where are you going now, boy?" Balor called after him.

"I have to close the Montana door. It's not safe. If there's anyone out there in the human world, I need them called in."

"Faolchú! Help Talies — er, Diego. Call them home."

The scene through the stable doorway looked peaceful enough, but Diego wouldn't let Faolchú step through, just in case. Faolchú raised his head to the sky and howled, a long keening that could have carried through several worlds. A few little fairy lights answered his call and rushed through the doorway, but otherwise everyone seemed to have known of the danger and had returned to the Otherworld already.

"That's everyone?"

Faolchú nodded. "There are no stray voices, Diego. We are all home."

"Back up a step, hon. I don't want you caught in any backlash." Diego reached out to the doorway and grasped the lower right corner, where his magic had melded with Balor's. He yanked hard, a sickening jolt running up his arm as the magic bond tore. Destabilized, the quadrangle of magic collapsed in a howling vortex. He had shut out the human world. For the moment, they were safe.

Chapter Twenty-One

A Place to Stand

Finn stayed in the Dreaming for three days. Diego suspected it was due to more than physical ailments. He tried several times to find Finn in his Dreaming, to speak to him, but Finn refused to answer. His pain and guilt seeped through clearly enough, but any more than that, Diego couldn't get from him.

On the third night, Finn suddenly appeared in the *sidhe* bower Diego had been using, crawled in beside him, and curled up with his head on Diego's chest.

"Finn?" Diego stroked the thick silk of his hair.

The arms around Diego tightened and Finn's body heaved with silent sobs. Feeling helpless, Diego held him close and rocked him until he settled into an uneasy sleep.

The damage to his body had healed, but the wounds to his soul seemed unable to close. Finn spent his days at Cian's Ford, lying in ankle-deep water and staring at the sky. In the evening, he allowed Diego to coax him into eating a bit, then he would curl up with his head in Diego's lap, silent and still.

The world, unfortunately, could not stop for Finn, and Diego still had work to do. The fae needed a safer place to cross over into the mortal world, a secure place, a more permanent solution. Diego discussed it with Balor and Danu, their Champions, Heralds and Seers, and decided a good temporary fix would be Miriam's house in New Brunswick. From there, he could contact Miriam and hash out the best plan of action.

Finn refused to help build another doorway. Not that he actively refused, he simply didn't react when asked. A water sprite had to be recruited to take his place, and Diego had to fight her wild water magic every inch of the way when he built the New Brunswick door. This one he hid inside the house, in the back study that had once been Finn's art studio. They would be more cautious, and the Canadian government tended to be more tolerant of oddities, so he felt they had a reasonable amount of time.

The house, large enough for a family of ten, stood unchanged, right down to the key inside the little decorative turtle by the garage. Zack, who had been fussed over endlessly by both *sidhe* and Fomor alike, was installed in the largest guest room, where Diego hoped he would have some peace. He put Finn to bed in their old bedroom, hoping that familiar surroundings and happier memories would soothe him. Unfortunately, he was sadly mistaken. Finn grew worse. He even refused to go to the river, spending his time on the porch swing, rocking.

A skeptical Miriam arrived the next day, and Diego felt a surge of hope when her tank-solid frame trundled up the front steps, as if the cavalry had finally arrived.

"Okay, kiddo, what's the hush-hush emergency, and why the hell is our Finn sitting in the cold in nothing but his damn jeans, looking like the poster child for catatonia?" she demanded before he even got out a hello.

"It's a long story." Diego ran his hands back through his hair. "And you'll think I've lost it at first. But Finn's condition's part of the story, and I have some people I want you to meet who'll bear me out."

"Well, that just puts me right at ease. Fuck, Sandoval, you disappear for days and weeks at a time, you miss meetings, you miss deadlines, and now you want me to give you the benefit of the doubt? Are you into something illegal here?"

"No, not illegal," he reassured her. "Maybe a little dicey immigration-wise, but mostly it's a touchy…diplomatic situation."

"Sounds like we better go in and sit down." She stomped over and took Finn by the hand. "Damn it, sweetie, stop rocking. Come in out of the cold."

Finn came meekly enough and let her shove him into a chair in the kitchen.

"Want coffee?" Diego asked as he poured a mug.

"I think I'd better have a beer instead," Miriam muttered.

Diego knew better than to think she was kidding. He opened a bottle, plunked it down in front of her and pulled Finn into his lap when he sat down.

"I guess the best place to start is to tell you that Finn's…well, I've been lying to you about Finn all this time."

"He's not your lover?" Miriam's dark brows drew together.

"He is, but he's not an Irish immigrant. That is, not in the normal sense."

"So what is it, kiddo? Passport expired? No working permit? Stop beating around the bush. We can fix this stuff."

"It's more complicated than that. That first book we got published, the pooka one, the one where I used Finn as the 'model' for the pooka?"

Miriam made an impatient gesture.

"It was all the truth disguised as fiction. Finn is the pooka. That is his life in that book."

"Look, sweetie, if this is some kind of pitch for some weird publicity stunt, you need to tell me straight up." Miriam took a long pull from her beer. "This isn't like you. None of the last couple of months has been like you."

"Okay, you're really not hearing me yet. I understand. Finn had to work hard to get me to believe, too. Here's the plain, simple truth — magic is real. Fairies are real, and I'm not talking about the gay pride kind. Nonhuman beings share this planet with us arrogant humans who were always so sure we were alone, it's all real. I'd ask Finn to show you, but he's not feeling himself today."

Diego twisted his head to shout toward the back of the house. "Angus? Are you back there?"

Of course he was. Diego had prepared the fae for the necessity of showing Miriam. Angus appeared in the doorway, wearing only his kilt, un-glamoured and undisguised. He hesitated at the kitchen tiles, still unable to walk confidently on a floor containing black lines.

"Well, he's a hottie, I'll give you that." Miriam's eyes swept up and down Angus' tall, lean-muscled frame. "Interesting eye color. Theatrical contacts?"

"No, those are his. He isn't human. Would you mind, Angus, showing Miriam your other form?"

"If it will help." Angus raised his arms and closed his eyes. The golden glow of his magic danced over his skin. The kilt dropped from him as his limbs melted and transformed until the golden eagle stood in the kitchen.

"Holy shit," Miriam murmured. "That's some wicked special effects."

The eagle screamed, hopped to Miriam and pecked at her foot.

"Ow! Damn it!"

"I am not some illusion created by a machine," the eagle said indignantly. "I am quite real."

One by one, Diego called his friends out until Miriam had seen them all—Sionnach with his bushy tail back in its full-furred glory, Lugh with his hoofs and his bull form, Nathair with his scales, Scath and Croi, who could never be mistaken for human, and finally Faolchú, who found the whole thing rather amusing and let Miriam stroke his ears and muzzle to assure herself that he was real.

"Holy. Fucking. Hells," she finally spat out, no longer able to deny the evidence of her own senses.

"So you believe?"

"Either that or I've gone completely bugfuck nuts."

Diego managed a dry chuckle. "And to top it all off, there's an injured Marine upstairs who was a lot less difficult to convince than you."

"So I'm a hard sell." Miriam shrugged and polished off her beer. "I need another one of those. Like you wouldn't believe. And then you better spill. A story comes with all this, and I think it's time you told me, Sandoval."

With the fae perched on various pieces of furniture and counters, Diego told her everything, from his first encounter with Finn to the escape from the IER. Miriam listened with only an occasional expletive or sharp question interrupting the flow. By the time Diego finished, she held the neck of her third empty beer, showing no sign that the alcohol affected her in any way, with a thunderous frown aimed at the table.

"And here I thought you were settling down," she finally said with a snort. "Shit." Miriam heaved her bulk out of the kitchen chair and swung her gaze around the room. "Okay, boys and girls, stop staring at me. Let me go unpack and think about all this. I won't make any promises, but, kids, you've come to the right woman."

Of that, Diego had no doubt. With everything done that he could at the moment, Diego put Finn to bed. He hadn't said a single word during Diego's telling, not one interjection, not one correction, and given how much Finn loved to tell stories, this was the most worrisome of all.

Finn offered no resistance while Diego peeled him out of his jeans and settled him under the covers, but he offered nothing else either, no caresses, no heated glances, no teasing words. Diego stripped down to his boxer briefs and crawled in beside him, hoping, somehow, to reach him.

"*Mi amor*, please talk to me," Diego urged as he let his fingers travel over Finn's chest. "Tell me what hurts so badly that you've shut your mind away."

"Useless," Finn whispered, trembling.

Diego let out a long breath. "*Corazón*, I know you've been hurt. They betrayed the trust you wanted so badly to give humans and brutalized you. I hate them for it. But what we do here is not useless. To believe that is to damn every magical creature with a single word."

"No," Finn choked out. "*I'm* useless."

"What? *Mi vida*, no. Don't say such things."

"Couldn't keep you safe. Couldn't save you. Again. Someone else had to. Real heroes. Lugh. Zack. Faolchú."

"If you weren't feeling so poorly, I'd slap you," Diego said, completely exasperated. He grabbed Finn by the chin to lift his head, staring into anguished black eyes. "It took more than forty people to save us. Lugh helped and Faolchú. Zack, too. But they sure as hell didn't do it alone. Remember that I couldn't keep you safe, either. These are my people, my time, and I should have been able to, but I failed you. That stabs at my heart and gives me nightmares, but I can't let it stop me from doing what needs to be done."

He leaned in to press his lips down-soft against Finn's. "And you did help save us."

Finn jerked his head away, a spark of anger joining the pain. "How?"

"Because of what you did, trying to use your dragon shape to rescue me, one human believed in us. Because of who you are, and your brave, loving heart, another human found compassion for us. Without you, we would never have made it out." Diego took Finn's head between his hands, forcing his face back around. "Without you standing beside me, I'm lost. I need you, my strength, my anchor, my life."

"Diego…"

"Stand beside me. Say you will."

Finn searched his face for a long moment, eyes brimming. He slid a hand up Diego's shoulder, across his jaw to trace his lips. "As long as you need me. Yes."

"I need you, God, yes, I need you," Diego murmured. "Touch me. Please. I've been alone too much these past couple of months."

Finn's long-fingered hands slid down his back and slipped inside the waistband of his briefs. A wave of heat rushed through Diego as those fingers kneaded his backside and slid the material down to mid-thigh. Finn's lips captured his, caressing in tender kisses which soon caught fire with Diego's rising need, his tongue plunging in to plunder Finn's mouth, stroking the roof and ridges.

With a soft moan, Finn shoved a hand between to run a fingertip along the length of Diego's shaft. Half erect already, the simple touch finished the job, and Diego reveled in the feel of another cock sliding against his, silken skin over hard marble. Finn took both erections in his hand, stroking them both together. A sharp cry escaped him and his hips rocked forward when Diego's finger teased the pucker between his cheeks.

"Shh, hush," Diego whispered, peppering kisses over Finn's lips and jaw. "We have a whole house full of people."

"Ah. Best keep kissing me then," Finn panted out. "To keep me quiet."

"Not a problem." Diego seized his lips again.

His conquest of Finn's mouth became desperate as Finn's fist pumped them both from base to crown, stopping every few strokes to palm the engorged heads and share the pearl drops leaking out between them. Diego's balls drew up tight in a sudden rush, his breaths labored as the pressure increased to where he felt like a steam valve with no outlet.

"Finn...*Dios*...I'm coming," he gasped out.

"Yes," Finn hissed and leaned in to fasten his teeth on Diego's shoulder.

That sharp, bright point of pain hurled Diego over the edge. He gripped Finn's head with both hands, grinding his hips hard against the fist around his cock. Teeth clenched, he bit back his ecstatic cries as his orgasm thundered through him in breathtaking hammer-pulses.

Growling, hips bucking, Finn followed him over a moment later, his moans muffled against Diego's skin. Aftershocks zipped through Diego at the hot splash of Finn's seed against his chest and stomach.

"Better?" Diego asked when the black spots faded from his vision. "Ready to face the world?"

"Ready for a nap," Finn muttered, stroking Diego's back. "Stay with me?"

Diego kissed him tenderly, for once not at all concerned about the sticky mess between them. "Always."

They had time while Miriam made phone calls and pondered through everything. For Finn, there would always be time.

* * * *

In the evening, Miriam emerged from the den, which she had been using as her impromptu war room with her cell phone, her PDA and her little black book. While some people kept phone numbers in little black books, this would have been far too antiquated for Miriam. Diego had called the black book her 'web of intrigue' since in it she kept track of relationships and favors, who had access to what and to whom.

She asked that they convene in the dining room, with all the principal players present.

"Zack, too," Diego insisted.

"I don't think so. That boy should be in the damn hospital," Miriam snapped.

"Too risky. The minute we check him in, he's exposed. They'll come arrest him for desertion, even across the border, I'm sure," Diego said as calmly as he could. The whole issue of Zack upset him, that he had destroyed the young man's career and possibly doomed him to a life of exile. "Besides, the fae healers have his ribs knitting, probably faster than human doctors would."

She grumbled a few rude words, but conceded, and soon the cavernous formal dining room table held Balor at one end, Danu at the other, and their respective Champions, Heralds Seers and Healers lining the sides. Diego took the middle next to Eithne, Finn at his side, while Miriam took the seat across with Zack next to her. It didn't escape Diego's notice that Lugh shooed Morrigan up the table so he could claim the seat on Zack's other side.

"All right, everyone." Miriam slapped both palms on the table. "Seems to me you have two problems — one of security and one of sovereignty. In the end, they boil down to the same damn thing and your biggest problem of all — secrecy."

"We have kept apart and hidden for good reason," Danu said. "Nuada's death, the attempt at Finn's execution, the increasing desire over the centuries of humans to use us to gain power and wealth."

"Right. I hear you, Your Majesty." Miriam nodded, but forged on. "Thing is, though, the secrecy causes a lot of these misconceptions and misunderstandings that bring humans to do terrible things to you. The boys here" — she waved to Sionnach and Angus — "have told me there used to be regular diplomatic contact between your courts and the human rulers. Angus knew King Brian Boru personally. Sionnach remembers drinking with King Conchobar. And in those days, fairies weren't being killed or hunted."

"Those days are gone," Balor growled. "Long past."

"Sure. Things change. That's the only thing you can count on." Miriam looked from one ruler to the other and Diego recognized the signs. She was moving in for the kill, about to do the reveal. "But secrecy breeds suspicion and the wrong conclusions. You let people have only rumors about you, they'll make up lies to fill in the gaps. What you need is for everyone to know. For everyone to understand, so you have allies and supporters. You need a press conference."

Zack, still pale and exhausted, choked on the water he'd been sipping. "You've got to be kidding."

"What is this...conference?" Lugh asked as he rescued the water glass.

"It's... You've seen the news broadcasts by now, right?" Zack leaned back so he could look up at the *sidhe* champion. "That's what they call 'the press' — all those folks who gather the news from the day and write about it and show it to everyone on the TV. Ms. Thorpe is saying you should go on TV, expose yourselves to the world."

Diego cleared his throat. He always found it difficult to disagree with Miriam. "I'm not sure it's such a good idea. The issues of exploitation, the — "

"Your pardon, but these conflicts arise when a single group of humans believe they can lay claim to us," Nathair interrupted softly. "Sovereignty, Miriam said. We need to be...our own nation."

"Yes!" Angus pounded on the table. "With our own governance."

"Whoa, hold on." Diego held up both hands. "Unless you're thinking about moving to Antarctica, all the land in the world belongs to someone. Where would this nation be? Certainly, you have the Otherworld, but you still need a place here to call your own if you want to be free of obligations to human governments."

Miriam chuckled. "Governments need money, kiddo. You bet your nuts real estate can be had, for a price."

"We have no human currency," Danu said, her delicate fingers drumming.

"Not yet, you don't. But I hear his huge majesty can call gold from the ground, and that you, unless I've heard wrong from these boys, have stockpiles of gems that would put the Smithsonian collection to shame."

Danu's brows drew together. "Diego says humans do not barter with such things any longer."

"Not directly, no." Miriam leaned forward, her chair creaking. "Not like you could waltz into a grocery store and plunk down a handful of gold. But these things can be exchanged for money. Invested, so you have shitloads...sorry, *piles* of money."

"You will help us with this, Miriam," Danu said, in a tone just shy of an order.

"I will help you, my cousin the investment banker will help you, my father the jeweler will help you."

"Back to this press conference," Diego prompted.

"Right. It's the perfect way to let everyone see you, let them ask questions and let the world's governments know you're looking for some property to call your own." Miriam gestured toward the ends of the table. "I'd say their majesties should be in front of the cameras. And this handsome lug over here." She waved at Lugh, then down the table to Sionnach and Angus. "Plus those two fast-talkers. And Finn."

Beside Diego, Finn jerked back as if struck. "No," he whispered, shaking his head frantically.

Miriam fixed him with her sharp gaze. "Sweetie, I know you've had a rough road lately. But you've got a face lots of people will recognize. From the book illustrations. You've already got fans. They just don't know you're real yet. You don't have to say anything. Just sit there with your friends and look pretty."

Diego took Finn's hand, concerned by how hard he shook. "*Mi vida*? You don't have to. Miriam's just making a suggestion."

Finn ripped his hand free and bolted from the room.

"Off he runs again." Morrigan's caustic remark drew more than one dark look.

"Keep talking." Diego rose. "I'd better check on him."

The retching sounds guided him to the powder room off the kitchen where Finn knelt, heaving up the little bit of dinner he had managed to get down. Diego held his hair for him and waited patiently until he finished. Then he snagged a washcloth from the stack, soaked it with cold water, and pressed it to the back of Finn's neck.

"Anxious about being in front of so many humans?" Diego asked gently.

"Terrified."

"You can stay here, you know. Or go back to the caverns. No one would force you." Diego knelt behind him and eased Finn back against his chest.

"No, I must do this." Finn's voice shook but he still managed a fierce edge to his words. "It is time to stop hiding. To do the things that need to be done, no matter how hard or how frightening."

"I'll leave it up to you. Your decision, *caro*. Are you all right now?" Diego kissed his temple, hoping Finn's words weren't as ominous as they sounded.

"Well enough, my hero. Your pardon. My stomach has been a bit touchy of late."

"Obviously. Get cleaned up, *querido*. Come join us again when you're ready."

With a last hug, Diego rose and returned to the dining room, where the discussion had grown lively.

"So I should appear dressed in something like Miriam wears?" Danu asked with a little smile.

"Oh, no, Light of the World!" Sionnach sprang up, searched the room, and sat back down. "You should be adorned as a queen."

"I don't think they wear gowns any longer." Her soft laugh cascaded through the room.

"As a *modern* queen," Angus broke in. "We will help you. There are books with smooth, shining pages that show how people dress."

"What the hell is he talking about?" Miriam turned to Diego as he resumed his seat.

"Catalogs. So they want to go through with this?"

"Looks like it. They're working out the details and I'll just need to set it up, say, four, five days from now. Should be enough time to get the buzz going."

"Where, Miriam?" Diego said on a weary sigh. "You can't put them on a plane to New York and I'm not sure I want to risk another doorway right now."

"Nah, you worry too much, kiddo. We'll do it right in town. I'll head in tomorrow and see if we can borrow the meeting hall. Is your handsome hunk okay?"

"He's managing. He wants to be there."

"Good." Miriam huffed as she stood. "I got a hunch it's important to have him there."

* * * *

When the day arrived, a gray mist shrouded the house. Diego shivered as he stared out of the floor-to-ceiling windows in the front room. He had stood at these same windows to confront an ancient, evil being, had gazed out on this same landscape months later at an astounding, ethereal work of ice art, had seen more impossible, bizarre things than any man had a right to, yet somehow taking the fae to a press conference struck him as more surreal than all the rest put together.

"*Y los sueños sueños son*," Diego murmured into his coffee mug. The line from Calderón had never seemed more appropriate.

"Diego…" The soft, melodic voice drifted into his thoughts, and he turned to see Eithne behind him.

"Good morning. Are you coming with us?"

She came to join him at the window. "No. I will leave such things to those better suited." She slid her arm through his and rested her black-furred cheek on his shoulder. "I would ask that you have a care. Morrigan has foreseen sorrow stemming from this day."

"Whose?"

"I do not know." She was quiet for a long moment, then spoke even more softly, "You will have my son with you and my father, as well as several people I love."

284

"I'll be as careful as possible." He tried to reassure her through his own mounting dread. "And return them all to you."

"Have a care for yourself as well." She reached up to touch his cheek. "There was a time when you were mine."

"So I'd heard. Eithne…I'm sorry I can't be that person for you in this life."

"I would not ask it of you. You cannot change your nature any more than I can change mine." She stepped away so he could watch as her form shimmered and changed. A beautiful woman in a long, black gown stood before him, her raven hair cascading to her waist, her almond-shaped eyes staring at him steadily. "We may have the illusion of change, but we cannot change who we are." Another shimmer and she was Eithne again, pointed ears swiveling atop her head. "I am content."

Diego turned back to the window, thinking to change the subject. "Have you and Morrigan always been friends?"

"We have an understanding, she and I," Eithne answered with a little smile. "Morri prefers the female form."

"Ah. I had wondered." The steam rising from his mug mimicked the curling tendrils of mist outside. The flows of magic tugged at Diego as if urging him to see some pattern there, its meaning remaining stubbornly out of reach. "Was I ever able to see the future?"

"There have been lives where you had the sight, yes."

"I wish I could still. To see what today holds for us."

Eithne leaned her head on his shoulder again, purring. "The seers are only given warnings. How things will play out is hidden even from them."

A tread on the stairs pulled Diego's head around and his heart sped at the sight of Finn descending in the gray suit Miriam had bought him. He would be the only fae at the press conference in actual clothes, since his talents did not extend to glamours. His blue-black hair, brushed to a glossy sheen, lay loose in a heavy curtain against his silk jacket. The tailored slacks flattered his long, lean body and the rose-colored shirt supplied the perfect complement to his complexion.

He held his tie out in one hand. "Could you help me with this blasted thing, love? Miriam showed me how the damned knot is done — rather too reminiscent of a noose, I'd say — but it won't come out evenly for me."

Diego chuckled, relieved to hear Finn finally sounding more like himself. While they dealt with the tie, the rest of their party arrived in ones and twos. Angus and Sionnach had opted for suits as well, though Sionnach had arranged his glamour so his tail remained visible, proudly waving beneath his jacket. Balor, Lugh and Faolchú, who insisted he would not be excluded, all appeared in human guise, wearing military dress uniforms worthy of European royalty.

Danu glided in last, commanding every eye in the room. Her clothes, a formal, low-cut dress of deep bronze, stunning heels and a tasteful diamond tiara, were all illusion, but her own physical appearance remained unaltered, her green hair, pointed ears and bear eyes all on full display.

"We are ready, Diego." She extended her hand for Diego's, regal and elegant, every inch the queen. "Lead on."

The limos Miriam had hired pulled up the drive as if on cue. Diego led them out, Danu on his arm and Finn at his side, to seats covered in silk sheets to mitigate the effects of the vehicles' steel components. Miriam had taken Zack and gone ahead to make certain all was in place. Throughout the ride into town, Finn rubbed at his wrist, where his hand had been repeatedly severed, but otherwise he appeared calm.

News vans lined the streets as they pulled into the town's sleepy main street. All the major Canadian players, both local and national, and most of the US networks had taken Miriam's hook.

Cameras descended on the limos, preventing their getting out, until a chiseled figure in jeans and T-shirt hustled them back, barking out orders in a voice that even the most stubborn news hounds would obey. Zack to the rescue again.

A path cleared and they made their way inside amidst shouted questions. Miriam raised her voice to a congenial roar, "Come on in, boys and girls! You'll get your answers inside like civilized people."

She directed them to the long table at the front of the hall, where the town council usually sat, while the reporters and camera operators filed in to fill up every folding chair and last bit of good viewing space. The fae settled in the chairs, their anxiety filtering to anyone with the least bit of sensitivity.

Diego took the lectern and cleared his throat. "Ladies and gentlemen of the press, thank you for coming and for your indulgence. We realize arrangements are a bit unusual and appreciate your patience. I have a statement prepared, then we'll allow questions directed to our guests.

"My name is Diego Sandoval. Some of you may know me as an American novelist, but today is not about fiction. Nearly two years ago, a figure stepped out of myth and into my life, forever transforming my view of the world. These beautiful people to my right are fae royalty and members of their court. Fairies, if you need a more familiar term, nonhumans who have lived beside us in secret for centuries. They choose to reveal themselves now because their lives are in great peril. They must reach out to the human world or face extinction."

He went on to explain the connection between the two halves of the world, the consequences of their temporary separation and the need for the fae to have a foothold in the human world to survive. Statement complete, he introduced each of the figures sitting at the table and respectfully turned the conference over to their majesties.

"I cede the right of first address to you," Balor said with a nod to Danu. He shifted uncomfortably in a chair much too small for his massive frame.

"I thank you, Heart of the Earth," she said with a little smile. A wave of gratitude washed over Diego that they managed a united front in public. "To you, the heralds of this human world, we wish to say that we have no designs on your lands or your—"

"Queen Danu!" a blonde reporter called from the center of the pack. "Is there a trailer available for this movie yet? Who's the director?"

"Yeah, when's the release scheduled?" called another.

"Is it Peter Jackson?"

"Is there a title?"

Danu turned bewildered eyes to Diego. "What do they ask, Taliesin? They speak words I know, but I cannot fathom their meaning."

Before Diego could answer, Finn slammed both palms down on the table and rose. He stalked around to stand in front, the blazing red of his eyes giving away his anger.

"Listen!" he shouted over the din of questions. "This is not a movie. We are not here to promote any sort of story. This is real!"

Someone in the back shouted, "You're the model from *A Pooka's Life,* aren't you? Are you reprising that role?"

Finn buried his face in his hands and Diego held his breath, waiting for him to fall to pieces. Instead, a roar from behind him shook the building. An ominous rumble shivered through the floor.

"Bloody idiots!" Faolchú snarled as he came to wrap Finn in his arms. "How dare you upset him like this! Do you have any idea what you people have done to him?"

With a nod from Angus, Sionnach came around the table as well, where everyone could see his tail. His melodic, soothing voice filled the hall. "This is no movie. We are not human. Several days ago, a human government mistook us for beings from a distant planet. Four of us were captured and tortured in the name of scientific experimentation."

"Which government?" someone shouted and was quickly shushed.

"I do not think it wise to say which one," Sionnach continued. "Finn has not yet recovered from his ordeal. They treated him as if he were no more than a rock or an interesting bit of driftwood."

"My dears," Danu spoke up from the table. "Perhaps it is time to do away with illusions. Let go of the glamours. Shift, if you like."

"They will run screaming," Balor said with a snort.

"Then let them run." The chill in Danu's voice signaled her patience wearing thin. A white light suffused her skin, pulsing outward as her body blurred and expanded until a huge, brown bear sat in her place.

Balor grinned and abandoned his human features for his tusks, his royal uniform fading away to reveal his massive, heavily muscled frame, covered only in his kilt. A black bull soon stood tossing his head at Danu's side. A golden eagle mantled and shrieked atop the table. Sionnach stood before them clothed only in fur from the waist down, graceful and beautiful. Faolchú turned his wolf's head to the watching reporters and licked his jaws in a less-than-friendly fashion.

"Faolchú?" Diego murmured. "Please don't eat anyone."

"Disgusting thought." Faolchú's muzzle wrinkled. "Who knows where these humans have been?"

Finn shook free of his arms and faced the stunned gathering. Blue light danced over his skin as he raised his arms and melted out of his clothes. A moment later, a bright-eyed otter sat where Finn had stood.

"Wow. Those are some *wicked* effects," one of the younger reporters said on a whistle.

"These are not effects," Otter-Finn said as he rose up on his haunches and shifted to raven. "This is magic. True, actual magic, not illusion." The raven shifted to a black turtle, then a panther. "The sort of magic humans have long thought the stuff of fiction. Try me, test me. Ask me for any animal and I will shift for you. If I did this with machines or computers, I would not be able to anticipate *all* of your requests."

The shouted requests came fast and furious.

"Sheep!"

"Horse!"

"Hummingbird!"

"Chicken!"

Finn complied with each and every animal request. In buffalo form, he snorted, "You have no imagination! Harder ones!"

"Octopus!"

"Bird of Paradise!"

"Pangolin!"

Finally stumped, Finn turned his bird head to Diego. "What is a pangolin?"

"Those armored anteaters," Diego reminded him. "You saw them on National Geographic once."

"Oh, yes." Finn flipped his wings and expanded to become the strange, Asian mammal.

The reporters had, *en masse*, jostled closer, most of them no longer in their seats, wide-eyed and fascinated. A voice startled them all from the side of the hall.

"Finn! Do the dragon!" Zack called out.

Pangolin-Finn lifted his head. "I will frighten them."

"They need to be scared, Finn. They're not getting it."

"Heart of the Earth? Could you move the table back a mite?"

Balor picked up the eight-foot table with ease and moved it to the back wall. A shiver ran through Diego as the flows of magic shifted, Finn pulling what he needed from the air. The hair on the back of his neck stirred and the blue glow around Finn grew star sapphire bright. Finn's body expanded and expanded, until his head brushed the ceiling on its long, sinuous neck. Black wings snapped out to either side in a span wide enough to cover a city bus. Dragon-Finn filled his lungs and let out a bone-shaking roar.

The front rows scrambled back, creating chaos as they became entangled with the people behind them.

Someone screamed and a panicked stampede seemed inevitable. The stampede had nowhere to go, though. Miriam's solid bulk blocked the only door.

"Settle, you ninnies!" she bellowed over the din. "He won't hurt you!"

Diego held up his arms, his heart bursting with pride for his love's courage and persistence. "Finn…"

The dragon head lowered to nudge at his chest. Diego wrapped his arms around Finn's neck to rest his cheek against the cool dragon hide. A careful claw-tip stroked through Diego's hair, then Finn lifted his head to his audience again.

"Come. Touch me. Prove to yourselves that I am as real as you, that a dragon stands before you." He pointed a claw to the blonde who had spoken first. "You, beautiful lady, you strike me as braver than most."

She stepped forward, wobbling on her heels as she picked through overturned chairs, a tiny woman with sharp, blue eyes. "Melissa Hawkins, Channel Seven News." She squared her shoulders and reached a shaking hand up to touch Dragon-Finn's nose. "Oh! It's so soft…" Her hand slid down to stroke his muzzle. "So smooth. Could I see your…foot?"

Finn lifted a clawed forefoot for her to touch.

"Ow! Damn! Those claws are sharp."

Eyes round as saucers, she turned back to her colleagues. "This is the real deal."

"Yes, real. We are magical beings, and we are as real as you." Finn flipped his wings to settle them on his back, standing still and patient while several other intrepid reporters came to touch him. "We are here to appeal to you, to your governments, to the people of the world. We do not need your houses, your money or your cars. We have no designs to rule the world. We ask for one thing only. A place to call our own. We have existed on this earth for thousands of years, lived beside you, often helped you. Now we need help so that the fae and the world's magic do not become so much dust and memory. All we ask is a place to stand."

"Sounds like a sound bite if I ever heard one," Diego whispered to him.

"You like that? I thought it sounded impressive," Dragon-Finn whispered back as his forked tongue flicked out to lick Diego's temple.

With the flummoxed reporters satisfied and doing their level best to absorb what they had learned, everyone settled again and the press conference began in earnest. To their credit, several of the reporters were old pros and recovered quickly enough to ask relevant questions. What requirements did the fae have in a land purchase? Were any negotiations already ongoing? Finn shifted back to his fae form behind the lectern, where he pulled his pants and shirt back on, apparently content to listen.

After an hour, Miriam called a halt, citing the fact that some of the fae were still recovering from their ordeal, and thanked everyone, the signal for them all to please leave. Sionnach accompanied them out to answer any last questions and give them some final photos.

Diego let out a slow breath. "I think, all things considered, that went rather well."

Whoops and cheers erupted from the fae as they congratulated one another. Enthusiasm overflowing, Lugh seized Diego by the biceps, lifted him up against the wall and captured his lips in a crushing kiss. Too stunned to react, Diego simply let it happen a moment, surprised at the softness of his mouth when the rest of Lugh was so hard.

Then he pulled back with a little laugh. "Stop that, you big lug. Go find someone else to manhandle."

Lugh gave him a wink and a grin. "Your pardon, I was carried away in the moment." He turned from Diego and shoved Zack against the wall instead. Zack's gray eyes opened wide in shock as Lugh plundered his mouth, then he closed his eyes and gave in with a little moan.

When Lugh came up for air, Zack slid his arms around Lugh's neck and said, "Do that again."

Now that looks promising. Diego turned to find the one he truly wanted to kiss. "Where's Finn?"

Faolchú's ears twitched as if searching. "He was just over there."

"Diego!" Sionnach rushed back in, clutching Finn's clothes to his chest, his eyes brimming with tears. "I'm so sorry… I couldn't stop him."

"What do you mean? Where's Finn?"

"He's…"

Diego seized the little Fomorian by the shoulders, a cold hand squeezing his heart. "Where is he?"

"He said that what he does now, he does for you," Sionnach whispered, the tears trickling down his beautiful face. "He shifted to raven form and flew away. He's gone."

Chapter Twenty-Two

On Tearmann Island

"We appreciate your position, Mr. President." Diego placed the delicate china coffee cup down. "And I do understand why there can be no public apology."

"Thank you, Mr. Sandoval. My staff and I are grateful for your understanding, and for Prince Lugh's, in this delicate matter of national security." The President nodded to Lugh, sitting in the wing chair across from him.

Meeting with the President of the United States had been the furthest thing from Diego's mind a year ago, and yet here he was, acting as unofficial human attaché to the unofficial royal fae ambassador. The meeting had been scheduled for the President to issue a private apology for the incarceration and mistreatment of fae citizens.

"Have you had a chance to look through the land grant proposal, Your Highness?" the President addressed Lugh directly.

"Yes, I've discussed it with my grandparents." Lugh settled one ankle on the opposite knee, his hooves clearly visible below his gold-piped trousers. "We hope that there will be no offense taken, but we feel, given the current global climate and certain...internal considerations, that it would be best for us not to be directly tied to the US."

"No offense taken, Your Highness. But I am concerned over where you will find a home."

"As to that..." Lugh broke out his most charming smile. "The Canadian government has offered us what we feel is a fair price for the Isle de St. Genevieve."

"I'm not familiar with that island..."

"It's primarily been a bird sanctuary, Mr. President," Diego supplied. "About five hundred square miles of dunes and cliffs with one usable harbor, east of New Brunswick. There's no fresh water supply, hence the lack of human habitation."

"Won't that cause resource issues? I assume the fae do need water, and the human staff certainly will."

"I've been assured by King Balor that he'll be able to remedy the situation," Diego said.

"Our human staff will be minimal," Lugh said. "And visas, for the moment, will be granted only at their majesties' discretion."

"Is there anything we can do for you or your people?"

"We have three requests. The first involves Mr. Sandoval, whose possessions and writings have been left behind, with your government and in his house in Montana. We would like his belongings returned to him intact. The second involves a Sergeant Zachary Morrison, whose courage and insight have proven invaluable to us. We request a full Presidential pardon for him and an honorable discharge from the service.

The third involves the status of humans who have been granted Otherworld citizenship. We would request that these humans be permitted dual citizenship."

"All easily done, Your Highness. I'll make sure of it myself."

* * * *

Eight months later, Diego turned on the TV in the lounge at the back of the embassy. "Guys, it's coming on in two minutes! If you want to see it, you need to get in here!"

Scath and Croi flew in pell-mell, chattering excitedly. Sionnach, Angus, Nathair and Faolchú followed at a run, with Eithne and Morrigan arriving at a more sedate pace.

The Isle de St. Genevieve had been renamed Tearmann Island, the old Irish word for sanctuary, and the embassy had been built entirely by fae hands and magic. Aboveground, the structure appeared nothing more than a country cottage with a reception desk and offices, a meeting room, kitchen, formal dining room and lounge. Most of the embassy existed belowground, with the infirmary and living quarters for as many as a hundred fae at a time. Hidden deep in the smooth rock tunnels also lay the Doorway, the only open door between the worlds, secure and safe from human eyes. Diego's broken heart had shattered a little more when he'd had to build another doorway without Finn, but no one else could do it, and it had to be done.

News clips of the press conference had quickly gone viral, with video feeds, websites and blogs all discussing and rehashing. Diego wasn't surprised that the most viewed and disseminated clip was the one of

Finn, as the beautiful black dragon, making his plea for "a place to stand", but every time his voice came over the net or the TV, Diego fought despair.

There had been no word from Finn since the day of the press conference. Every morning, Diego crossed the Veil to call to him, every evening he reached into the Dreaming to search for him, but there was no trace of Finn. He had hidden himself too well. Lugh had apologized over and over for the kiss he believed had driven Finn away. Though it might have been part of the reason, Diego knew there had to be more to it.

He spent his days helping the fae deal with the human world, learning to act as a diplomatic liaison along the way and finding himself *de facto* head of the only fae embassy on the planet. The ferry arrived twice a day to bring supplies and mail. There were a few human staffers who manned the embassy's phones, computers and security, which Zack oversaw when he wasn't in Washington or New York with Lugh. While human cities weren't the healthiest places for a sidhe prince, Lugh didn't exhibit the asthmatic reactions Finn had to pollution. Some countries still refused to acknowledge Tearmann Island as a sovereign nation, but most of the world had, which kept Lugh away in his ambassadorial status much of the time. Zack rarely left his side, acting as security, human liaison, personal assistant and perhaps lover, though Diego didn't ask.

The work Diego did was important as well, he knew that, and yet he felt as if his insides had been scooped out and he moved through what was needed and what was polite like an empty puppet. Every night, he trudged up the stairs to the living quarters the fae had built for him on the second floor, and every climb up to that lonely bed caused the despair to fall like a black stage curtain again.

Diego pulled Scath into his lap to settle him, and Croi happily perched on the arm of the wing chair. "It's coming up on this next break." He pointed to the TV with the remote. "Everyone here?"

Everyone certainly seemed to be — all those who were on the island that evening. The medical drama faded to commercial, to a shot of a green field with apple trees in blossom. Sionnach walked toward the screen wearing a pair of cargo shorts and a golf shirt, Croi beside him, hand in hand. They had found a backless sundress in a soft cream with a delicate floral pattern so she could keep her wings free. Diego had been at the shooting and knew Scath was there as well, just off-camera. Otherwise the shoot would have never worked.

Sionnach took a seat on a moss-covered rock, his tail curled around him, and Croi, wings fluttering, settled beside him. He gave the camera a congenial smile. "Hi, I'm Sean Silver and this is my friend, Croi. We're not CGI renderings or the product of hours of makeup. This is who we are."

Croi fluttered closer.

"We're fae," Sionnach went on. "Magical beings who share the Earth with humans. I know it's hard for some people to accept, but you're not alone. We've always been here, and now, we've decided to come out into plain sight."

He put his arm around Croi's waist. "We're not here to steal your children or change the way you live. We just want to live healthy, happy lives, just like you. So if you see one of us, or something we've made, don't be frightened. We may look different, but we want the same things. Please, treat us as you would any other citizen of this planet."

Croi leaned her head on his shoulder, looked straight into the camera, and with her childlike face and bell-sweet voice, spoke her one line, "Because fae are people, too."

A voiceover came on to say, "This has been a public service announcement from the Fae Cooperative Council."

Those watching applauded. It couldn't have been more perfect.

"Well done." Diego leaned in to kiss Croi's cheek, then set Scath aside so he could stop by Sionnach and congratulate him, too. That was all he had the energy for, though. He wandered out to go to bed.

On his way out, he heard the hushed whispers.

"He is no better?"

"No, every day is the same. And every day he still says Fionnachd will come back, that he must have had reason for leaving."

"Our poor Taliesin, I wish we could help…"

There was no help any longer. The light had gone from the world.

* * * *

Finn stared at the Doorway. He heaved a long sigh, his heart aching with the knowledge that this door would not take him to either of the houses he had called home, but to an unfamiliar place that might never hold happy memories for him. His hip brushed a tree limb, and he winced. Blasted burn refused to heal.

When he had returned to the *sidhe* court, Danu had told him about the island and the embassy, but she had remained cool and distant, and ended with, "Be wary of your welcome there, Fionnachd."

Armed with that cryptic warning and clothed in nothing but the little leather pouch on a thong around his neck, he stepped through into a room of smooth, gray stone. The room was empty, a silver door on the opposite wall the only other way out. Anxious thoughts chased each other as he grasped the handle and went out.

The stone hallway, carved in Fomorian glyphs and artwork, gave him no indication of where to begin.

"Your pardon." With a little bow, he stopped the first person he saw, a *sidhe* female with nut-brown hair. "Would you be able to tell me where Diego is?"

Her eyes swept up and down his body. Then she pointed with her chin to a spot on the wall with a harp carved into the stone. "Through there. Up the stairs. He is often occupied with many things at once and may not be able to speak with you."

"Thank you, beautiful one." Finn turned to the bit of wall and cocked his head to one side. The harp wall was a clever glamour, whoever had done it, with a staircase hidden behind.

At the top of the stairs, he found himself in another little room, this one with a wardrobe and a desk with a pretty human girl sitting behind it.

She smiled. "Welcome to the embassy, sir. Is this your first time here?"

"Yes. I…I'm looking for Diego Sandoval."

"He's in his office on a call right now, but we'll be happy to set something up for you." The girl rose, opened the wardrobe and pulled out a silk dressing gown of deep blue. "If you wouldn't mind, sir.

Embassy protocol. The Consul discourages nakedness aboveground. Just in case there are visitors."

The Consul? "Ah, yes, of course."

She frowned when she caught sight of his hip. "Do you need medical attention, sir? There are healers downstairs."

"I'm well enough, m'dear, don't fret." He gave her what he hoped was a dazzling smile as he shrugged into the silk. "This is days old now. If you could just point the way?"

"He's down at the end of the hall on the right but...sir, wait! You can't just go in there!"

Finn ignored her, prepared to set her gently aside should she get in the way. Another young woman hurried toward them but bypassed him to intercept the first human.

"Let him go, Cheryl."

"But Mr. Sandoval's on the phone with—"

"I know. But that's *him*."

"Him?" The first girl's voice grew hushed. "*Him*...the picture on his desk?"

"Yeah, that one."

"Oh."

Good gods, this place is confounding. Finn pressed his ear to the door at the end of the hall. Diego's voice rose and fell in a one-sided conversation. Oh, that beloved voice, it pierced his heart and nearly took him out at the knees. *Courage, you cannot turn coward now.*

He eased the door open. Diego sat behind a desk of dark wood in a button-down shirt of deep burgundy, as breathtakingly beautiful as Finn recalled. *More so*, the ache in Finn's chest insisted. Those deep, expressive eyes rose from his papers and widened in shock.

"Finn? Holy—" For a moment, Diego just stared. Then he spoke into the phone. "I'll have to call you back."

"Good morning, my heart." Finn tried a smile, but it quickly faded when Diego's anguished expression didn't change. "How do you fare?"

"Not very well over the last eight damned months, thank you," Diego answered. "Finn...where the hell have you been?"

"My love, I had to go." Finn spread his hands in front of him, pleading for understanding. "To give you time and space. Without me. To choose what you truly needed."

"I chose some time ago." Diego's voice caught. "I thought I made that crystal clear."

Finn dared to take a step closer. "Yes, but I have wondered whether that was the best thing for you. That if, separated from me for a time, you might make a choice better suited to you."

"How dare you? By what right do you make decisions like that for me? Without a word of warning? Without discussion? Damn it, Finn!"

"I only thought to—"

"I've waited eight months for you! Called for you every morning and every night! Agonized over why you left and *this* is the best you can do?" Diego buried his face in his hands. "*Ay, Dios*...Finn... I can't stand the sight of you right now. Please go away. Leave me alone."

There it was, then. Diego had asked him to leave. Further explanations about where he had been and what he had been doing no longer mattered. Diego had told him to go, and he had promised if Diego ever said it, he would respect his love's request and do exactly that.

"As you wish," he murmured as he backed out of the office. He staggered down the hall, no longer certain of his balance or if his heart still beat.

"Didn't go so well, did it?" the girl at the desk asked, her eyes filled with concern.

"No. He tossed me out." Finn's voice shook so badly, he wondered how he could form words.

"Is there anything we can do to help?"

Finn leaned on the desk, willing his legs to hold him. "Water... I need running, fresh water. Is there a river on the island? A stream? A trickle of creek?"

"There's a fountain out back in the garden. It's the start of the stream King Balor called up for the island. Do you need...help, sir? You don't look very well."

"No!" He jerked back when she reached for him. *Don't touch me, please gods, not now. I'll shatter into a million pieces.* "No. Thank you. I'll manage."

Her directions took him out a back door and into an enchanting garden filled with flowers and fruit trees. He trudged down the path, unable to enjoy the beauty before him, hardly aware of anything but the need to place one foot in front of the other. He had done what he thought he must, had known the risks, and lost his love, perhaps for all time.

Where do I go now? How do I continue on without you, my heart, my light? Sweet Mother, if I weren't a pooka, I'd drown myself...

A sudden rush of footsteps interrupted his thoughts. A hard blow slammed into him and hurled him to the ground. Clawed hands seized him and flipped him to his back. He caught a glimpse of raven-dark hair and sharp teeth before a fist hit his jaw with the force of a war hammer.

"You lying, craven worm!" Morrigan hissed, her claws around his throat. "What have you done to him now?"

Finn coughed, struggling for a breath, and wheezed out, "I might follow your words better if my poor head didn't spin like a whirlpool…"

"*Diego*, you slug! He sits at his desk weeping as if his heart has broken all over again." She shook him like a terrier with a rat. "What have you done?"

Her claws and her weight suddenly lifted from him. Finn gasped after air, the black spots clearing from his vision in time to see Faolchú tuck a struggling Morrigan under his arm.

"Let me loose, you mangy, misbegotten hound!" Morrigan rasped.

"Uncalled for, Morri." Sionnach appeared on the path, shaking his head. "Faolchú is simply trying to prevent a tragedy. Somehow, I don't think killing Finn will make Diego any happier."

Nathair crouched beside him and stroked a hand over his hair. That gentle touch nearly caused Finn to lose his composure. "Fionnachd, he has wept every night for you, though he tries to pretend not. Where have you been?"

All the things he had wanted to tell Diego spilled out in a desperate rush, where he had been and why. By the end of the telling, Angus had joined them, and even Morrigan listened with interest, her head cocked to one side.

"You told Diego all this?" Sionnach asked.

"No." Finn choked on his words. "He told me to go away. So I am."

Angus threw his hands up in exasperation. "You colossal fool! He cannot mean for you to go away for good and all, he means for an hour or two, perhaps until this evening so he might collect himself."

"This evening..." Nathair murmured with a speculative expression. "It occurs to me that Diego is too often alone with his dinner. I believe we should make dinner for him tonight."

* * * *

Diego pulled a brush through his hair in a half-hearted attempt to tame the curls. He hadn't bothered with things like haircuts in a number of months. What did it really matter? He was in no mood for dinner guests, either, in no mood to face anyone, but Nathair had said this dinner was vital to the peace of the island. Duty called—he had to go.

Why the mystery, he couldn't understand. Maybe there was some piece of fae politics he hadn't seen yet, some secretive faction he had yet to deal with.

But, *God*, he was tired and aching, wanting nothing more than a stiff drink and bed. Finn had taken his demands literally, it seemed, and had vanished again, and Diego was left, once again, to carry on as if his heart hadn't been ripped from him. His hand stole to his chest where the agate ring nestled against his skin on its chain. He was a great fool to keep it with him still, but he couldn't bear to part with it.

He made his way down the stairs, still toying with the idea of making his excuses, saying he was ill and engineering a quick escape. Sionnach met him in the hall to take his arm and walk with him, leaning his head on Diego's shoulder. What Diego took for sympathy, he realized was merely distraction when he reached the dining room.

Soft candlelight shimmered from every surface. A light supper of roast chicken, boiled potatoes and asparagus graced the table. Only two places had been set, and one was occupied already…by Finn.

"I think I've been set up," Diego said as he looked around at the expectant faces by the door.

He extricated his arm so he could turn and leave, and ran into a massive chest.

"Oh, no," Faolchú growled. "My beloved spent all this effort to get you two in the same room, so you will stay in the same room." He spun Diego back around. "Sit down, please."

Diego sat, certain the alternative was Faolchú forcibly placing him in the chair. Cleaned up and dressed in a black oxford shirt and black dress pants, Finn sat across the table, hunched over, staring at his hands, obviously unhappy with these forced arrangements.

"Now, I have bespelled the door." Faolchú crossed his arms over his chest. "When we leave, it will lock behind us and only I will be able to reopen it. Fionnachd has things to explain to you, and you, Light-wielder, need to listen. Two hours. Surely that will be enough time to talk things through. Then I will open the door again."

"But —" Diego tried to protest. Too late, the other fae had made their escape and shut the door. He sighed and leaned back in his chair. Finn wouldn't raise his head and made no move to speak. Dark hollows lined his eyes. His cheekbones stood out too prominently. He looked so miserable, it would have been easy to feel sorry for him and forgive him.

"You should eat," Diego said into the long silence. "You look like you could use it."

Finn shook his head. "I cannot."

"When's the last time you ate?"

"I…don't recall."

Well, this is going just perfectly.

"You needn't…" Finn still stared at his hands twisting in his lap. "I'm certain you could break through Faolchú's spell. If you don't wish to be here."

"Probably. But I think I'd hurt the big guy's feelings." Tired and heartsick, Diego abruptly ran out of patience. "You broke my heart."

"Ten thousand apologies aren't enough."

"So explain, damn it. Faolchú said you have things to tell me."

"I have not… That is, I…" Finn shook his head and wiped a sleeve over his eyes.

A flutter of worry ratcheted around Diego's stomach. He had never seen Finn at a loss for words, so flustered and forlorn. "I won't yell at you. Just tell me."

"I wanted you to be proud of me," Finn forced out in a cracked whisper.

Diego drummed his fingers on the table. "I was proud of you. Damned proud. When you swallowed your fear at that press conference and made them see the truth, made them listen…for one, amazing, brief moment, I was bursting with pride. Then you saw Lugh kiss me and you got ticked off and ran away."

Finn buried his face in his trembling hands.

Now come the tears…

But Finn surprised Diego. He drew in several shaky, hitching breaths and reached for the saltshaker, which he uncapped and dumped out on the table.

"That kiss stabbed at me, I will not say otherwise." Finn stared at the salt as he drew a finger through it in a spiral pattern. "I had determined to go some time before, though. That Lugh still showed a preference for you only shored up my resolve."

"You'd *planned* on leaving me?" Diego choked out.

"Not leave you, my heart, not in the sense that one leaves a lover for another. I left your company for a time. To see if I could stand on my own. To see if you would choose another when I no longer hovered over you."

"You can toss me at Lugh all you want, it won't—"

Finn raised a hand to stall him. "I still wished to give you the choice. But I have not simply been hiding, waiting for you to fall into someone else's arms. I have been on a…mission."

"For whom?"

"All of us." Finn sighed, tracing the outline of a horse in his salt pile. "I'm not explaining this well at all. Forgive me. From the moment you rescued me from the bridge in New York, I have been allowing others to do the things that were necessary. You saved me from a slow death. You made me see the beauty in this life again. You defeated the wendigo. You are the one who has saved the world's magic, built the doorways, schemed, plotted and fought your way through every obstacle. Yes, you had help, you will tell me. Certainly. But precious little from me. I did aught else but blunder about and cause you trouble and worry."

"Finn…"

"I am explaining. Let me explain. Please." Finn raised his head for the first time, and though anguish still swam in his eyes, determination had joined it.

"I'm listening."

Finn nodded and went back to his salt drawing. "I wished to do something myself. Something good and important. Something that would help. It occurred to me that during all the discussion about saving the fae, only the courts had been consulted. There are others, the wild fae, who do not associate with one court or the other. No one had thought of them. No one had asked them if they wished to rejoin the human world. Who better to speak to them but one of their own?"

"So this was your own diplomatic mission? To the wild fae?"

"Yes."

Diego ran his hands back through his hair. "And you didn't tell me, didn't discuss this with me beforehand, because *why*, exactly?"

"It was not the safest thing to do. You would have tried to dissuade me, tried to come with me. I had to do this on my own, and you were needed here."

"*Dios*, Finn…why didn't you at least answer me when I called? Why let me think you were gone forever?"

"To give you the time and space—"

"To choose, yes, damn it, I got that." Diego flung himself up and away from the table to pace. "I would have died first rather than take another lover to my bed. I've *been* dying, every fucking day! Some message, some word, some hint, *anything* would have kept me whole."

Finn ducked his head, his voice small and full of misery, "I was so certain… I'm so sorry. My light, please believe that I thought I did the right thing. The honorable thing."

"Honor is overrated," Diego muttered and returned to his chair with a huff. "Look, I understand someone, or maybe more than one person, told you that you weren't good enough for me. Maybe even told you it would be a good idea for you to stand aside. But when it comes to what's between us, the only person you should have listened to besides yourself is me."

"I'm sorry. I've hurt you so terribly." Finn's whisper cracked and wavered.

Diego slammed his palm on the table. "Damn it, *don't* cry! You haven't earned the right, and you haven't told me anything about where you've been."

Once again, he watched Finn struggle for calm. Even through his anger, it tore at his heart. He wanted to strangle Finn and take him in his arms all at once.

"I went to the wild ones," Finn said on a long sniff. "The wood sprites, the *bane sidhe* who live under the hills, the spriggans, who haunt the lonely places, the selkies who are salt-water folk, the other pookas—"

"There are other pookas? A pooka community you never bothered to mention?"

Finn shook his head. "No, hardly a community. We are all male. There are only four of us, each solitary, each taking on some aspects of those who live closest to them. One spends most of his time as a seal, another resembles tree bark and the last one has adopted scales since he lives near the dragon caves—"

"Dragon caves? I guess next you'll tell me you went to talk to dragons."

"Yes. I could not very well exclude them."

"Oh." The gears in Diego's brain ground to a halt. He had never considered there might be others, had simply assumed Balor and Danu spoke for all of the Otherworld since they acted as if this was understood. Guilt pried its fingers into his thoughts. He should have realized. His anger at Finn faded in the face of more far-reaching concerns. "So all of these people you spoke to, what did they say?"

"The selkies are pleased. They have missed the Atlantic. The spriggans are...less so, but they owe old debts to Danu and will not gainsay her. The wood sprites understand the necessity. The *bane sidhe*..." Finn hesitated, his brow furrowed. "They agree because of you. They have been watching you and say that they have sifted your dark from your light. That you are balanced."

Diego blinked. "What does that mean?"

"I have no inkling. The only fathomable thing I got from them was 'yes'."

"And the other pookas?"

"They tell me I am a great fool for sticking my nose in where it has no business. But they have no objections. They pretend not, but they miss the human world and all its possibilities."

"The dragons...you saved them for last."

Finn returned to his salt, drawing strange, amorphous patterns. "Out of necessity, yes. One never knows if an encounter with a dragon will leave one unscathed."

"Are they...feral? Half-sentient?" Diego leaned forward, drawn into the story despite himself.

"Hmm, not that so much. They are reticent by nature and...wary from long and terrible experience." Finn blew out a slow breath, his gaze unfocused and distant. "They are beings for whom everything is a puzzle to be solved. They thrive on puzzles...riddles...arcane knowledge. They must be approached slowly, over several days, so they are certain of your intentions. Gifts are important. Any polite interaction with outsiders involves gifts."

"What did you bring them?"

"I went to see the oldest surviving dragon, Hssetassk, with the gift of a pen."

"Just that?"

"Yes. You must have left it behind on one of your jaunts across the Veil, the red, plastic one where the point appears and disappears when you click the top. He was fascinated by it and required that I explain how the material was made. I tried. I wish you had been there for that. But he agrees with me that pulling solid, colorful material from pitch must require some form of magic."

"Science, Finn. It's not magic."

"To a dragon, they are one and the same." Finn pulled a leather pouch from beneath his shirt. "He demanded stories of the human world and my involvement in it. This was...difficult. Dragons cannot abide falsehood. Any embellishment is dangerous. I was with him for two weeks before he gave me two things — his answer and a gift for you."

"What was his answer?"

"He says the halves should not have been separated, that you have prevented a great calamity by opening the way again. But he must think further on whether dragons will ever come here to the island or interact with humans in any way. Humans decimated his race over the centuries. There are so few left. They do not hate, but they remember all too well." Finn opened the pouch and pulled out a crystal sphere, small enough to fit in his palm. A dull silver liquid swam inside the little globe, twisting and turning in a mesmerizing way. "Quicksilver. He says it is a seeing orb, for one who can feel its energy."

Diego stared at it, filled with wonder. "How do I thank him for such a gift?"

"He does not expect it. A gift for a gift. I told him the pen was from you, which was true." Finn reached across to hand him the orb, which required him to rise from his chair. He flinched and cried out, panting as he leaned on the table, eyes squeezed shut.

"Finn!" Diego ignored his outstretched hand and dashed around the table to support him. When they touched, Finn's mental walls crumbled, all his anguish, his uncertainty, his physical pain stripped naked. "You're hurt. *Dios*, you're burning up. Let me see."

"Don't fret so. Naught but a —" Finn tried to fend his hands off when Diego undid his fly. "Please…it's not so terrible."

Diego hissed through his teeth when he peeled Finn's pants down to his knees. Charred skin covered him from waist to mid-thigh on his left side, the black punctuated with lines of red where the burn cracked and bled. "That looks bad. God, what happened?"

"I mentioned, I think…" Finn swayed. Diego caught him and pulled him down onto his lap. "Mentioned that falsehoods make dragons angry? Hssetassk asked me why I rubbed at my right wrist so often. I tried to concoct some story, not wanting to tell him the truth. It was a small lick of flame. He apologized. But dragon burns heal so slowly."

"All right." Diego stroked his hair, trying to calm him. *I should call for Faolchú to open the damn door and take him to the healers.* But it felt so good to hold Finn, to have his water-rush and spice scent fill his head, that he couldn't bring himself to get up.

He slipped a hand under Finn's hair to the back of his neck where the skin was on fire, his other hand hovering over the burn. With the magic flowing through his fingertips, he concentrated on cooling, soothing images, dark forest pools and chuckling streams, willing Finn's body temperature down. A strange tingling ran through his fingers, not unpleasant but as if an army of tiny sunbeams raced through him.

Finn moaned and rested his head on Diego's shoulder. After a moment, he twisted to look at his hip. "My hero...when did you learn how to heal?"

"I haven't—" Something in Finn's voice pulled Diego's gaze down. The charred skin had closed over, the black faded to the angry red of a sunburn. "I guess...just now." He put a finger under Finn's chin to turn his head back around. "Feel better?"

"Yes," Finn breathed out in a husky murmur. "And no. Are you still angry with me?"

"Of course I'm still angry with you. You put me through hell, and though I'm willing to forgive you. I can't just forget all those god-awful days without you."

"Your pardon, my heart, I'm—"

Diego put a finger over his lips. "Sorry. Yes, I know. Do you think you can promise me you won't do anything like that again? If you have something to do, you tell me. If I call for you, you don't block everything out so you can't hear me. Can you do that for me?"

"Yes." Finn's lips closed over his fingertip for a soft kiss. "I promise."

"Good. Now I have another promise I want from you."

"Ah." Finn sighed. "Is it some sort of penance?"

"Some might see it that way." Diego reached inside his shirt to pull out the agate ring on its chain. He went on as he worked it free. "I wanted to do this some time ago. I don't know, maybe you would've felt more confident if I had, more sure of yourself and us, so in a lot of ways, I've blamed myself for all this."

He took Finn's left hand and slipped the ring onto his finger. "I love you, more than life, more than breath. I want to be with you always, to have you by my side, to wake up to you, to go to sleep with you. You and no other, my Fionnachd, *mi vida*."

"Diego..." Finn whispered. "It's beautiful, but I don't think I understand."

"I'm asking you to marry me. To be my husband, mine for all the world to see."

Tears swam in Finn's eyes and this time Diego didn't berate him when a few fell. "What do I say? Is there an accepted form of response?"

"Yes or no usually works."

Finn wiped at his face and managed a smile. "Yes, then. A thousand times over if you need it."

Warmth spread through Diego, the frozen iron bands falling from his heart. He gave Finn a smile and slid his hand to the back of Finn's neck. "Once is good."

He pulled Finn's head down, a heated spark leaping between them as their lips met. What he had meant as a tender thank-you caught fire, his mouth besieging Finn's, his tongue demanding entrance. Finn surrendered with a soft whimper, melting against him.

"*Cariño*, I've missed you so," Diego whispered against those soft lips. He placed tender, sucking kisses along Finn's jaw while his fingers made short work of the buttons on his black shirt. There was something incredibly vulnerable and sexy about that lean, gorgeous body dressed in nothing but the pants around his knees.

Finn's head fell back on a hard groan when Diego swept his fingers lower to stroke the inside of his thigh.

"I've missed you, too, my light, my heart. Please —" Finn gasped when Diego ran a finger up the underside of his erection. "Oh, please...I need you so badly I might go mad."

Diego patted his thigh. "Up. Turn around."

Oh, that beautiful, muscular butt...

He made Finn wait while he stripped out of his own clothes and folded them neatly on the chair. With a tender, reverent touch, he traced along Finn's shoulder, down his spine and over the globes of that perfect backside. Finn shivered, obviously keyed up and more than ready.

"Bend over the table," Diego murmured, his hand still stroking Finn's ass. His knees turned to water when Finn bent at the waist and laid his top half flat on the table amidst the dishes. The erotic sight of those gorgeous globes offered up to him so readily sent firefly sparks of need zipping through him.

Diego reached over and snagged the bottle of salad oil from the center of the table, fascinated by the golden stream on Finn's pale skin as he drizzled a generous amount down Finn's crease.

Finn squirmed, rubbing his cock against the rough linen of the tablecloth. "Take me love, please."

"No need to rush," Diego said with a little smile. "Faolchú gave us two hours."

He spread Finn's cheeks and teased at the puckered entrance with the pad of his thumb. Slowly, wanting to prolong Finn's pleasure, he slid the tip inside, only to withdraw it right away. He repeated this until Finn squirmed and begged breathlessly for more. Finally, he sank two fingers into that tight sheath, and a hard shot of desire slammed through his groin. While he stroked that sweetest of spots inside Finn, he slicked olive oil over his shaft, hypersensitive after his long months of celibacy.

Finn tensed when he withdrew his fingers. "Shh, relax, *querido*." Diego kneaded the muscles along Finn's spine while he positioned himself. He bit his lower lip, fighting the urge to plunge inside and hammer away. Instead, he eased just the head inside on a harsh, tortured groan. *God, oh, God, it's almost too much...*

He stopped and held still, only his hand moving gently along Finn's back.

"My heart? I love you with every fiber of my being, but you're driving me stark raving mad," Finn said in a strangled voice. He whimpered when Diego pushed inside just a hair further. "Please, Diego, take me. Now. Please."

"Soon, soon." Diego pulled out a fraction to prolong the delicious torture. "What will you do, *mi amor*, the next time you feel uncertain or less than you should?"

"What? Love, this isn't the time for questions! Fuck me!" Finn's hips lifted in a desperate attempt to push him inside.

Diego pulled out almost to the point of withdrawal. "What will you do?"

"Oh...sweet Mother...come talk to you? I'll come to you." Finn's hands fisted in the tablecloth, his body trembled.

"Yes. Right. You promise me? No more disappearing, no more running off without a word?"

Finn made a sound half-groan, half-sob. "Yes, yes, I promise! Wrack and storm, love, I'm yours, yours alone! Whatever you wish, it's yours!"

"Good." Diego thrust hard, burying himself halfway. "Mine," he said in a fierce whisper as he withdrew and plunged in again. Buried to the hilt, the silk of Finn's

Diego

sac rubbing against his, Diego slid his hands under Finn's shoulders and kissed his neck. "Mine," he murmured more tenderly. "As I am yours."

He set an unhurried pace at first, reveling in the feel of Finn lying under him, wrapped around him. Enveloped in Finn, the scent of his arousal, the heat of his tight sheath, the heavenly touch of skin against skin, Diego wanted the gradual thrust and retreat to last forever, this delicious, tender assault. The self-enforced celibacy had taken its toll on them both, though, and the slow pace soon had Finn writhing and bucking.

Finn's wild desperation overturned glasses and rattled plates. Diego had no choice but to ride along with him. He wrapped his arms around Finn and held him close, nuzzling at his shoulder. A sudden desperate urge of his own hit him.

"*Caro*, wait...stop, please."

"Water goddesses help me, what now?" Finn whimpered, though he did his best to still.

"Turn over, *mi amor*. I need your arms around me."

"Ah. For that, I'll gladly halt a moment." Flexible to a contortionist extent, Finn pulled a leg up onto the table and turned slowly in Diego's arms, never losing the connection between them as he rolled to his back. He wrapped his long legs around Diego's ribs and his arms around his shoulders. "Better, love?"

"Much, thank you," Diego whispered as he stroked Finn's hair. "I'm still mad at you, but I'm so damn glad you're home."

"I will wait on you hand and foot, my heart, cater to your every need." Finn lifted his head to steal a soft, lingering kiss. "Until you feel reparations have been made, until you feel whole again. I love you so. If I had come back and you had chosen another, I think I might have died on the spot."

"Would've served you right." Diego nipped at Finn's jaw. "But I love you, too. Only you."

Diego picked up his rhythm again, impaling Finn in long, sure thrusts which increased in force and speed as Finn moaned and arched beneath him. He clenched tight on the muscles of his core until Finn's face contorted in ecstasy. Diego gasped as his balls drew up tight in a sudden rush. His bellow echoed off the walls of the dining room as he came in cannon-fire pulses. Finn's cries of pleasure joined his. Diego's cock squeezed tight as the walls of Finn's back channel contracted through his orgasm.

Panting, his vision dark around the edges, Diego collapsed atop Finn, riding the aftershocks down.

"Oh, damn, I needed that," he muttered against Finn's shoulder.

He received a contented sigh for an answer.

When Faolchú poked his head in a little while later, Finn sat snuggled in Diego's lap again, both of them still stark naked. Diego fed him bits of chicken and potato from his own plate.

Diego glanced up. "Sorry, we made a bit of a mess."

"Easily remedied." Faolchú sniffed at the air. "Everything settled, then?"

"Yes, thank you."

Faolchú's teeth showed in a wolf-grin. "There, you see? I knew it would work. Perhaps I should act as an ambassador, as well."

"I think we'll save your diplomacy for last-ditch efforts," Diego said with a wry chuckle. "Everything's fine. My Finn is home. Better than fine."

"What do you mean?"

Finn held up the hand with the ring. "Diego has asked me to be his husband. Because I am not quite the fool people think me, I have agreed."

"You —" Faolchú's husky-blue eyes widened, then he turned to shout down the hallway. "Nathair? Don't go down to bed just yet, love. Seems we have a wedding to plan."

Epilogue

Miriam took credit for the weather. She claimed she had ordered the picture-perfect fluffy clouds and seventy degrees just for the occasion. The fae knew her well enough not to take her seriously and instead treated the statement as a metaphor for all the things she truly had accomplished.

At that moment, she mingled with the guests in the garden, while Diego stared out of the window at the ever-growing gathering.

"Diego, *siéntate*." Carlita pushed him into the nearest kitchen chair. "You've gone all white."

The Sandoval clan had arrived the night before, granted special visas for the week. Diego's sister, Carlita, had jumped at the chance, as curious about the fae as she was eager to see her big brother. She was divorced, again, so she had no need to drag a husband along, but Diego's niece and nephew, ages seven and five respectively, came with her, as well as Diego's somewhat reluctant father. Enrico Sandoval had taken some years to come to terms with his son being gay. Now he had to sift through the added facts that not only was his son gay, but he was about to marry another male, and that other male wasn't even human. He'd accepted the invitation all the same, and had even spoken to Finn on the phone several times before the trip, patiently helping Finn through his less-than-perfect Spanish.

"Just a dizzy spell." Diego accepted the glass of water she handed him and took a small sip. "I guess I'm a little more nervous than I thought."

"You fight monsters and big, bad government agencies and *this* scares you?"

"I am a man, *hermanita*. I think we're hardwired to be afraid of marriage."

Her laugh soothed him, a sound from his childhood and the happy memories there. "Not many men die from wedding jitters. You did take your medicine, right?"

"I did. I made sure."

"*Bien*, you're golden then."

* * * *

Finn twisted around again to glance out of the bedroom window at the garden below and the guests milling about.

Eithne swatted his shoulder. "Sit still. Worse than a little eel."

"Your pardon. I'm a bit…overexcited."

She let out a little growl and he straightened to face the mirror, trying his level best to stay still while she finished his hair. Diego liked to brush his hair out, but had never done…*this*. It was a new experience, but then, most everything that day would be, hence his nerves jumping like spring frogs.

Nervous, anxious, uncertain, he was supposed to do something about these feelings. Ah, yes. *"Beloved? I feel as if I might come out of my skin at any moment."*

Diego's thoughts came back to him in a song. *"'It ain't no sin to take off your skin and dance around in your bones...'"*

Finn laughed. *"That would be quite a sight."*

"Is it all the people?"

"Yes, that. And I am terrified I will forget what I am to say. I will make a fool of myself and embarrass you."

"That's why the minister's there, mi vida. *If you forget, she'll prompt you. A lot of people get nervous and have sudden attacks of wedding senility at the altar."*

"Very well, then. For you I will be brave, my hero."

"Finn?"

"Hmm?"

"I can't wait to see you. And you'd never embarrass me. I love you. I'm so proud of you."

"Now what is that besotted smile for, Fionnachd?" Eithne brought him back to the physical world as she finished his hair.

"Diego." He glanced up at her when she snorted. "That is, he was bespeaking me, telling me...well, that's a private matter."

She leaned in to kiss his cheek. "I have never seen you so happy as when you are with him. A moment more, I have something for you." When she waved her hand, a carved box materialized on the dresser. From this, Eithne drew a silver disc on a long chain, which she looped over Finn's head.

"It is lovely." He rose to view it in the light. Fomorian glyphs winked in gold and copper along the disc's rim, its center occupied by an oak etched into the silver. "What is it?"

"The Champion's seal," Eithne told him with a soft smile. "You were our champion but for a short time, but Father decreed you should have one to match Faolchú's."

"Truly? But I'm naught but a —"

"You are our champion, Fionnachd." She stood on tiptoe to kiss his lips. "Our hero."

A strange feeling swelled in his chest, making him want to stand taller. After some reflection, he thought it might be pride.

* * * *

Diego pulled at his tuxedo jacket again, regretting the formalwear in light of the day's warmth and the relative informality of the setting. Tia Carmen said the gray cutaway made him look like he had stepped off the movie screen, though, so he supposed it wasn't all bad.

The guests in all their varied finery filled the chairs and grass. Apple blossoms drifted through the air in a miniature snowstorm. Lugh and Zack, acting as his groomsmen, waited under the wisteria-covered pergola, with Faolchú and Angus, as two of Finn's oldest friends, standing on the other side, all of them in the royal military dress uniforms of pine green and gold that the fae had adopted for human occasions.

With Carlita on his arm, Diego made his way down the aisle, through this beautiful tableau. He hoped he wouldn't faint. Carlita handed him off to his groomsmen with a kiss and took her seat with the family.

"Don't lock your knees, Mr. S.," Zack leaned in to whisper. "Or you're gonna do a face-plant right into the roses."

"I'll do my best." Diego managed to crack a smile. "But I have you two here. I have every confidence you'd catch me."

"We would never let you fall, little man," Lugh murmured, a rather suspect quiver to his voice.

Diego had no chance to ask if he was all right, since the fae musicians at the back struck up a tune, a curious mix of harmony and discordance played on reed, wind and percussive instruments he couldn't name.

All heads turned toward the embassy and into this anticipatory atmosphere, accompanied by the ethereal, haunting music, strode Finn. Tia Carmen walked with him, the closest person he had ever had to a parent, beaming up at him.

Diego's knees threatened to buckle at the approach of this vision in silver and cream. Putting Finn in a tux had seemed a crime against nature, so Diego had left him to choose his own wedding attire. *Madre de Dios*, it was barely legal. Finn wore a pair of leather pants, slung low on his hips and so tight and soft, it looked as if he had been poured into butter cream. His long, elegant feet were bare, as many of the fae's were, and up top, he wore only a cream-colored leather vest, short enough to leave a tantalizing bit of skin exposed. His hair hung loose except for a few artfully crafted, slender braids woven with silver filigree and white starflowers.

"My angel," Diego breathed as he held out his hands to receive Finn's. The guests, the embassy and the garden all faded from his vision.

Finn leaned close to whisper in his ear, "I take it you are pleased?"

"I think I might be having a stroke," Diego answered. He went on when he saw Finn's concern, "You're so beautiful."

"So are you," Finn said with a long look up and down Diego's body.

The minister cleared her throat. "If our grooms are finished admiring each other…"

Laughter rippled through the guests and Diego chuckled, too, even as he felt himself flush. They stood with hands joined, gazing into each other's eyes as they spoke their vows. Finn didn't forget a single syllable, though his hands shook so badly when it came to exchanging rings, Diego had to help him as he slid the ring on his finger and spoke the words, "With this ring, I thee wed, and pledge my faithful love."

Finally, the minister spoke the words, "You may kiss."

Diego turned his face up to Finn's and blinked in surprise. "*Cariño*, you're glowing." The blue light danced over Finn's skin, as it did sometimes when they made love.

Finn took Diego's face between his hands. "So are you."

When their lips met, a visible spark leaped between them. The blue of Finn's magic met Diego's blinding white, and the two melded into one.

* * * *

A strange fae stood at the back of the company. No one knew him, but he had come from the Otherworld, so no one questioned his presence. As tall as any of the *sidhe*, as massive as the largest of the Fomorians, his golden skin seemed to attract the sunlight as he stood with his arms crossed over his chest.

When the wedded couple kissed, he raised his hand and whispered, "Fionnachd of the Shannon, may you have times of peace now. May your heart heal and your days be filled with joy. Long life to you, Diego Sandoval, and a pooka's own luck."

A golden ball rose from his palm to join the glow under the pergola, nestling softly in with the blue-white nimbus surrounding Finn and Diego. The golden fae toyed with the odd pendant around his neck, a red, plastic pen on a gold chain. A sharp-toothed smile lit his face as he finished his spell. "The blessings and thanks of my people go with you, oh Knight of the Pen."

Want to see more from this author? Here's a taster for you to enjoy!

Fireworks and Stolen Kisses
Angel Martinez and Freddy MacKay

Excerpt

Back straight, back straight. Is this person my social equal? Tally offered a *futsurei* to be safe while the evening's host introduced him as the new Urusar from Wisconsin. He wished Dad had come with him. As hard as he tried to think of this as just another business conference, the names and places had started to run together. Back home, he might have reached for the worry stone in his pocket. Here, that might be rude.

The ballroom was gorgeous, with the doors to the terrace rolled back to reveal the view of Mt. Fuji. Tables groaning with food lined the walls. Arrangements of blood-red flowers decorated every table. Everyone seemed to know everyone else, though that might have been an illusion created by nerves.

"Wisconsin?" the middle-aged woman inquired with reserved decorum. "That is the state of cheese, yes?"

"Very true." Damn it, he'd forgotten her name. She was the Uruma, the village mother, to one of the larger cities to the south. "Though thankfully the state is more than just cheese."

She laughed politely, turned to greet another conference-goer, and Tally hoped it had been a dismissal. He shouldn't have felt out of his element. Employees depended on his decisions all day, every day. Meetings were his lifeblood, or at least took up most of his life. Not to mention these were *his* people. The perfectly draped Global Lijun Alliance banner dominated the front of the room—there for anyone, human or lijun to see. For the humans, it was simply a trade organization. For the lijun, it was survival, a shared bond of secrecy and a way for lijun communities to thrive.

Except Tally would always stand outside, which simply made diplomacy that much more important. When his father had gleefully announced his retirement as Urusar, village father of their community in Wadiswan, Tally knew his duty. He'd been groomed for it all his life. He'd taken up the leadership mantle with the sobriety and respect it deserved, even though some of their lijun neighbors had whispered about another deadly serpent leading them.

Uktena.

Tally couldn't escape his heritage or his lijun type, but he was here at this conference to continue his father's work—to ensure his community thrived, that the lijun under his care were safe, and to fight against the ancient prejudices that branded him as *dangerous*.

He retreated to one of the buffets to nibble on sectioned oranges with his back to the wall so he could observe. Not everyone at the welcome dinner was as bound by formalities. The younger attendees had dressed in a variety of styles and more or less appropriately. Nearer the terrace, a young woman in a leather miniskirt tapped her boot heel to music only she could hear. On the other side of the room, a handsome young man in a strange mix of business formal and rebel-casual lounged against the bar. The suit jacket and expensive jeans fit in well enough. The faded T-shirt and rainbow suspenders? Not so much.

Tally thought he would introduce himself to this interesting person, but an older gentleman beat him there and spoke urgently to the young man, who made an impatient gesture and stalked off.

Too bad. He'd been an...otter? Tally surreptitiously flicked his tongue out to taste the air. Difficult to tell in such a large gathering, but he was sure he was right. Something beyond the rainbow suspenders drew him to the otter, a yearning that he didn't want to deny. He was about to follow when someone touched his arm.

"Herr Bastille, is it not?" A man with flame-red hair, an educated European accent and a calculating smile stood at his elbow. "I am Gerhard Klug. I understand you are a hotelier?"

Tally offered his hand rather than a bow and smiled in return. "Good to meet you. Tal-tsu'tsa Bastille. Everyone calls me Tally. Yes, I run the family business back home. Several properties."

"Good. Good." Herr Klug put an arm on his shoulder and steered him toward the bar. "I'm hoping we could discuss a possible business arrangement."

"I'm always interested in discussion, Herr Klug." Tally signaled the bartender. "What are you drinking?"

"Gerhard, please." The fox lijun laughed. "You'll make me feel old. And they have a pear brandy here that is good."

Tally ordered the brandy and a whiskey sour for himself. Yes, Gerhard was obviously here to woo him, but Tally didn't like being put at a disadvantage right from the start, even with something as small as who paid for drinks. "What is it you do?"

"I have glassworks," Gerhard said as he hopped onto the stool next to Tally's. "My family has been in glass for several centuries. While we have commercial lines, we have sites dedicated to custom work, as well."

Tally had the oddest image pop up at the phrase *in glass* of littles foxes running about under cheese domes. Of course he knew what Gerhard meant and the more focused part of his brain perked up at the mention of custom work. "Oh? What sort of custom work?"

Gerhard pulled a small tablet from inside his suit jacket. "For restaurants. For hotels. *Erholungsort*...what is the word? Resorts."

Tally answered the fox's calculating look with a soft laugh. "I have the feeling you've brought a portfolio. Please, let's have a look."

"Thank you. It's very kind of you to give me a hearing." Gerhard opened the tablet between them as their drinks arrived. "We have contracts across Europe. This first set is work we recently added for a winter resort in Sweden."

They leaned in together to inspect the photos, Tally nodding and asking questions here and there. The images showed wine glasses, water goblets, tumblers and beer glasses in beautiful shapes and colors, with the property name and logo etched discreetly into each piece. Tally particularly admired the champagne flutes with the snowflake-shaped feet. Lovely, though he gave no outward indication that he reacted to any one set more than another.

When they reached the end of the photo samples, Tally sat back, sipping at his whiskey and making Gerhard wait. "It's a very interesting thought. Though I imagine a certain percentage of that pretty glassware vanishes from the properties as souvenirs."

"Ha. I'm sure some of it does. Though not offering the prettiest glasses in the guest rooms most likely reduces that number."

Gerhard's eyes twinkled as he laughed and if Tally had been someone who craved casual sex, Gerhard might have been a candidate, but his heart would only be half in it. The other half had already left the room with the handsome otter. The suspenders were a beacon, a flare sent up, and Tally was going to speak with the otter of definitely-not-straight orientation that evening if it killed him.

"I'd like you to work up some samples with the resort manager at Sapphire Lake." Tally didn't mention immediately that the manager was one of his sisters. "We'd need to see physical pieces, of course. Then we can discuss the possibility of starting a small contract there first. I do have properties in Europe, but allow me to begin closer to home."

"Very good. A pleasure, Tally, surely." Gerhard extended a hand and they shook—a gentlemen's agreement to further negotiations.

When Gerhard Klug finally let him go with an exchange of business cards, the otter was nowhere in sight. Uncharacteristically disgruntled, Tally left the main ballroom to check some of the smaller venues where different sorts of food were on offer. The first meeting room had been set up as a sushi bar, which seemed a good place to find an otter. He wasn't there. The second was a room dedicated to international cuisine, offerings from host countries of previous years. No otter.

The third was a paradise of desserts which had drawn the children since the beginning of the evening with its siren song. Tally hurried his steps when he picked up shouting from that direction and he skidded to a stop in front of the door.

About the Author

The unlikely black sheep of an ivory tower intellectual family, Angel Martinez has managed to make her way through life reasonably unscathed. Despite a wildly misspent youth, she snagged a degree in English Lit, married once and did it right the first time, (same husband for almost twenty-four years) gave birth to one amazing son, (now in college) and realized at some point that she could get paid for writing.

Published since 2006, Angel's cynical heart cloaks a desperate romantic. You'll find drama and humor given equal weight in her writing and don't expect sad endings. Life is sad enough.

She currently lives in Delaware in a drinking town with a college problem and writes Science Fiction and Fantasy centered around gay heroes.

Angel loves to hear from readers. You can find her contact information, website details and author profile page at http://www.pride-publishing.com.